MIDAS

This is for Pat and Maxine

Piers Kelaart

Midas

Macdonald Futura Publishers

A Futura Book

First published in Great Britain in 1981
by Macdonald Futura Publishers
Copyright © Piers Kelaart 1981

ISBN 0 7088 1988 5

Typeset, printed and bound in Great Britain by
Hazell Watson & Viney Ltd
Aylesbury, Bucks

Macdonald Futura Publishers Ltd
Paulton House,
8 Shepherdess Walk,
London N1 7LW

CHAPTER ONE

Sandro Munari sat with the back of his chair tilted against the wall of the customs shed listening to the angry rasp of the car travelling quickly through the hairpin bends that traversed the fertile hillside in giant steps. He sat with his peaked cap tilted over his eyes, his grey-uniformed legs stretched straight in front of him so that the shadow of the roof incised a sharp line across his knees and left his boots gleaming smartly in the sun. As the speeding car drew nearer, its wasp-like buzzing becamed a muted roar. Sandro heard the thin screech of writhing tyres and thought the fellow must have the devil up his tail pipe. But never mind. He would still have to stop at the customs post. Everyone had to do that. And with that profound thought, Sandro turned his attention to more serious things – like Maria, like food.

In Sandro's heat-drowsed mind Maria and food were inseparable. First the *gnocchi* then the knocking, lunch and the siesta afterwards, with the smoothness of her belly pressed against his, the touch of her sweat-damp flesh sweetly prurient through the hairiness of his own body. Which made him think of Father Lorenzo. If Father Lorenzo knew, would he say that too-frequent sex in the afternoon was sinful, even though Maria and Sandro had been married only three months and were still very much in love?

The silver-grey car heeled round the last corner and Sandro's thoughts moved abruptly from the problems of theology to the problems of duty. The car's nose dipped sharply as the driver saw the sign and the customs shed at the same time and braked hard. The circular red and blue warning sign was too close to the customs post. Two years ago a speeding Maserati had impaled itself on the rear of a Citroen and a French woman passenger had been injured, but they still had not done anything about moving the sign further back. They never did anything about anything, Sandro thought, taking somnolent steps into the centre of the road and extending a large, brown hand with dirty fingernails.

The tyres streaked black along the tarmac and spattered tiny stones as the car shed speed. It was a BMW 3-litre coupé, low and sleek, painted in metallic silver. 200bhp, a top speed of nearly 250kph, a 0–100km time of under eight seconds. It had six cylinders and consumed 9·9 litres of gasoline every hundred kilometres. Sandro knew all about BMWs, the knowledge compensating for the realization that he would never own one.

He rested his hand against the fly-spattered windscreen and waited while the window moved down with a soft hum of electrics. The driver's face was shielded by an outsize pair of Raybans. He had tight curly brown hair, a sun tan that looked as if it had come from a bottle, and a long nervous jaw that twitched as if he were chewing gum, even when he wasn't. It was the head of a serpent, a head full of guile and bitterness, Sandro decided, taking the limply held out passport and car documents to the accompaniment of the Rolling Stones in full blast from the eight-track cartridge player.

'*Qualcosa de dichiare?*' Sandro asked, fingering the documents.

'Nothing,' the driver replied quickly, the heavy gold ring on his finger tapping impatiently against the steering wheel, but not in time with the music. The green-covered passport said his name was Jacques Duval, American. He was five feet ten inches tall and twenty-seven years old. How on earth did someone only twenty-seven years old find eleven and a half million lire for a car like this?

'*Sigarette, profumi, whisky?*' Sandro asked perfunctorily.

An impatient shake of the head in reply.

'*Da dove venite? Milano?*'

'Yes.'

If he was in a hurry and he had come from Milan, why had he not used the *autostrada*? 'You have cigarettes, perfumes, whisky?' Sandro asked, this time in English, so far only vaguely suspicious.

'No. Nothing. Nothing.' The voice with a twang like a snapping violin string, the face looking straight ahead, tight with anger and impatience.

'You have any Italian money?'

An impatient shake of the head, a hard look from behind the dark lenses, the small mouth curling with long-suffering forbearance. Sandro had come across people like Duval before – young, spoilt, imperious, with no idea of how to treat a working man. Sandro could tell what Duval was thinking. Just because Sandro wore a uniform, Duval thought he was beneath contempt. Duval was thinking that Sandro was a *fascista porco*.

Duval handed him a slim leather wallet. In it were 1,500 lire and the same number of Swiss francs. Sandro sighed and handed the wallet back.

'Satisfied?' Duval asked provocatively.

'Not yet,' Sandro said and thought that he was no fascist, that he was no pig. His father had been a partisan and fought against Mussolini, and Sandro remembered his older brothers talking of how they had been taken to Mezzegara, the tiny village which overlooked the Lago di Como, to see the bodies of the dictator and his mistress, Clara Petacci. Sandro placed his hand on the door and said, 'Kindly step out, signore.' Sandro had decided that his lunch could wait. He had decided to do his job very thoroughly and very well. He had also decided to teach this arrogant young man a few manners.

Behind the dark glasses, Duval's face twitched with alarm, and Sandro lost all interest in educating the man. He felt a quickening of the senses, the excitement of discovery. It was almost like finding a prize-winning *lotteria* ticket in the street.

'What? Why?' Duval asked.

'Now we look inside the car,' Sandro said.

Duval didn't move. Sandro unlatched the door with his left hand and held it open, while unfastening the flap of his revolver holster with his right. He stood there watching Duval's face, listening to the footsteps of his colleagues coming up behind him.

His colleagues were in a boisterous mood. It had been Luigi's birthday and they had spent the morning drinking Chianti. 'Hey Sandro, you going to confiscate the automobile?' 'Sandro, you mustn't be late for Maria.' 'It isn't only the *gnocchi* that will get spoilt!'

Sandro felt his face redden, and tried to ignore them while he studied the car. It had German export plates and was a year-old model with 75,000km on the clock. Two years' mileage in one year. Duval must be a commercial traveller, but Sandro didn't think that was likely.

'I am a tourist, man,' Duval protested. '*Tourista Americano*.' He still didn't get out of the car.

The other customs men crowded round, their jokes less strident. Someone said it was too hot an afternoon to strip down a car.

'I am in a hurry,' Duval said, repeating it in Italian, using the word '*fretta*' as an indication of his urgency. 'I have an important meeting in Lugano,' he added, tapping his wristwatch with the ring.

'In such a fast car you can get there in no time,' Sandro said, avoiding Duval's eyes, and easing the revolver two inches upwards in its holster.

Duval got out, still wearing the expression of long-suffering patience.

Sandro tilted the seat forward and looked into the rear. Nothing there. Leaving his colleagues admiring the car, he marched Duval round to the boot and gestured to him to open it.

Inside, expensive carpeting and a Louis Vuitton suitcase in leather so expensive it looked like plastic. Inside the case, suits from Blades and a Cardin pullover, a quilted jacket by Dimitri of Italy and shirts by Hathaway. A widely travelled gentleman, obviously, complete with Brut after-shave and *two* Philips electric shavers. Pity there was nothing criminal in travelling well or expensively. There was no false bottom to the suitcase, either.

Sandro twisted his fingers in the pile of the carpet. A car like this could lap Monza at over 180km an hour. It had a boot big enough for family holidays too. His idling fingers felt the fold at the end of the carpet and pulled it out. Strange, he thought, the boot was rectangular and the carpet was made to fit something of a slightly different shape, almost as if there was a space at the far end between the bulbous protrusions of the rear wings. He lifted up the carpet and looked underneath. Black metal all round and an alloy spare wheel with 'Michelin XAS' painted in white letters. *Elegantemente!* Sandro let the carpet flop back and looked at the far end of the boot underneath the overhanging sill of the body. That was black, too, no space beyond the uncompromising rectangle. Funny, he could have sworn that normally there was a space where there was now a sheet of black metal. Fastened with Philips screws too. Sandro tapped the panel with his knuckles. It sounded hollow, decidedly hollow. He paused and looked up at Duval. There was no arrogance now, only fear, sweat ribboning the upper lip.

Sandro picked a Philips screwdriver from the tool kit and unfastened the panel. It came off as easily as the top of a can of sardines. The space inside was stuffed full of Italian currency notes.

CHAPTER TWO

Carmody shut the door of the interrogation room and leaned the backs of his shoulders against it. He was a leathery-looking man of about fifty, with grizzled white hair, a square, battered face, and eyes that were red-rimmed, steady and expressionless as holes in a sheet. He'd picked up the squeal on Duval's arrest on the midnight news, left Geneva at four, and driven for six hours across Switzerland to the Italian border near Menaggio. Sweet Jesus he was tired!

'Hey man, it's good to see you. I thought you were never coming.'

Carmody rubbed his eyes, lit a cigarette and studied Duval through the smoke. Young, fashionably slim, creased and frightened. Carmody knew he would break. He'd spent much of his life breaking dudes like Duval.

'Now you're here, let's fix up how you get me out,' Duval said. The Cacharel velour shirt was crushed, the pre-faded denims marked, the twitching of the jaw nearly rhythmic. Duval didn't look as if he'd slept much the previous night, either.

'I got shafted,' Duval was saying. 'It's the biggest fucking frame up you've ever known.'

Carmody looked about the room. It was neither large nor small, very institutional, with a scarred wooden table in the centre surrounded by six straight-back chrome and plastic chairs. Paint peeled off the green walls and the panes of the barred windows were cracked and grimy. Carmody pushed himself away from the door, walked into the room. The yellowing picture on the noticeboard was of a heavily moustached Sicilian, wanted for armed robbery in Reggio Calabria. No chance he would have travelled so far north.

'It was the fucking garage that did it,' Duval was saying. 'The bastards worked on the car just before I left. They stuffed the boot full of lire. I can show you the garage. It's a small place on the Via Beloti in Milan.'

Duval was standing at the end of the table, watching Carmody carefully and twisting his fingers together. Carmody decided he was frightened and not very bright. There was no chance that anyone would believe Duval if he didn't believe the story himself. Carmody said, 'You've made mistakes like that before.'

'Mistakes . . . What do you mean, mistakes? I'm telling you I was shafted by that fucking garage.'

Carmody said, 'I know your record. Six months in 1973 for smuggling hash into Germany. A Bureau of Narcotics and Dangerous Drugs warrant for peddling snort by the ounce in San Anselmo. So cut the bullshit.'

Duval sat down, looking mean and frightened. 'What are you, man? You from the embassy or what?'

'I'm from the embassy,' Carmody said.

'Are you a lawyer?'

Carmody shook his head.

'What the hell good are you then? I need a lawyer, man, a mouthpiece, not some mother who sits on his ass all day pushing papers around.'

'You've got me,' Carmody said, as if that finished the matter. 'I'm a right motherfucker.'

Duval went on the defensive. 'No need to take it personally, but I mean, what the hell good are you if you aren't going to spring me?'

'I don't give a fuck about springing you,' Carmody said. 'All I'm interested in is the preservation of your constitutional rights. You can stay here and rot for all I care.'

'That's a hell of a way for a government man to talk. I

mean that's a hell of an attitude for a government man to take. You're supposed to take care of me, friend. You're supposed to help me.'

'Help you do what?' Carmody asked. 'Help you get on the streets so you can peddle a little shit maybe?'

'You're supposed to help,' Duval repeated slowly, as if he was speaking to a retarded child. 'You're supposed to take care of me. I'm a United States citizen for chrissake!'

'Then you shouldn't try to beat other countries' laws,' Carmody said. 'What's happened to your friends?'

'Friends? My friends have nothing to do with this. It was that fucking garage that screwed me up, and that's the truth, man.' Duval looked angrily out of the window.

Carmody said, 'You made the news last night. Every hour on the hour. Your friends should be here now, talking to the *carabinieri*, arranging lawyers, fixing up bail.' He waited till Duval was looking at him again. 'All you've got is me.'

'I don't need friends,' Duval said softly. 'I don't need any fucking friends. I can handle this myself. I've got all the bread in the world, man.'

'Sure,' Carmody said. 'Sure. You can handle it. You want to get yourself a lawyer?'

Their eyes met, moved to the old-fashioned black telephone with the frayed cord. Carmody nodded. Duval hesitated, then said, 'Yes, I want d'Annunzio from Milan. He's the best. He'll show these mothers what to do.'

Carmody waited while Duval dialled, and the operator made the connection. He waited while Duval spoke, hesitated, spoke again, flushed. Duval put the phone down and said, 'The bastard won't even talk to me. He doesn't want to know.'

'Friends,' Carmody said. 'They bury you. They've buried you, Duval. You'll get three years for this. And after that the BNDD will have you shipped back to the States and make sure you get a seven to ten.'

Duval looked at Carmody in horror. 'Ten years! Man, you must be crazy!'

'It's your life,' Carmody said, stubbing out a cigarette. 'You'll be an old man when you come out. No use to man or beast. Not much good to a woman either. You would have jerked it all away in ten years.'

'That's a lot of crap,' Duval said. 'That's a lot of bull-shit.'

But Carmody was looking at him and could see that he was thinking about ten years. Ten years in a ten-by-eight cell with no fast cars, no silk shirts, no classy hotels and no good-time broads.

Duval asked, 'Will I really go ten?'

Carmody nodded.

'Shit, man. That's a lot of time.'

Carmody lit a fresh cigarette and let Duval think about that. It wasn't yet noon and he was nearly through the pack. Carmody had been a sixty-a-day man for thirty-five years and he knew one day he would die of lung cancer. One day; not yet – and he couldn't kick the habit.

'Hey, aren't you going to do anything about it? You aren't going to let them—'

'I'm not a lawyer,' Carmody said. 'They only sent me to see if you were comfortable.'

'But I need a lawyer!'

'You'll get one on the day.'

'Is that all you motherfuckers can do? Get me a lawyer on the day! Is that what we spend billions of dollars of tax-payers' money for? So you can get me a lawyer on the day!'

Carmody sighed. 'You want a lawyer, you get one. You can't get one, then we'll find one. But that's it, friend.'

'But ten years, for chrissake!'

'It's a long time,' Carmody agreed and coughed. He pulled hard at the cigarette and said, 'I'll tell you some-thing for free. They picked up two more people like you

14

last night, all making for Lugano, with their trunks full of lire.'

Duval said softly, 'It isn't true.'

Carmody shrugged. 'So you're surrounded by friends. They'll be waiting for you in ten years.'

Duval shook his head helplessly. 'What do I do?' he asked. 'What do I do?'

Carmody got up and walked to the door. 'It's your life, your decision.'

Duval followed him. 'Hey, man, where are you going?'

'See you around. I've left some cigarettes and chocolate with the guards. Have a nice day.'

The twitch of Duval's jaw was like epilepsy. He scratched himself and said, 'Look, man, I'll tell you about the money. I'll make a deal.'

'I'm not a cop,' Carmody said.

Duval turned and walked back to the table. 'If I were to tell you something, would you help me?'

'Depends on what you tell me.'

'It's big,' Duval said. 'It's very big.'

Carmody moved back into the room. 'If it's that big, it will help,' he said. 'If it's very, very big, I might even spring you.'

Duval twisted his head round and looked Carmody in the face. 'How do I know I can trust you?'

'You don't,' Carmody said. 'What have you got to lose?'

Duval remained silent for some time, his eyes studying Carmody's face. Finally he shrugged and said, 'Okay. It's a bank job.'

'There's nothing big about hitting a bank,' Carmody said. 'I'm political.'

'This is political,' Duval said, '*and* it's a bank job, *and* it's bigger, *and* it's different.'

Carmody lit another cigarette, drew up a chair and sat down. Duval didn't look at him as he began to talk.

15

CHAPTER THREE

Carmody just made the 18.15 Swissair DC-9 out of Zurich. The aircraft was full and he was slotted into one of the window seats at the rear, where he had the dulcet experience of a Pratt and Whitney JT8 D-7 turbo screeching out 14,000 pounds of thrust inches from his left ear. Not that the noise made much difference to Carmody. He never slept on planes.

An hour and a half later he was at Heathrow. Customs and Immigration cleared him cursorily, taking no account that all the luggage he had was one battered briefcase. Outside the customs area were hordes of expectant people crowding in the space between the doors and the brightly lit Rent-a-Car counters. Carmody pushed his way through them, making for the rendezvous area. Already he could see Martin Pelham's thatch of blond hair like a helmet rising above the crowd milling before the defunct Arrivals board. Standing lopsidedly, the weight of his body twisted over the right foot, Martin ranged above the crowd. His lanky frame was covered in a suit of grey denim. He twisted angularly as Carmody approached.

'Hi, Lew. Good to see you.'

'You too, Martin.'

Martin's hand reached to take the briefcase from Carmody. Instinctively Carmody tightened his grip.

'Okay, okay,' Martin said. 'I only wanted to help. I'm only half crippled, you know.'

'It's all I have in the world,' Carmody replied, avoiding the confrontation with Martin's infirmity, trying to make a joke of it.

Martin pointed and started moving towards the glass-sided walkway that led from the Terminal Building to the car park. He walked with a pronounced twisting of the body, advancing his right foot, throwing all his weight onto it, dragging the left behind him in a half shuffle. Carmody forced himself to walk slow.

'Good flight?'

'In an hour twenty, you don't notice.'

They went up the ramp to the walkway. An incorporeal female voice announced the departure of Air France flight 601 to Paris. Carmody and Martin exchanged information about their families. Martin's wife and two children were well. They were staying overnight at his mother's, so Carmody wouldn't meet them unless he stayed over Sunday. Carmody told Martin that his wife, Hilda, was looking for a house for them in the States, that he was retiring in the fall.

'That'll be the day,' Martin said. 'What will you do with your time?'

'Sleep,' Carmody said. 'Mainly sleep. That's the one thing I haven't been able to do for twenty-eight years.'

'Twenty-eight years is a long time in our business.'

'A damn sight too long, as every rookie in the Section reminds me. It's not been too bad a life, Martin, but I'm getting too old to learn the new ways.'

'Rubbish,' Martin said. 'You're always teaching us new tricks.' He stopped at the entrance to the car park, slightly out of breath, and pointed to where his car was parked.

Martin Pelham lived in a four-bedroomed, detached house set well back off a quiet street in Maidenhead. It was only half an hour from the airport and built on a hillock, with a two-car garage, a gravelled drive, and flowerbeds verdant with geranium, petunia and fuchsia.

While Carmody washed, Martin went to his den. It was a small masculine room with antique Japanese daggers over the fireplace, model soldiers on the mantelpiece, smelling

18

strongly of worn leather and cigars. On a table between the sofa and the unused fireplace were plates of cold meat and salad, bottles of Côtes du Rhône and Sancere. Martin opened the red, filled two glasses, lit a panatella and sat down at one end of the sofa, waiting.

'I thought we would eat here,' he said, hearing Carmody enter. 'It's quiet and we can talk.'

Carmody came round and sat on the sofa, lighting another cigarette. 'Nice,' he said. 'Being kicked upstairs suits you.' He picked up the glass of red wine and placed it well away from him. He said he hadn't slept for thirty-six hours and was too tired to drink anything but iced water.

Martin got him the water and said, 'Well, what's brought you here so suddenly?'

Carmody picked at his food, put the plate down and drew at his cigarette. 'Yesterday,' he began, 'someone called Jacques Duval was arrested on the Italian–Swiss border. He was driving a 3-litre BMW coupé. His trunk was stuffed full of lire notes.'

'I thought that sort of thing happened all the time,' Martin said.

'It does. But we've had tabs on Duval for a while. He is a small-time smuggler. He used to carry for the Movement. He's done time in Germany, and the Bureau of Narcotics and Dangerous Drugs have a warrant out for him. He's stayed in Europe ever since and it seems he's switched from running dope to running money. Now he's down for a seven to ten.'

Martin sipped at his wine and ate. The leanness had gone from his face, Carmody noticed; the cheeks were now plump and he was becoming quite heavy around the jowls. Carmody also noticed that Martin ate heartily, drank his wine in deep draughts. Carmody wondered if the shooting had changed him that much.

'I spoke with Duval this morning. His people had taken

19

a powder and he wasn't keen to look a seven to ten in the eye on his own. I offered him a deal. And he sang. He was carrying the dough for someone called Siccoli. Siccoli is a wealthy Italian industrialist who lives in Menaggio. But even though Siccoli had given him the money, Duval wasn't putting it into Siccoli's account in Switzerland. He was paying it into a bank in Lugano for the credit of someone called Marc Landi. Marc Landi is the chief foreign-exchange dealer of the Banco Lattoria d'Lugano.'

'Edgar's bank?'

Carmody nodded.

John Charles Edgar was an insurance broker, who had become a rentier, who'd become a property tycoon, who'd become a share dealer, who'd become an asset stripper and founder of conglomerates. Edgar Holdings was one of the best known if not the best run company in the country. The City had never forgiven Edgar Holdings for buying out a conservative and sleepy merchant bank and going into banking.

Carmody said, 'There are rumours that the Banco Lattoria is in trouble because of its foreign-exchange dealings.'

'I've heard those rumours too. And not only about the Banco Lattoria.'

'The Banco Lattoria is special,' Carmody said. 'Duval has been running currency for a weirdo gang called Midas. As far as I can gather they are a bunch of young people, pretty deep into radical politics, and organized on the principle of separate cells. Each person only knows three others and no one knows who heads the group. All they know is that he is called Midas. And Midas is going to smash the Banco Lattoria.'

'Why, for God's sake?'

'Duval seemed to think it would be a supreme and sophisticated act of terrorism.'

'That's rubbish, Lew. These people don't play with banks

and currencies. Their game is letter bombs and hijacking aircraft.'

'Maybe,' Carmody said. 'But if they smash the Banco Lattoria, they smash us. We've been using the Banco Lattoria for the past few years for collections and pay-offs, especially pays-offs to informers and infiltrated agents.'

'So change your bank.'

'That still leaves records of the transactions with the Banco Lattoria. True, a number of the payments were made under cover, but anyone with time to spare and access to the records could discover a lot of names. A lot of our people within subversive organizations might get wasted. Our whole network might be destroyed.'

Martin laughed. 'And I thought you wanted to help save the pound.'

Carmody said, 'I need help, Martin. I dare not clear this with my people.'

'Why, for heaven's sake?'

'Because I'm scared. I'm scared that we've been penetrated.'

'Rubbish,' Martin exclaimed. 'Your Anti-Terrorist Section is the best ground—'

'Look at it my way,' Carmody said. His eyes were sore from lack of sleep, his throat was rough from too many cigarettes. He felt a terrible lethargy creeping over him. 'There are fifty banks in Lugano the same size as the Lattoria. Five hundred in Switzerland that are no bigger. If Midas are only interested in this sophisticated act of terrorism, why pick the Lattoria?'

'Any bank that was picked could ask that question.'

'Sure, but the fact remains; they have picked the Lattoria. And I can't take any chances. Martin, I want to use Dominic Cain.'

'Oh boy,' Martin said. 'Oh boy. Dominic Cain! Dominic hasn't worked for us in two years, Lew. He hasn't worked for us since . . .'

For a moment the two men stared at each other, remembering that time when Martin's hip had been shattered by a .44 Magnum.

'The Department retired him after Chagny,' Martin continued. 'The official view is that Dominic Cain is an uncontrollably violent person, usable only as an extreme measure, as a matter of last resort. They ran a psychological profile on him after Chagny. It's something to do with his childhood.'

'I still want him,' Carmody said. 'He's the only one who can do this job. He's the only person with the knowledge to check the bank's books and the ability to deal with Midas, whoever he may turn out to be.'

'You'll need Edgar's permission to let Cain into the bank.'

'There is such a thing as an old-boy network,' Carmody said. 'I am asking you to use it.'

'Lew, don't you think you are presuming too much?'

'No,' Carmody said. 'If the Banco Lattoria goes under, someone – Edgar or the Bank of England – will have to find a few million pounds. My contact in the bank tells me the loss could be as high as fifteen million. That's money out of England, friend. That's money into the pockets of Midas. Think what a terrorist group could do with that kind of bread.'

Martin frowned. 'I'll need evidence—'

'Do yourself a favour,' Carmody said. 'You've got the evidence. If Midas pulls this off and has fifteen million pounds, no institution is going to be safe. They're going to be bigger and much more dangerous, much harder to fight. Talk to your economic boys now. Have them tell you how many banks have gone under in the last twenty-four months. Have them tell you why and what havoc each bank failure causes. Then talk to your people about Edgar and about Cain.'

'You're getting edgy, Lew.'

'Of course I'm getty edgy. I'm running scared. I've got four months to go and I'm sitting on the biggest operation in my life. And I am going to stop them, Martin. You're going to do this for me, or I go somewhere else. Either way, I get Cain and Edgar.'

Martin leaned back in his chair and laughed. 'Lew,' he cried, 'Lew! Of course I'm going to help you. Why don't you get some sleep while I go and talk to some people.'

Carmody relaxed and sipped at the glass of red wine. 'You do that,' he said. 'I'll make a few phone calls.'

CHAPTER FOUR

The four apartments were in a small block, neatly stacked one above the other, like shoe boxes. They were of identical shape and size, each with one bedroom, kitchen, living room, lobby and bath, a small balcony and an identical view of what had once been the Great North Road. There was no lift, and the stairs were bare and narrow.

Martin Pelham dragged himself onto the second-floor landing and clung to the white wooden globe at the head of the bannisters. He was breathing heavily and irritatedly aware of Carmody standing patiently on the step below him. At 8.30 on a Sunday morning, the only sound was that of his own breathing. Opposite him, the doormat of Flat 2 was bereft of Sunday newspapers, and it certainly didn't say 'welcome'.

Martin limped across the landing and pressed the doorbell. There was a brief silence, then the sound of feet crossing the parquet hallway that Martin knew lay behind the door. The footsteps stopped; silence, and Carmody breathing into Martin's ear. They waited for a whole minute, then Carmody leaned past Martin and pressed the bell again. No immediate reaction from the apartment, then a surreptitious rustle. Martin felt there was someone standing silently on the other side of the door, and hoped he wouldn't do anything too damn stupid. Then he saw the light go behind the head-high spyhole and he forced a placatory grin. He was rewarded by a rattling of chain and the clunk of a lock turning back. Then Dominic Cain was holding the apartment door open.

Even at 8.30 on a Sunday morning, Dominic was very much awake. Martin remembered how, when they had worked together, Dominic had always come awake at first light; it was something to do with a childhood spent in the tropics. Now Dominic was not only wide awake but wearing a thigh-length judo jacket, whose crossed lapels were held together by a brown cotton belt. In his hand was a two-inch-barrelled Colt Python.

'Martin,' Dominic said. 'Lew!' – eyes moving flatly from one to the other. 'What a surprise!' He still held the gun in his hand, and the eyes were expressionless. Dominic Cain was a tall man, a fraction under six foot, lean, with wide swimmer's shoulders and flat pectorals. He had a long Aryan face, with the attendant sharp nose and large black eyes that looked like dried pools of ink. His hair was long, curly and also black; his complexion neither dark nor light but perfectly in between, with good smooth skin that had turned a deep bronze in the sun. It had been rumoured in the Department that somewhere in Dominic's ancestry there was a touch of the tar brush.

Dominic moved back into the hallway, with its framed Van Gogh prints and a poster from the Budokwai. 'Sunflower' and 'Cornfield at Arles' – the first and the last of Van Gogh, Martin thought; anyone who liked them both was capable of wild extremes. He watched Dominic moving across the hallway with the gracefulness of a natural athlete. He'd always admired the way Dominic moved. At one time he'd even tried to imitate that easy, lithe walk. But that had been light years ago.

'Come into the kitchen,' Dominic said, waving the gun at a door on his right. 'I was just making coffee.'

The kitchen was a rectangular room, bordered with cupboards, a fridge and a sink, smelling of freshly brewed coffee. At the end of the room was a gas cooker; beside the door, a small table with four chairs. The kitchen was neat, orderly, with none of the clutter of a man living on his own. Dominic went over to the stove, while Martin and Carmody sat at the table. The Sunday papers all confirmed that, according to the Prime Minister, there was no sterling crisis.

Dominic asked, 'How do you like your coffee?'

Carmody said cream with no sugar and Martin wanted his black. Dominic poured, carried the coffee over to the table, and sat between them.

'How you been, Martin? I hear you've got your own anti-terrorist section now.'

Martin avoided Dominic's glance. 'That's right. They had to put me someplace where I wouldn't have to run.'

He sipped at his coffee and forced himself to look at Dominic. 'I wanted to keep you, you know.'

'I know,' Dominic said, shrugging. 'But not to worry. I've begun to like the quiet life.'

'Then why make with the gun?' Carmody asked.

'Eight-thirty on a Sunday morning is too early even for Jehovah's Witnesses. I thought it might be old enemies calling.' Dominic took the gun from his belt and laid it on a cupboard, within easy reach.

Carmody eyed the gun carefully. The Colt Python was chambered for the ·357 Magnum as well as the milder ·38. He asked Dominic what he used.

'The Magnum, of course,' Dominic said. 'I don't believe in second chances.'

'And you still worry about the Movement?' Carmody asked.

'We didn't finish them off,' Dominic said. 'We should have.'

'We couldn't,' Martin said. 'Not after the fuss over . . . You got a licence for that thing?'

'No,' Dominic said. 'Should I?'

'You know damn well you should. If you are being threatened, you should go to the police.'

'And you know damn well that all I'd get is a routine check from a noddy car and a request to call 999 if some-

27

one started shooting at me.'

'The Movement was two years ago, Dominic,' Martin said. 'It doesn't exist any more.'

'Not in that form it doesn't,' Carmody said.

Dominic felt a slow prickling of the hairs at the back of his neck. 'Is that why you came?' he asked.

Slowly Carmody nodded.

Martin said, 'Banks – it's to do with banks. Have you any idea, Dominic, how many banks have gone under in the past year?'

'If you include the fringe banks, I'd say eight or nine.'

'Seventeen,' Martin said. 'That's what our economic unit tells me, and some of them were not so fringe either. Franklin National in the States; Bankhaus Herstatt in West Germany; ICB and Fina in Switzerland; Israel–British, and London and County here in England. That's something like one thousand million pounds up the spout in twelve months.'

'Inevitable,' Dominic said. 'Some borrowed short and lent long, some invested for a boom and hit a slump, some were badly run, and some simply got taken. A slump always sorts out the men from the boys.'

'We're interested in some of those that simply got taken,' Carmody said. 'We believe that someone is deliberately trying to ruin banks. We've got positive evidence.'

'But why?' Dominic asked.

'Look at it this way,' Martin said. 'If you want to fuck up the system, I mean really fuck it up, there isn't much point whining about the multinationals. ITT and General Motors are too big and powerful. They can look after themselves and the most you can hope for is a dent in their PR man's credibility. Banks, especially small banks, are different. They're more vulnerable. They're more get-at-able, and much more dangerous.

'Wrecking a bank is like throwing a stone into a pond. The ripples go on forever. You ruin a small corporation and who suffers? The shareholders, the employees, the creditors. In other words a small and defined group of people. But with a bank there is no such precise grouping. There are depositors, there are businesses who have borrowed from the bank, the creditors of those businesses, their employees and shareholders, there are strangers who've accepted letters of credit and bills of exchange, there are institutions that try to mount a rescue operation. You hit a bank and you're hitting everybody.'

'Very clever,' Dominic said. 'The domino theory of banking.'

'Right. If enough banks fall, people will stop putting money into banks and start stuffing it into their mattresses. If banks don't have deposits, then they cannot lend. If business cannot borrow, then it must retrench and stagnate. If business stagnates, governments are unable to raise taxes. So they create inflation or they themselves stagnate.' Martin clapped his palms together. 'Recipe for prolonged depression and ruin of Western society and end of lecture.'

Dominic turned to Carmody. 'You said you have positive evidence?'

Carmody lit another cigarette. Counting the number he smoked was no help. It only made him more aware of the damage he was doing to himself. 'It started on Friday afternoon,' he said, 'with someone called Jacques Duval trying to smuggle five and a half million Italian lire into Switzerland.' Slowly and clearly, with the aid of two more cigarettes, Carmody told Dominic about Duval's arrest, about the money destined for Marc Landi, about his own section's accounts at the Banco Lattoria, about his suspicion that his own Section had been penetrated, and about Midas.

'I've got news for you about Midas,' Carmody said. 'I've had London do a records check on the members of Duval's

29

cell. Kit Garnham, Kevin Cormack and Morrie Ellis – all former members of the Movement.' He handed Dominic a manila folder containing photographs and record print-outs.

Christopher (Kit) Garnham was a small, lantern-jawed individual, twenty-seven years old, and even in the photograph the eyes that were described as brown were watchful. He had spent a great deal of time in the Middle and Far East, and was reputed to have organized supplies for the Movement. He'd returned to Europe after the organization had collapsed. While at university he had received a suspended sentence for possession of drugs.

Kevin Cormack was a long-time friend of Garnham's. They were reputed to have run a dope-peddling ring at university, and while working for the Movement Cormack had been known to travel extensively, purportedly organizing transportation and collecting pay-offs for the shipments. He had no criminal record and was known to have a fondness for luxurious living. He was a year older than Garnham, Irish, and, according to the photograph, extremely good-looking. For a while after the collapse of the Movement he had lived as an informer, thus becoming known to Carmody.

Morrie Ellis was the most dangerous of the three. Physically quite small, with a square head and a heavy moustache, he stared implacably back from the photograph at Dominic. He was American, twenty-six, and had missed Vietnam because of his puny stature. He'd had convictions for violence and possession of firearms, and was known to have been an enforcer for the Movement. He was suspected of having shot and killed a New York distributor, who had been three weeks late in settling a debt to the Movement.

Dominic returned the file. 'Does this mean that the Department wants me back?'

'Not quite,' Martin said. 'This is a oncer. We're helping

Lew – if it works.' He shrugged. 'I want you back, Dominic.'

'Has it occurred to you fellers that I am presently gainfully employed?'

'I spoke to your gainful employer last night. For the sake of Queen, Country and Lew Carmody, he is prepared to release you indefinitely, on full pay. That's provided you want to do the job.'

'Very noble,' Dominic said. 'What do I have to do?'

'Nothing too audacious,' Martin said. 'We'd like you to get on the first available flight to Switzerland and check the books of the bank.'

'That's all?' Dominic asked. 'Just like that?'

'That's it,' Carmody said.

'You've forgotten something. The bank belongs to Charles Edgar. He isn't going to let me get into his bank on a Sunday, let alone go through his books.'

'Right now,' Martin said, 'Mr Edgar is being interviewed by two very persuasive gentlemen from Her Majesty's Treasury. By the time they're finished, Edgar will even let you count his grandmother's grey hairs.'

Dominic raised the coffee cup to his lips, then realized the coffee was cold. He walked over to the cooker and poured himself a fresh cup. 'You think of everything, don't you, Martin,' he said over his shoulder. 'You've become a right Mister Fixit.'

'All part of the job, dear boy, all part of the job.'

Dominic came back and stood looking at both of them. 'How much?' he asked.

Martin and Carmody looked at each other. 'How much what?' Carmody asked.

'Henry Nash. Bees and honey.' Dominic rubbed his thumb and middle finger together.

'Oh,' Martin said. 'You mean money. Your firm is releasing you on full pay, dear chap.'

'No need for you lot to make a profit out of that, though.'

Martin grinned. 'The usual, then?'

'Twice that,' Dominic said. 'In Swiss francs.'

'Twice is steep,' Martin said.

'Twice is inflation.'

Martin said, 'Rubbish. We'll go elsewhere.'

'Twice is fine,' Carmody said. 'In US dollars.'

Dominic held out his hand. 'We've got a deal.' He reached over to the cupboard and stuck the gun into his waistband.

'Dominic . . .' Martin said. 'No guns.'

Dominic looked from Martin to Lew. 'What the hell do you mean, no guns? You haven't picked me because I'm an accountant. You picked me because I am the only one who can understand the bank's books and deal with Midas. If Midas are who you say they are, there will be shooting.'

'I'll take care of the shooting,' Carmody said. 'I'll take care of all the back-up information, all the expenses, all the body-clearing. I'll take care of everything, except the bank.'

'Are we travelling together then?'

'No, but I'll be around.'

'How do I make contact?'

'I'll find you.'

'What happens if I need you?'

'I'll know about that before you do, I promise.'

'I don't like it,' Dominic said. 'But for twice the usual and a crack at the Movement, I'll do it.'

CHAPTER FIVE

Dominic Cain sat very erect in the window seat of the British Airways Trident and stared out of the window. The flight was not full and he had a whole row of seats to himself. The captain announced that they were flying at 28,000 feet and approaching the French coast. In a few minutes, those passengers on the right-hand side of the aircraft would be able to see Paris. Dominic, seated on the left, stared at the ragged cottonwool clouds and thought about his sister.

Sarah had died in a warm bath, the blood from her slashed wrists swirling gently into the water, feeling nothing except lassitude. Though she'd been a tall girl, she'd weighed barely six stone when she died, her arms riddled with injection scars, unable to kick the habit or willing to live without it.

She'd been twenty-two, in her final year at university. The last time Dominic had seen her, she'd been in the secretive phase and he had suspected nothing. They had spent a week in the Lake District and talked about James and Lawrence and Proust, about Mozart and jazz, and she had promised to come and stay with him in Beirut as soon as she'd sat her examinations. Then, she had said, she wanted very much to begin her first novel.

Dominic's involvement with the Movement had begun then. The Movement was a group of men in their late twenties, with middle-class backgrounds, revolutionary ideals, and access to the dope markets of the world. Dominic didn't give a stuff for their ideals. He'd learned a long while back that politics was a power game, and whenever he faced a man who claimed he was struggling for a better world, he invariably asked, 'Better for *whom*, brother?'

After Sarah's death, Dominic had not returned to Beirut. He'd resigned from the finance division of the oil company, turned in his part-time job with the Department. For three months he'd moved around south-east England, searching. He made contact with the ring of puerile pushers who supplied the students. He dealt in a small way, made it known that he had access to supply and means of shipment, that he too wanted to change the world. When the Movement offered him work, he took it eagerly. And when he had enough evidence, when he knew that Sarah had been introduced to the habit by an older student called Gavin Thirstone, he went to Martin Pelham and offered him his knowledge and his services.

For two years, they had hunted the Movement. They hit their supplies, their laboratories, their couriers. They worked in a small unit, pooling information and personnel with Carmody's group. The end had come that day in Chagny, two years ago.

Dominic remembered Martin walking up to the door of the farmhouse as if to palaver, remembered hearing the heavy bark of the Sturm-Ruger Blackhawk as the .44 Magnum smashed Martin's hip. He remembered what had happened afterwards, too; there had been no pleasure in the killing of Gavin Thirstone, because there had been no time to tell Thirstone why.

The Department had retired him after Chagny. Arrests were easier to explain than corpses and the police of more than one country had been involved. And afterwards, though Dominic lacked neither for work nor money, he had been left with a curious emptiness. Not the emptiness of revenge satisfied, but of a need unfulfilled. Dominic had known for two years that he was as addicted to the hunt as Sarah had once been to heroin.

'A drink before lunch, sir?'

Dominic turned and looked flat-eyed at the stewardess.

'Coffee,' Dominic said. 'Now.'

She brought it straightaway. Women frequently mistook the expressionlessness of his eyes for passion.

Europcar had a Renault 5 waiting for him in Zurich. The drive to Lugano was mainly autoroute, skirting lake and mountain and the breathtaking scenery of the Valley of the Russ. Traffic was light, travelling well within the oil-embargo-influenced speed limit of 130kph. Dominic drove easily, thinking that Chagny had changed Martin too, physically and mentally. Martin was no longer easy to be with. He inflicted you with his infirmity. He laughed less easily these days and his attitude to life was no longer casual. He seemed committed to something that made him less approachable, as if pain had brought not compassion but bitterness. Dominic recalled that they hadn't seen much of each other after Chagny. Dominic's enforced retirement had been an embarrassment, and they had been both concerned about revenge. Perhaps that was a pity, Dominic thought, because he had always liked Martin.

He'd liked Edgar too, when they'd met earlier that day – a dapper, alert man, smaller than Dominic had expected from the newspaper photographs. He had been precise and aggressively charming, accepting interference in his business by government busybodies with resigned humour. He'd known of the bank's loss for twenty-four hours and admitted freely that anything in excess of twelve million pounds was more than they could sustain. The staff would be working in the bank all that Sunday, and Dominic was to meet with Herr Alfred Doppler, the titular head of the bank, and Brian Keith, his assistant. Doppler, Edgar said, was pedantic, boring and very Swiss. Keith was the person Dominic should relate to. He would do anything to help Dominic if it would also help Edgar. He gave Dominic a letter appointing him his personal representative, and inviting anyone who may be concerned to give Dominic all necessary cooperation. Edgar made one condition however. On all financial matters Dominic was to report to him first. He treated Midas as a joke. 'If you find him,' Edgar had said, 'bring me his head on a platter of gold.'

Dominic decided to miss out on the scenery in order to save time, and drove through the St Gotthard Tunnel instead of over the Pass. He reached Lugano about five in the evening, glimpsing the lake as he breasted the Monte Ceneri, feeling the heat as he drove down the mountain.

Lugano was situated in the central bay of the lake, Italianesque buildings crowding the shore and the gentle hills above. The Riva beside the lake was clogged with traffic and Dominic checked into the Splendide-Royal before driving to the Piazza della Riforma and the bank.

Brian Keith greeted him warmly. He was a burly Scot with a florid complexion and thinning, sandy hair. He was in his late thirties, and had worked with Edgar for six years. The bank was in good shape, he said. He still felt it was all some ghastly mistake.

Doppler was less cordial. A narrow, formal man in his late fifties, with neatly parted grey hair and square-lensed rimless glasses. Despite the fact that he had been working all day, he still wore a dark suit, and he made it quite clear that Dominic's presence was not only an imposition but an insult.

Keith defused the situation rapidly. There was a lot of work to do, he pointed out, and even with the three of them it would take all night.

Dominic sat before the teletypewriter and tapped out, 'PRINT T'. His mouth tasted sour and his shirt was stiff with dried sweat. There was a heaviness around his eyes and a dull ache across his shoulders from sitting stooped for too long. Dominic desperately wanted to stretch, to stretch long and high. Then he wanted to sleep. He cast

36

bleary eyes at the figures in the carriage of the teletype. £34,252,107. Grimly he typed in, 'BYE', and tore off the sheet.

It was five o'clock on the Monday morning. The room was acrid with the smell of Doppler's Schimelpenicks and Keith's Dunhills. Remnants of pizza and bottles of red wine stood on their desks. The atmosphere was smoky and heavy and tired.

Dominic looked from the paper in his hand at Doppler, who had found an all-night session exhausting enough to force him to remove his jacket and roll up his sleeves, revealing braces and hairless forearms. Doppler had made no effort to hide his resentment of Dominic and now he stood there glowering, with his hands on his hips and a cigar stuck between his teeth, his square-lensed glasses glinting in the lamplight like pieces of ice. Across the room from them, Brian Keith was slumped across his desk, red-veined blue eyes staring doggedly at Dominic, a patch of blond stubble covering his chin and his sandy hair hanging in tousled streaks across his forehead.

Dominic cleared his throat. 'The figures are correct,' he announced, with a kind of regret. 'The bank has lost over a billion Swiss francs, approximately thirty-four million pounds sterling.'

Doppler gave a harsh laugh. 'So we were right,' he said, pleased to have proved his point. He'd never understood why Edgar had chosen to send his own accountant to Lugano. It was almost as if Edgar didn't trust Doppler or the Swiss.

'Now we *know* you were right,' Dominic said dully, too tired to argue, hoping Doppler would see the subtlety of that.

Doppler coughed into his handkerchief. 'Tomorrow we talk to the Banking Commission and appoint a Receiver.'

Dominic looked across the room at Keith, saw him shake his head slowly, and said, 'No.'

'But we have not the money to pay these debts.'

Dominic was reminded that he was in a land where financial integrity was paramount, and financial morality clearly defined.

Brian Keith said, 'The decision to liquidate must come from London.' He looked at Dominic. 'Will you talk to Charles or shall I?'

'I'll do that,' Dominic said. 'He'll be expecting me to call him anyway.' He leaned back in his chair and looked at both men. 'The losses are all on foreign exchange. How come this dealer, Marc Landi, speculated so heavily on a rise in sterling?'

'On the principle, I suppose, that what goes down must come up,' Keith replied. 'Sorry. That was a bad joke. The foreign-exchange section was Marc's responsibility. He made the decisions.'

'But didn't anyone check the daily summaries? Didn't you see we were going short on the Swiss franc and the dollar?'

'I pointed it out to him on two occasions,' Doppler said self-righteously. 'He explained that the Swiss franc was overvalued and the dollar was due for another fall because of the elections.'

'And you okayed it?'

'It was not my responsibility.'

Dominic reflected that Landi's theories had had a glimmering of sense, but the timing had been horrendously out. The phone shrilled in the momentary silence. Keith picked it up and lolled his head towards Dominic.

'It's for you,' Keith said. 'Someone called Carmody.'

For the barest instant, Dominic hesitated. Then he said, 'Don't know anyone called Carmody,' and turned to Doppler. 'Who gave Landi authority to deal forward?'

'Charles Edgar.'

'Without limit?'

'The limits were made by Mr Edgar.'

38

'Have you evidence of this?'

'Only my own memoranda.'

'Nothing from Edgar?'

'No.'

Keith smiled and said, 'You don't know Charles very well. He hates putting anything in writing. He's the original phone freak.'

'And what about you, Brian? Did you check what Marc told you with Edgar?'

'I had no reason to. Foreign exchange was Marc's baby.' He hesitated as if searching for the right phrase. 'Charles was high on foreign exchange. He liked the element of gambling in it and rationalized it as a hedge against devaluation of his sterling assets. He and Marc were like this.' Keith held up two crossed fingers.

A statement of fact, Dominic wondered, or jealousy? Think over it later, he told himself. He was too tired to think clearly now and he was anxious to get back to the hotel to see what Carmody wanted. Perhaps it had been a mistake to have denied knowledge of Carmody. His reflexes were sluggish with disuse and fatigue, and denial came easier than affirmation. 'Let's get together at nine,' he said and stuffed his report into his briefcase. 'Could you make sure that Landi is here then?'

Keith looked shocked. In a low voice he said, 'That won't be possible.'

'Why not?'

'He's dead. He was killed in a car accident last – on Saturday night. Herr Doppler identified the body.'

'Yes, yes, I did. It was most sickly. He was driving back fast from Menaggio when the auto flew from the road.'

'That was very unfortunate,' Dominic said, feeling a shiver run through him, as if someone had walked over his grave.

CHAPTER SIX

Outside, the Piazza della Riforma was covered with silvery-grey pre-dawn shadow. Empty tables and chairs stood in front of the pavement cafés, and ash-white neon indicated the presence of the Union Banque Suisse and half a dozen other banks, their lighted windows showing listings of Friday's stock market prices and foreign exchange rates. To the left of the Banco Lattoria d'Lugano was a cluster of motor cycles – Nortons, BMWs, Triumphs – parked beside a black maria and an illuminated sign saying *Polizia*. Across the square, there was a car, a huge black Mercedes, with its parking lights on. Dominic thought nothing of it as he climbed into his hired Renault and drove quietly onto the Riva Caccia that bordered the lake, and headed towards the Hotel Splendide-Royal.

Landi had been careless – worse than that, reckless – but so far Dominic had found no trace of fraud, unless you could say that Landi's death itself had been fraudulent. Suicide was the ultimate sin. He'd learnt that in the Catholic school at which he had been boarded. Oh yes, he knew all about the cheating of life and the final betrayal of hope. The question was, however, had Landi committed suicide, or had he been murdered? Neither Keith nor Doppler had seemed overly surprised at the accident. Maybe Landi had had a reputation for driving too fast, perhaps even for drinking too much, both not uncommon vices in the young. But what made him think Landi was young? Keith's empathy or Doppler's sense of retribution?

Dominic parked on the hill leading up to the marvellous Romanesque pile of the hotel and went through the magnificent deserted lobby to his room. He'd taken a small single on the first floor, a long, narrow room with a marble-floored entrance, a baby chandelier, a Giradoux print, and a tiny balcony with a view over the Riva Caccia and the lake. He dropped his briefcase on the floor, took off his jacket, and flung open the french doors that led to the balcony. The lake gleamed dark and silent and the mountains beyond were pin-pricked with light. A cross kept flashing on and off through the light dawn mist.

If he called Edgar now, he could get a couple of hours sleep before returning to the bank. He poured out a shot of duty-free Chivas, took the notes out of his briefcase and spread them on the bed.

At that hour he got London straightaway. Edgar's voice was clear and crisp, sounding as if he were in the next room and very wide awake. Dominic gave him the exact figure of the loss, in Swiss francs and in sterling. There was a moment's silence on the line while Edgar assimilated the information. 'That's more than I thought,' he said at last, 'but that isn't your problem.'

'Doppler wants to appoint a Receiver.'

'You are to stop him doing that. Tell him it is my direct order.' Another pause. Then: 'How much time have we got before we have to make the loss public knowledge?'

'I'd say about a week.'

'Fine. That gives me enough time. I'm owed some favours and I think the Bank of England will support me. They're going to like losing thirty-four million in sterling as little as I do. Do you know the cash position? Can we meet our normal requirements till Friday?'

'Brian Keith thought so.'

'Good. That's very good. The main thing, Dominic, and I would like you to impress this upon Brian and especially upon Doppler, is that there must be no panic. No panic and absolutely no publicity. If people know we're in trouble not only will we get screwed in the foreign-exchange markets, but it could start a run on the bank and no one will or can help us then.'

'I understand,' Dominic said.

'Call me if there are any other problems. Now you'd better get some sleep. You've done a grand job, Dominic. Thank you.'

Dominic replaced the receiver and put his notes away in the briefcase. The phone began to ring again. He picked it up thinking Edgar must have remembered something else.

'Dominic, this is Lew.'

'Hi, Lew. Where are you?'

'I'm in a phone box near your hotel.'

Dominic remembered the phone boxes. Two brightly lit columns on the opposite side to the lake, standing in front of a concrete abutment, about a hundred yards from the hotel on the way into town.

'You've got to get back to London, Dominic. They know about you. Cormack told me they want you out. Morrie Ellis—'

Dominic heard the explosions through the open french windows – sharp, separate cracks like, but not identical to, a car's backfire. At the same time he heard Carmody's scream over the wire, a single expelled 'ah' which thickened into a rich gurgle. Then the solid thud of something heavy falling, followed by the sinister rhythmic knocking of the phone as it swung against the sides of the call box.

Dominic slammed down the receiver, hearing as he did so the sound of a car accelerating hard along the road below, in the direction of Morcote. He raced out of the room, along the corridor, down the stairs, across the lobby and along the gravel drive that led to the road.

Traffic lights winked from red to green in derisory silence. No moving traffic, the only cars parked. He began to run along the pavement towards the phone boxes, moving with the staccato, high-kneed stride of a sprinter, feeling his clothes stretching and snapping against his body and the air rushing in and out of his lungs, hearing the movement of his swinging hands and pounding feet as he sped

43

towards the yellow rectangles of light that spilled across the pavement like congealing wax.

The first phone box was empty. Carmody was in the second. His body had twisted backwards from the velocity of the bullets, and his face had smashed through the glass pane of the door and now stared eerily out into the street, blood still trickling in lazy, slow drops from his face onto the pavement. They had got him twice, in the spine and in the back of the neck. He had died quickly.

Dominic reached past the blood-stained face and felt under Carmody's coat. Carmody hadn't been carrying a gun. Then, with a sensation that bordered on guilt, he stood up and looked both ways along the street. It was empty and he felt his body tremble.

He stepped back and looked for the last time at Carmody's face, square and bloodied, the mouth hanging open in death. 'Goodbye, Lew,' he muttered and turned and walked quickly back to the hotel.

He had to get control, he told himself; he was too slow, too automatic. He should never have run out into the street like that. If they had seen him come, they could have picked him off like a duck in a shooting gallery. No, he had to get control, he had to freeze his nerve and his emotion and get back into the game again.

Despite his resolve, Dominic was still shocked, still groggy with lack of sleep. So, when he entered his room, he only half glimpsed the figure standing in his bathroom doorway. He was starting to move sideways, drawing his palm into a fist, opening his mouth to cry out when the sap caught him on the side of the head and he felt his knees snap like worn elastic. Then the marble flooring was pressing against his cheek and the last thing Domonic remembered was a feeling of mild surprise that the marble was not at all cold.

CHAPTER SEVEN

There was bile in his mouth and the smell of vomit in his nostrils. His head felt as if it had been trapped between the pressure plates of a metal crusher. There was a tender lump behind his left ear, a lethargy in his legs, an all-consuming nausea that made him want to curl up and die.

Dominic came out of the bathroom, blinked painfully at the day and collapsed on the bed. His watch said it was twenty past eight. He'd been unconscious for nearly two hours. Very gently he touched the lump behind his ear as if probing fingers could detect a hairline fracture or a depression of the cranium. He remembered he knew nothing about the effects of concussion.

His passport was where he had left it, in the drawer of the bedside table. His wallet, stuffed with currency and travellers cheques, was still in his trousers pocket. So what had the intruder been after? He focused his gaze on the Giradoux print, on the table and dresser, on the loose change lying on the chest of drawers, on the air ticket and library book on the bedside table. Everything was there. Everything was normal. Only his briefcase was missing.

He lay back on the bed and decided there was no great loss in that. The briefcase was old, the papers in it were only to do with the bank's accounts. If anything, they would prove that he was what he was supposed to be. Besides, assuming the intruder was a representative of Midas, the information in the briefcase would hardly be news to them. If they were sophisticated enough to have defrauded the bank, they would expect the bank to be in serious financial difficulties by now. His papers would confirm their expectations, and he could see no disadvantage in that.

But why had they not killed him? They'd killed Carmody easily enough. Were the papers more important than he'd thought they were, or was this simply their belief?

He thought for a while about Carmody. Carmody had been a professional, fully aware of the risks of his occupation and the kind of end he was likely to have. Whatever else he did, Dominic determined that he would not get emotional about the manner of Carmody's dying. Being affected by that death could only hinder him, perhaps even help to cause his own death. He had to think of Lew as a casualty, as meaningless as a unit in the figures of road deaths. It was the only way he could act with decision and clarity, and it was only by acting with decision and clarity that he could hope to find Midas.

He slipped off the bed and sat cross-legged on the floor, placing his feet on opposite thighs, forcing his spine erect. Staring at the light through the french doors he began to breathe slowly, deeply, in and out, in and out, until he felt the tension inside him ease, the pain and the nausea mingle and dissolve in the vision of the candle flame that danced in his mind's eye.

Some time later he stretched one leg out and rested his forehead on his knee. Then, having spent one minute standing on his head, Dominic went into the bathroom and took a cold shower.

Afterwards he felt much better. He was twenty minutes late at the bank and driving there he noticed there were two policemen standing by the phone boxes and that the pavement had been roped off.

Brian Keith was in his office, puffy-eyed but freshly suited and shaved. 'Thought you weren't going to make it,' he said, waving Dominic to a chair.

'Me too,' Dominic said. 'I overslept.'

'That means you slept well.' Brian said and Dominic found himself looking for a hidden meaning in Brian's reply.

46

Brian was staring at the lump on his head. 'Looks like you fell out of bed...'

'I was mugged,' Dominic said.

Brian's eyes widened in disbelief.

'Kids,' Dominic said. 'I had to leave the car on the road outside the hotel. They jumped me while I was walking up the drive.'

'Did they take anything?'

'My case,' Dominic said. He fingered the lump on his head. 'I got this when I dived after them and hit a railing.'

'Jesus wept! You mean someone's got your figures? Your report on the bank?'

'They were kids,' Dominic said reassuringly. 'Just kids, not more than fifteen years old. They probably can't read Italian, let alone English.'

Brian reached across the desk for a phone. 'I'd better get the police.'

Dominic moved, his hand streaking out, pinning Brian's palm to the receiver, the rapid movement sending a sharp, rolling wave of pain through his head. 'No,' he said, screwing his eyes shut against the pain. 'No police.'

'We've got to get that briefcase back,' Brian said tersely.

'The police have a hundred other things to do, and the briefcase contained papers, not diamonds. They won't get it back. Snatches like this happen every day.'

'Snatches like this don't happen every day in Lugano. This isn't Rome or Milan, you know.'

'In any case, no police.' Dominic released Brian's hand and told him of his conversation with Edgar. No publicity. No police. No reports to the Banking Commission. No appointment of a Receiver. Within twenty-four hours, Edgar and the Bank of England would have alleviated the bank's crisis.

Brian looked at him suspiciously. 'If those are Charles's instructions, someone had better talk to Doppler.'

'You or me?' Dominic asked.

Brian said, 'It would be better coming from me. Doppler feels you're an outsider.' He grinned. 'Don't get me wrong – he thinks I'm an outsider too, and I've been here three years.'

'Your pleasure,' Dominic said deciding Brian was all right. 'What I'd like to do today is analyse Marc's accounts.'

'That's a hell of a long job. What do you expect to find?'

'Where the money went. Foreign exchange is a one-to-one transaction. That means that one person cannot make a profit without someone else making a loss.'

'In other words, capitalism.'

'No. Capitalism couldn't survive on that basis. Most people's profits aren't other people's losses. It's only when you get close to gambling that this happens.'

'Sorry I spoke,' Brian said. 'Forget it.'

Dominic wondered if Brian was being a little too self-effacing. 'As Marc's deals were one-to-one, and we know the bank has lost thirty-four million pounds, someone somewhere has made thirty-four million pounds. I want to find out who.'

'I can tell you that. The winners are other banks, and some of our customers.'

'I still want to find out exactly who and how much.'

Brian shrugged. 'Go ahead,' he said. 'You'll still be here tomorrow morning.'

'I'll need two hours,' Dominic said, 'if I can use the computer and have someone to help me.'

'Help is no problem,' Brian said. 'But Doppler is going to mouth horrid Swiss incantations about your using the computer. He's trying to get out a set of accounts for presentation to the Board, and he feels it morally wrong to use more computer time than is absolutely necessary when there is some doubt as to whether we can pay for it.'

'I'd rate this as necessary time.'

'Only if you win. If you lose—'

'He who fails is a bandit, he who succeeds is a king. That's an old Chinese saying.'

'Pre-Mao I hope. Doppler wouldn't like you feeding quotations from the Little Red Book to his computer.'

Dominic said, 'Talking about Maoism, tell me about Marc.'

'Why? Do you think there's anything funny about his death?'

'Not funny. Inconvenient. Tell me about him. What was he like?'

'To tell you the truth, I hardly knew him. The Swiss are a strange people. They spend all day working at the next desk to you, but afterwards, forget it.'

'Would you want to play with a Swiss?' Dominic smiled and asked, 'Landi – that's not a Swiss name?'

'Marc's father was Italian, born in Ticino. In other words, Italo–Swiss. In other words Swiss first and Italian afterwards. Like this town. A heap of sterilized pizza.'

'The lake's still polluted,' Dominic said.

'Oh, you know what I mean. I didn't see much of Marc during working hours. Occasionally we'd have coffee across the road, and even less occasionally, lunch. He was a bachelor, you see. Ate out a lot.'

'No loving mama cooking platefuls of carbonara?'

'If there was, he certainly kept her under wraps.'

'How old?'

'Pardon?'

'How old was Marc?'

'Thirty. He'd been four years at the bank.'

'Dealing is a pressurized occupation. How did he react to that?'

'Booze, birds and balling. Sorry, I was joking. I don't know. He used to drink a lot of coffee and he had a reputation for driving fast. He had one of those flash sports car things that keeps your bum six inches from the ground.'

'Was that the one he crashed?'

'I would imagine so. But Dominic, seriously, I think you're way off beam. Marc's accident is a coincidence.'

'Any money problems?'

Brian reached into his desk and pulled out a sheaf of papers. 'I have his bank statements here. Look for yourself.'

Dominic did. Marc Landi had been on a salary of 150,000 francs a year. His salary was credited automatically and there were few bankings of any other sort. He drew 500 francs a week in cash, paid 2,000 francs a month in rent, and had saved 102,214 francs, which he had divided equally between a deposit account and an investment in an unit trust run by the bank. He seemed to pay his bills on the same day each month and he made an annual donation of 2,000 francs to the Swiss equivalent of Doctor Barnardo's Homes. The character behind the bank account appeared conservative, cautious, honest, as if one could expect a Swiss banker to be anything else. But then, Dominic thought, if Marc had been on the fiddle, one wouldn't expect him to bank the proceeds with the Banco Lattoria.

CHAPTER EIGHT

Brian arranged for Dominic to use Marc's office and for someone who had worked with Marc to help him. The office was a large room in the basement, empty now, as the bank was using the excuse of Marc's death to stop further dealing in foreign currency. Such transactions as had to be made were being carried out by Doppler, in his suite on the first floor. With its shrouded typewriter and computer terminal, with the duplicated array of switches and lights for the direct telephone lines idle, the room already had an air of abandonment. Dominic walked straight across to an empty desk at the rear of the room, which must have been Marc's.

Dominic sat down at the desk, rested his elbows on the green metal top. There were two drawers, both unlocked. In one were pencils and biros, stationery, erasers and a pencil sharpener, all neatly arranged. Marc Landi had been an organized man. In the other drawer, an opened carton of menthol-filtered St Moritz, spare flints and lighter fuel, a box of Kleenex and a flat rectangular diary. Marc Landi seemed as anonymous as the room he'd occupied. Dominic opened the diary and looked.

Most days were blank with only the occasional lunch appointment or a note of a bank meeting. The only item of significance was that on the day Landi died he had an appointment to see Gianni Siccoli. Dominic remembered that it was Siccoli who'd sent Duval with the money for Landi. Had Landi gone to complain that the money hadn't come?

'What the hell do you think you are doing?'

Dominic twisted up from beside the drawers.

She was standing in the doorway wearing a white blouse tucked into pale blue slacks, twin spots of colour on her browned cheeks. She was trimly built, with long legs, narrow waist, small breasts, a resourceful face surrounded by heavy, shoulder-length brown hair. Large brown eyes, too, and an expression of outrage that could only be Swiss.

'What the hell does it look like I'm doing?' Dominic challenged.

'Whatever it is, it isn't very nice,' she said, walking into the room.

The outrage might be Swiss, but the accent was not. Dominic asked, 'You English?'

'Half,' she said. 'My mother is Swiss. I am Claire Denton. Brian Keith said I was to help you.'

Dominic leaned back in Marc's chair and asked, 'You know anything about foreign exchange?'

'Of course,' she replied curtly. 'I worked with Marc.'

The resentment in her voice was not only a reaction to Dominic's implied male superiority. She was jealous of her competence. 'Then you know the score,' Dominic said. 'You know the bank has lost money on foreign exchange.'

'I knew Marc was losing money. I don't know how much.'

Dominic said, 'I want to analyse the transactions over the last six months.'

'That's possible,' Claire said. 'But it'll take time.' She started to walk towards an alcove in which there were filing cabinets.

'Before we begin,' Dominic said, 'I'd like to talk about Marc.'

Claire kept on walking. 'Brian said you were in a hurry, Mr Cain. And I have a few other things to do for Herr Doppler.'

They began to work and Dominic had to admit she was good. She was fast and accurate, double-checked her own work, even wrote out programmes of her own. She knew how the accounts system was run and which department to get background information from. As they worked, she became a little less reserved, and once, when Dominic showed her a short cut, she looked grateful and told him she had read his book and hoped it would help her with the Banking Institute examinations.

They finished shortly after noon. By then, Dominic was able to see a pattern to the bank's losses. Rounding the sums off and working in sterling because it was the more familiar currency, twenty-two million pounds of the loss was scattered at random amongst other banks, industrial customers and a few long-standing personal accounts that had a history of speculation. Twelve million pounds had gone to three small Liechtenstein-based companies, Intra, Kastel and Sulden. All three had become customers over the last six months and all three had been introduced by Marc.

Dominic picked up the settlement accounts. The accounts of the three anstalts had been settled all right, and paid to the same bank, the Fieldhaus in Zurich.

Claire came round behind him and looked at his figures. 'Thirty-four million pounds,' she said. 'The bank can't stand it.'

'John Charles Edgar thinks it could, with a little help from his friends.'

She raised a quizzical eyebrow. 'They'd better be very good friends.'

'You worried about your job, then?' Dominic wanted to take her mind off the size of the bank's loss, remembering what Edgar had told him about secrecy.

She lit a cigarette. 'No,' she said. 'I leave at the end of this week. My work permit has expired. Though my mother is Swiss, I was born in England. I've spent all my life there.'

The phone rang. Claire picked it up and said, 'Denton.' She listened for a moment, said 'All right,' and put the phone down. 'Herr Doppler wants to see you in Brian Keith's office right away,' she said to Dominic.

'Did Herr Doppler say why?'

'No.' She gave him a small smile. 'You'd better go upstairs and find out for yourself.'

Which Dominic, collecting his papers together, did.

When Dominic had gone, Claire began to tidy up the room. So that was Dominic Cain, she thought, snooper, accountant, author of text books and something else besides. She knew something more about Cain that no one else in the bank knew, and because of that knowledge she wondered what Dominic Cain was doing at the Banco Lattoria, masquerading as an auditor.

The phone rang. Clicking her tongue with annoyance, she picked it up.

'Miss Denton, this is Interstellar Textiles.'

Claire recognized the voice with its gruff New York accent. It belonged to Tony de Marco, known to his friends as Turk, one of the signatories to the Interstellar Textiles account. Interstellar Textiles was Claire's special customer. Tom Haden, in London, had made her responsible for the account. All she had to do was ensure that any instructions that were given were carried out speedily and efficiently. For that, Interstellar paid her two hundred and fifty Swiss francs a month, and though she sometimes worried as to whether that was right, she knew the payment did not conflict with the interests of the bank.

'Hello, Mr de Marco,' she said, reaching for a pad and clicking impatiently at her pen. 'What can I do for you?'

'How's the bank, Miss Denton?'

Claire frowned. Interstellar did not usually waste time with small talk. 'The bank's fine,' she said.

'Miss Denton, I have some bad news for you. Lew Carmody was killed last night.'

Lew Carmody was another signatory to the account. 'Killed! I'm sorry—'

'We suspect that it might have something to do with

54

our business. Has there been anyone inquiring about our accounts?'

'No,' Claire said. 'No. Even if someone did, you know we couldn't tell them anything.'

'Anybody asking questions of any kind?'

Claire hesitated. 'Well ... It's nothing to do with Interstellar ... But we're having some kind of an audit. They've sent someone from London.'

'Just one person, Miss Denton?'

'Yes, an accountant called Dominic Cain.'

'Describe him, please.'

'Well, he's tall, English, about twenty-eight or so, good-looking. He's got strange eyes.'

'Has he been investigating our account?'

'No,' Claire said. 'No.'

'That's good,' de Marco said. 'We'd appreciate it if you keep us informed. We'd appreciate that very much.'

The phone went dead in her ear.

Dominic went up to the first floor, to Brian Keith's office. The door was ajar. He knocked cursorily, went in, and stopped, as if he'd walked into a wall.

Brian and Doppler were standing on either side of the desk. On the centre of the desk stood Dominic's scuffed and battered briefcase.

'This was handed to the police a few minutes ago,' Brian said.

'Oh good.' Dominic picked it up, his hand jerking as his tensed muscles, expecting a certain weight, encountered only lightness. 'It's empty,' Dominic said.

'Bloody right, it's empty!'

Beside Brian, Doppler opened an early edition of an afternoon paper, turned it round on the desk so that Dominic could read the inch-high headlines. 'FOREIGN EXCHANGE SPECULATION HITS LUGANO BANK.'

Under photographs of the bank and John Charles Edgar was a smudged reproduction of the first page of Dominic's report.

'You've screwed it up,' Brian said fiercely. 'You've screwed it up real good. We've had the Federal Banking Commission on to us already, the Bank of England and Charles Edgar.'

'We will have to declare bankruptcy,' Doppler announced pompously.

'You've been bloody careless,' Brian Keith said tersely. 'Too bloody careless and too bloody negligent. Those papers should have stayed in the bank, not carried about Lugano.'

'I only took them back to my hotel,' Dominic protested.

'Kids!' Brian snorted. 'Kids who probably couldn't read Italian, let alone English. I'm sorry, Dominic. I've spoken with Charles. We feel that you cannot do any more good here. Your appointment is terminated, as of now. You will leave the bank immediately.'

Dominic started to explain, then stopped short. 'I'm sorry,' he said.

Brian turned away and looked out of the window, his shoulders slumped. Doppler walked across the room and held the door open.

Dominic left.

CHAPTER NINE

Dominic raced back to the hotel. He'd postponed telling Martin about Lew's death until he'd established the connection with Landi. But he had to call Martin now. He had to get help and he had to get a gun.

He left the car in the driveway and ran into the lobby of the hotel and demanded his key.

'Signor Cain,' the clerk said in a loud voice, resplendent in his blue uniform with gold piping. '*Numero cento sei.*'

Dominic snatched the key and raced to the lift, jabbed at the button urgently. The door slid back. He stepped in, aware of a big, soft-fleshed man padding after him. The door slammed shut. The lift began to move. His companion kept staring at him.

He was a huge man, with a large head covered with spiky brown stubble, two chins that rested on his breastbone, and a pair of sleepy blue eyes that looked as if they doubted the very principles of hydraulics that were moving them so smoothly upwards. He introduced himself as Chief Inspector Wolweber of the Lugano *Kriminalpolizei*. He promised to be most grateful if Mr Cain would spare him a few moments in the privacy of his own room.

There was no help for it. Dominic led him up the corridor, opened the door, let him into the room. The bed had been made, the windows onto the balcony left open. A fresh breeze blew in from the lake.

Wolweber perched himself on the end of the bed and said, 'I think you know one American gentleman called Lewis Carmody.' His tone was direct, flat, giving no indication of whether it was a statement or a question.

Dominic felt a hot flush of shock and instant fear. 'No,' Dominic said.

Wolweber shook his head and made a sucking noise, through his teeth. 'Mr Carmody is dead. He was shot in a telephone box—' Wolweber pointed – 'over there.'

'Really? I saw two policemen standing near those phone boxes when I was coming – What has this to do with me?' Dominic leant against the writing table and wondered if he'd got the right mixture of innocence and outrage.

'There was a notebook in – on Mr Carmody. It had your initials, DC, the telephone number of the hotel, and *zimmer* number 106. This room.'

'Must be a coincidence,' Domonic said with what he hoped was conviction.

'I find coincidence very interesting. Do you?' Wolweber moved uneasily on the bed, as if dubious that it would bear his weight.

A heavy cloud of silence descended over the room. Dominic determined not to break it. He breathed in softly and just as softly breathed out, mentally counting five on the inhalation, five on the exhalation. It was midly soothing.

'You still say you do not know this Mr Carmody?'

'I do not know Carmody.'

'Where were you last night?'

'I was at the Banco Lattoria till about five o'clock this morning. Mr Doppler and Mr Keith will confirm that.'

Wolweber nodded slowly. 'At the Banco Lattoria,' he repeated. 'You are what, Mr Cain, to work all night in a bank?'

'I am an accountant. I arrived yesterday from London, to work with the bank.' Hopefully Wolweber knew that, where banks were concerned, even Chief Inspectors of the *Kriminalpolizei* should tread warily.

'And after you left the bank, what did you do?'

'I came back here and slept. I was alone' – as if that made the lie more convincing.

'Mr Carmody was shot—' again the hand pointed out

of the window – 'over there. You did not hear any . . . gunshots?'

'I was sleeping very deeply.'

'And you did not go out of the hotel after you came back?'

'Come off it! Even if I did, why would I go out and shoot a complete stranger?'

'Why indeed,' Wolweber said mournfully. 'That is what I have to find out. So you heard nothing, you saw nothing, and you came back here from the bank and slept. Also you do not know Mr Carmody.'

'That's it. In a nutshell.'

Wolweber glared at Dominic. 'This is a serious matter. A person has been killed. Here in Lugano we are not used to murder.'

Here in Lugano they weren't even used to dropping Kleenex on the street, but Dominic didn't say anything about that.

Wolweber sighed heavily. 'I see they have returned your briefcase,' he said. 'It was left at the police station this morning. We returned it to the bank.'

'And the bank returned it to me. Thank you very much.'

'But there is bad news about the bank, is that not right?'

'Rumours,' Dominic said unconvincingly. 'Just rumours.'

'Tell me about this . . . Mr Carmody. What was he doing in Lugano?'

'I've told you. I didn't know the man.'

Wolweber twisted on the bed and rested a beefy hand on the headboard. 'You had a telephone call this morning. From whom was that?'

'Mr Edgar. The owner of the bank.'

'And what did you talk about?'

'The bank.'

'And what about the bank?'

'The bank's business.'

'And then you went out of the hotel?' Wolweber had obviously been talking to the staff.

'I wanted some fresh air.'

Wolweber shook his head uncomprehendingly. 'But you had just come in and when you went out you were running.'

Dominic looked crestfallen. He stared down at his feet and said, 'You are right. I did hear what sounded like gunshots. So I went out, but I saw nothing. Please understand, I cannot afford to be involved. This matter of the briefcase has already cost me my job.'

'I am sorry,' Wolweber said. 'Of course I understand. You are a stranger and do not want to be involved in shootings in Lugano. What was this Mr Carmody doing in Lugano?'

'I've told you, I don't know.'

'Very interesting,' Wolweber said. 'An American dies, an Englishman runs out of his hotel and loses his document case and his job.' He stopped and peered keenly at Dominic. 'What happened to your head, Mr Cain?'

'I had a fall,' Dominic said quickly. 'In the bathroom. I slipped on the tiles and hit my head on the bath.'

Wolweber sighed. Quite clearly he did not believe Dominic. 'Before you came, we had no trouble in Lugano,' he said. It was an accusation.

'I'm sorry about that,' Dominic said. 'When does the tourist season start?'

'There are always tourists in Lugano,' Wolweber replied. 'Proper tourists. People who come for holidays.' He sighed again and looked sleepily at Dominic. 'I do not believe you, Mr Cain,' he said, standing and bringing his enormous head in front of Dominic's face. 'I think you are hiding something. So you will please give me your passport, until we have resolved the question of Mr Carmody's death.'

Dominic made a formal protest, but the choice was either that or being arrested. He gave Wolweber the passport.

Wolweber gave him a receipt, turned and walked heavily to the door. 'Stay around, Mr Cain,' he said from the doorway. 'You and I have a lot to talk about.'

Dominic watched him go and breathed a sigh of relief. In his experience, there were two kinds of cops. Those who were dull and stupid and tried to frighten the truth out of you, and those who let your fears work themselves out so that you were compelled to tell the truth. Wolweber was the latter kind. But his temporary freedom at least gave him the opportunity to deal with Midas.

Dominic walked across the room, picked up the phone and called Martin.

'Dominic, what the hell's been happening? I've just heard about Lew, and Edgar's been raising the most damn awful stink—'

Quickly, quietly and lucidly, Dominic told him everything that had happened. When he'd finished, there was a long silence at the other end of the line.

Finally Martin said, 'Dominic, you'd better come back.'

'What the hell for? It's all happening here.'

'With Lew dead and you blown, the operation's finished. It was Lew's operation, and I can't think where we go from here.'

'What about Midas?'

'We'll find another way of getting them.'

'I owe them. I'm going to finish what we started four years ago. I'm staying.'

'But man – they *know* about you.'

'That's why I'm staying,' Dominic said. 'They've got to come and get me. Don't you see, Martin, they've got to make a play.'

'Dominic, I'm ordering you to come back.'

Dominic laughed. 'It's Lew's operation, remember? So you can stuff your orders in a pigeon's hole. All I want from you is a gun.'

'There's no way I can get you that,' Martin said. 'After

the stink that Edgar's created, we have to abandon. You know what the Swiss are like about operations on their territory.'

'I'm still staying,' Dominic said and put down the phone.

Driving to the Italian border before Oria, Dominic tried to analyse why he'd decided to stay. Revenge for Carmody was part of it. He'd liked the man, and didn't think that a lifetime of service to his country should be rewarded by a bullet in the spine and marrow all over a telephone box in Lugano. He didn't like the idea of a network being blown, either. Whatever the operation, they were all on the same side, and the loss in manpower and money was something worth avoiding. There was also the fact that he had been beaten. And something else. He remembered the hillside bungalow and the bullets cascading off the metal shutters, his parents lying at the windows, shooting into the tropical darkness outside. Those people outside had wanted the same things Midas wanted. To destroy, to ravage, to take, to build a society in their own image, a society so powerful and dictatorial that it denied freedom and the human spirit. Those people had hurt him deeply, at the time when he was too weak and too innocent to fight back. Hatred, Dominic thought bitterly, lasts longer than love.

At the border he produced the duplicate passport that Martin knew about and Wolweber didn't and drove through the tiny towns of Mamete and Cima, already aware of Italy, of age and poverty, of old men sitting on stone bridges staring at the lake, of shabbiness. The road twisted high above the lake and just before Porlezza he saw the relics of the accident, a bright yellow streak of metal, crumpled against a tree one hundred feet below him.

The car had been travelling towards Lugano, gone straight on at a corner, slammed through the guardrail and plunged towards the lake, stopped short by the tree. A few elderly men and little boys were looking curiously at the wreck, and a few yards apart from them a young policeman leant against a tree, taking care to see they did not get too close. Dominic stopped the car, got out and walked towards them.

They looked at him with open curiosity, and the policeman moved away from his tree and shooed the onlookers away. A stranger might mean authority. In halting Italian, Dominic explained that he worked for the bank. He showed the policeman Charles Edgar's letter and the impressive letterheading, if not the content, convinced the policeman that he could allow Dominic to look at the car. But quickly.

The car had left a trail of raw earth in its plunge downhill. Travelling at a hundred, hundred and twenty kilometres an hour, it had come down, completely out of control, smashing dead centre into the tree, forcing the engine into the passenger compartment, thrusting the steering column against the flattened roof and folding about itself like an old can. It was difficult to imagine that this had once been someone's pride and joy. Difficult also to recognize that it was the latest model from Lotus, a specialist sports car. Certainly too flash and much too expensive for a conservative Swiss banker.

Dominic could see where they'd had to cut through the roof pillars to take out Landi's body. There were still clots of dried blood on the seats, shattered Triplex glass and snake-like strands of rubber. One front wheel had been collected and placed on top of an earth-stained wing. Dominic looked up at the swathe of the car's passage. There was a circular whorl at the top, as if the car had cavorted round on hitting the soft earth, and then almost a dead straight line to the tree. It seemed to have gouged more earth on the one side than the other. Dominic walked up, looked and came back to examine the wheel resting on the shattered wing.

The wheel had come off from the track-rod end. Not wrenched off, just off. Looking underneath the car, he could see where the bolt had sheared or come away.

He thanked the policeman, walked back to the road and looked along it, towards Menaggio. Brake marks were still there, and the nearside, just where the car had left the road, showed chipping of the road surface. Accident, or murder?

Dominic climbed back into the Renault and drove to Menaggio. Marc's Lotus had lost its steering. When the wheel came off, it had lost its braking, which accounted for the fact that there had been no attempt to avoid the tree. Travelling perhaps a little too quickly, once the track-rod end had sheared nothing in the world could have stopped Marc from hitting that tree.

CHAPTER TEN

Dominic reached Menaggio half an hour later, and found Siccoli's villa quite easily. Everyone in Menaggio knew where Gianni Siccoli lived. It was a splendid place, built during the Italian Renaissance in what had then been countryside and was now the outskirts of the town. The villa was wide and high and impressive, its clean lines overcoming its dignified shabbiness and even the unfriendly effect of being surrounded by high stone walls, barred gates and guards.

The guard refused to let Dominic inside until he'd produced the letters from the bank. After that it was all smiles and friendship. Dominic was shown into a high-ceilinged room with furniture that was genuinely old and at least one picture that looked like an authentic Raphael. Siccoli came in half an hour later. He was a plump, smooth-looking man in his early forties, heavy-jowled and balding, with black, slow eyes, a petulant mouth, an air of being well fed and well satisfied.

'I spend my weekends here to get away from business,' he said, sitting down opposite Dominic, as if to point out that the interview was informal and would not last long. 'The Banco Lattoria knows my habits. I can only assume your visit is important.'

'I believe it is,' Dominic said thinking that Siccoli usually took long weekends. 'Last Saturday afternoon a young American was arrested at a customs post near Arogno. He was carrying five and a half million lire.'

'Did he not know that it is forbidden to take such an amount out of Italy?'

'He did. He said he was paid to smuggle the money to Switzerland for you.'

65

Siccoli's expression did not change. 'Then why have I not been arrested? Why have I not been questioned by the police?'

'You know as well as I do that it would take more than the accusation of a suspected drug smuggler to make the police move against you.'

Siccoli spread his arms in a big shrug. 'So, it's a free country. What business is this of the bank's?'

'We are interested in what that money was to be used for.'

'That is none of the bank's business.' For the first time, Siccoli showed impatience. 'Even if I admit to assisting this American to break Italian currency regulations.'

'You know we have suffered heavy losses in foreign exchange. You also know Mr Landi, formerly in charge of our foreign-exchange department. What did he come to see you about on Saturday night?'

Siccoli was shaken. Paydirt, Dominic thought with elation, and added, 'Or would you like to call your lawyer?'

Siccoli saw the gambit for what it was. He could get angry, he could protest, or he could call his lawyer. Only guilty men called their lawyers when asked what they had been doing the previous Saturday night. 'Landi was here on Saturday,' he said. 'Early in the evening. I believe he was also calling on other people in the neighbourhood. I do not know their names.' Siccoli seemed more relaxed now. 'When I tell you why Landi came to see me, you will understand why he didn't tell me who else he was visiting. Landi offered to make a fortune for me in foreign-exchange speculation.'

'After his dealing had cost the bank a fortune?'

'That was exactly it. The system he used was this. He'd call other dealers and agree to buy or sell foreign currencies. Now, if the transaction resulted in a loss, he'd mark it down as acting on behalf of the bank. If it resulted in a profit, he'd mark it down for a favoured customer. Of course

66

sometimes he allowed the bank to make a profit, and sometimes the bank genuinely did make a profit. Landi suggested we work together and that I give him thirty per cent of my profits. Naturally I refused.'

If Landi had been on thirty per cent of thirty-four million pounds, he had eleven million stashed away somewhere. But, Lotus Elite notwithstanding, Landi's pattern of life hadn't betrayed an extra ten thousand pounds to spend, let alone eleven million. 'Why did you refuse?' Dominic asked.

Siccoli laughed. 'I am too rich,' he said. 'I do not have to steal. Besides, I am also a practical businessman. You do business with a rogue and he ends up stealing from you.'

Dominic stood up. 'Thank you for your help.' he said. 'I apologize for disturbing your weekend.'

'Pleased to have been of assistance,' Siccoli said, and walked Dominic to the door.

At the front door Dominic turned. 'There's one more thing,' he said. 'Do you know of an organization called Midas?'

Siccoli shook his head. 'No,' he said. 'What are they?'

'They are blackmailers and currency smugglers, political guerrillas. They are behind the bank's losses. I also believe that Landi has left a document explaining whom they are blackmailing and why. Pick your friends carefully, Signor Siccoli.'

Dominic hurried down the steps, climbed into his car and drove quickly into Menaggio. He waited by the lake, watching a tourist bus disgorge its occupants. Twenty minutes later he watched as a black Mercedes rushed through the town in the direction of Lugano.

CHAPTER ELEVEN

It would take the Mercedes ten minutes' hard driving to discover that Dominic was not in front of it. Another few minutes of waiting and confusion, of turning round and returning, before the realization that Dominic wasn't behind it either. Dominic grinned and drove off along the road that ran south beside the lake towards Como. Less than thirty kilometres away were the narrow, winding roads across the steep hills of the d'Intelvi, leading to the customs post at Arogno, the route Duval had taken the previous Saturday.

There had been no passengers in the Mercedes. Only Morrie Ellis, a small man with a face that was neither young nor old, heavy sideburns and a dark moustache, his body erect behind the wheel, hands at a rigid quarter to three. Dominic had recognized him from the photograph in Carmody's file. A precise man, undoubtedly, but only one? He must be very good, Dominic thought, if they had sent him alone. Well, he thought, Ellis would have to find him first.

The appearance of the Mercedes and the solitary hit man proved Siccoli's involvement. It was Siccoli's motive that puzzled Dominic. The man had money enough, and influence. So was he committed to some screwy political philosophy, or proving his manhood by vicarious involvement in terror? Or was he simply being blackmailed? It wasn't a problem Dominic could solve now. He did not know Siccoli well enough, did not know whether his parents had loved him or whether he felt guilty about privilege. Dominic settled down to driving, beginning to enjoy hurling the gusty little Renault along the corkscrewing road. At least he now knew what the enemy looked like and that was a small victory.

He reached Lugano two hours later and drove slowly down the Via Caccia, now clogged in both directions with rush-hour traffic. The roadworks near the Piazza della Riforma didn't help much and the city seemed to be full of black Mercs. Mercs parked, Mercs behind him, Mercs coming towards him – but, so far, no black Merc driven by a small erect man with heavy sideburns and a dark tash. He should have got himself a gun first, Dominic thought, remembering how they had shot Carmody, and calming himself with the thought that that had been at five o'clock in the morning, not in the middle of the evening rush hour.

He drove away from the lake, grinding up the hills at the north of the town. Here traffic was somewhat lighter, the streets less crowded. Landi had lived in a new apartment block cut into the hillside and painted pale green, its second floor level with the steeply inclined road. There was an air of smart prosperity about the block, the kind of place where wives used Fiat coupés as shopping cars. Before turning off, Dominic checked his mirror and saw a black Mercedes. But it was much too far away for him to positively identify it.

He parked in the clearly signposted visitors' area, walked across the scrubbed tarmac to the entrance. Apartment 18C was in the first block through the third entrance, up three flights of concrete stairs that twisted round the building so that each level protected the one below from the effects of rain and snow. 18C stood on an open terrace with a view of other apartment blocks and the lake beyond. 19C stood opposite, and the front door of 18C was locked.

But not, as Dominic soon discovered, bolted. The mortice deadlock was unlatched, the door held by a single Yale. Either Marc had left in a hurry on Saturday, or someone had been careless. Dominic stooped before the lock and fumbled with his Diners Card. It fitted snugly into the crevice between the door jamb and the tongue of the lock. Now a little pressure. That's it. The bugger was stiff as a flag pole and his card was creasing about the middle. He pulled the card back, then slid it in deeper and twisted. That was better. A slight click and the lock moved. Dominic pressed his foot against the door. It swung softly open.

He pocketed the card and pushed the door slightly more open, looked into a small lounge which had once been tastefully decorated and undoubtedly been very pleasant. Now the leather seats lay on their sides with their cushions split open, the Kashan carpet stood rolled against a bookshelf, pictures and books lay on the floor with their backs ripped open and spines broken. The place looked as if it had been hit by a tornado; even the curtains had been torn from their hangings. Dominic was still trying to evaluate what had happened when he heard the soft slurp of a footstep behind him, felt the warm kiss of an exhaled breath on the back of his neck. Then the barrel of a small calibre pistol was jammed into his spine, and a voice hissed, 'Go inside, friend. Very quietly.'

Dominic moved, taking one large stride into the room, easing the pressure of the gun against his back, pushing the door wide open with his left arm. Then he whipped sideways. He glimpsed the small man with the dark moustache and sideburns, and he slammed the door against the man's outstretched gun hand. Dominic grabbed the hand above the wrist, pounded his hip against the door, bounced back, threw the weight of his body against the door, locked his other hand about the man's wrist, pushed hard and fast and sharp. The gun exploded, the blast singeing his face, the sound of the explosion in that confined space almost deafening, annihilating the acute crack of bones snapping and the thump of the gun hitting cement.

Dominic opened the door. Ellis stood there white-faced, his eyes screwed up in pain, nursing his shattered hand, his mouth open in a long, soundless scream. He'd never be a gunman again, Dominic thought, and, hearing footsteps behind him, turned. There were two of them, coming out

71

of the room in the back, big and blond, wearing jeans and camouflage jackets, their eyes moving swiftly from Dominic and Ellis to the gun on the floor. Dominic dived. He fell on folded elbows, felt the skin sear as he stretched out an arm and twisted crabbing fingers round the gun barrel. He wrenched the gun round, turning on his side and knew relief as the butt snuggled against his palm.

The boot crashed into his middle without warning, lifted him six inches, folded him in two like a soft pillow. He gasped, pain welling within him, tears streaming from his eyes. His lungs felt as if they had collapsed and were touching each other with the blazing friction of pain, and he told himself he must not let go of the gun. A boot hurtled over his head. There was the sound of feet on cement, voices, the slam of a door. Then Dominic was pushing his back against the wall, trying to sit up, and the room was empty and the only sound was that of his own tortured breathing.

Dominic eased himself upright onto legs that felt like spaghetti, stood bent double, sucking air gratefully, his body covered with clammy sweat, thankful that he could still walk. And grateful that he still had the gun. Bent double, he tottered towards the back of the apartment, gun hand outstretched before him.

He was in a small corridor with a bathroom at the end of it and, on either side, a shut bedroom door and a study. A noise from the study, a faint whimper or the rasp of too rapidly inhaled breath. Dominic stood still, and tried to slow his own breathing. From where he stood he could see the desk with sagging drawers, papers and books strewn about the floor. Slowly he edged beside the doorway. There was someone in there – he was sure of it. Someone standing against the wall by the door.

Dominic straightened, wincing. He concentrated on what he would do next, and when the pain had subsided, moved clumsily into the room, turning on leaden feet, feeling the

72

pain grab him again, remembering to keep the gun up and pointed to where he expected the person to be.

'All right, motherfucker, get your—'

Claire Denton stood helpless against the wall of the study, staring at him in fear and bewilderment. Her arms were raised above her head and her trousers flopped around her ankles. Below the white panties, she had a great pair of legs. Dominic lowered the gun. 'It's only me,' he said. 'Get your hands down and your trousers up,' He leant against the desk, feeling very tired and out of breath.

He watched her dress with a rustle of cloth and a clanking of belt buckles. Good nubile body, he thought; pity they had to meet again like this. She was glaring at him red-faced, with none of the relief appropriate to a damsel rescued from distress.

'What happened to you?' Dominic asked.

After the initial shock and embarrassment, the suppressed hostility was returning. For a moment she wrestled with gratitude and an instinctive dislike, and allowed gratitude to win by a beltnotch. 'I came here to get something I had lent Marc,' she said. 'Then those two louts came in and made me stand like this while they ransacked the place.'

And saved time and rope, Dominic thought; standing like that she wouldn't scream and couldn't run. He wondered what they would have done with her afterwards. Witnesses were always a liability. 'How did you get in?' he asked.

'I have a key,' she replied.

Slam her, Dominic decided, slam her while she's still off balance and before she can think up any clever stories. 'Were you screwing Marc?' he asked.

A slight hesitation, but no embarrassment. 'Yes,' she admitted.

'And what was it you wanted back?'

'Oh . . .' She looked across the room. 'A book.'

She wasn't a very good liar. Dominic glanced about the dishevelled room. Books on banking, Che Guevara and Mao, Keynes and Reich, a murder story by Durenmatt, and *The Greening of America*.

'What book?' he asked.

'I couldn't find it . . . It was a book of poems, by Mac-Neice.'

Unlikely reading for a serious economist like Marc. 'What were the others looking for?'

'I don't know. They ripped everything apart and kept making crude jokes while they did it. It was horrible.'

'Let's look again, shall we,' Dominic said.

The books gave him a new angle on Marc and perhaps there would be something else. Couldn't tell much about the way Marc had kept the apartment, after the mess the men had made. But there was no doubt he liked pictures. There was a whole store of unframed prints, and Marc had liked cars. There was a pile of *Quattroruote* magazines in a strangely undisturbed pile by the window. In the bedroom a photograph taken on holiday, three young men standing outside a forest inn holding steins of beer. Also a wardrobe full of modish and expensive clothes. The hi-fi in the lounge had been smashed but there was a good collection of classical records, mainly Vivaldi and Mozart, also some late Beatles and Deep Purple.

'You haven't found your book?' Dominic asked. She had followed him around the apartment like a guilty conscience, growing more contemptuous and hostile by the second.

'No,' she replied. 'Haven't you found what you're looking for?'

'I'm looking for Marc,' Dominic said. 'I'm trying to find out what he was like.'

'Why? He's dead. Or does your kind never let the dead rest in peace?'

74

'Marc's dead and he wouldn't even know,' Dominic said and added provocatively, 'I'm only doing my job.' He was rewarded by a sharp exhalation of disgust. Before she could launch into her tirade, however, the police siren started, a keening wail from far down the hill.

'That's it,' Dominic said, grabbing her arm. The fighting had disturbed the neighbours and the neighbours had called the police. He'd spent too much time in the apartment already. 'Let's go.'

She wrenched her arm free. 'You go if you want to. I've got nothing to hide from the police.' There was a malicious gleam in her eyes.

Dominic grabbed her shoulder and raised the gun. 'We're going together, my love, even if I've got to stuff this up that sweet little ass of yours.'

She gave him a look that would have frozen an eskimo. 'Bet you'd enjoy it too,' she sneered and allowed him to push her before him to the door. The wailing of the siren became louder as the car neared the top of the hill. Dominic pushed her. She broke free and, turning, kicked him in the ankle. He lifted the gun and then she was past him, running towards the back of the apartment.

'You stupid bitch,' he cried after her. 'There's no way out there.'

But she hadn't been trying to get away. She was in the study, rifling quickly through the stack of prints.

Dominic stood in the doorway and eased back the safety catch, audibly. 'In three seconds you could be dead,' he said quietly.

She looked up at him and he whitened his knuckle across the trigger.

'Come on,' he said. 'Move it.'

She had no way of knowing if he would shoot her or not. She found what she wanted and said, 'I'll come with you. Just let me take this. Marc wanted me to have it as a memento.'

She was still a bad liar, but she was rolling up the print and they were moving through the lounge, onto the terrace. They went down the winding concrete stairway as the police car flashed up the road beside them with an ear-splitting shriek and a flash of blue lighting. They ran down the stairs onto the tarmac and across to the Renault. Dominic clambered into the rear and pressed himself to the floor.

'You drive,' he said, listening to the wild scrubbing of tyres as the police car screeched through the entrance. 'Try anything and I'll blast you. I'm a lot closer to you than they are.'

Claire started the car. 'Drive where?' she asked in a low voice.

'Anywhere. Just get the hell out of here.'

She reversed and turned the car. Dominic sat very still, feeling the sweat break out all over him, hearing the slam of other car doors. She accelerated sharply and turned right. At least, he thought with relief, she was doing what she was told. They were leaving Lugano.

CHAPTER TWELVE

It was absurd, Claire thought, unbelievable! Here she was driving uninsured in Switzerland of all places, while a man lay on the floor of the car and pointed a gun at her back. In Switzerland, land of peace and order, where private property was sancrosanct and neutrality was guaranteed by the Treaty of Paris, she had seen men burst into an apartment and rip it apart. In Switzerland, she had been made to stand facing a wall with her hands in the air and her trousers over her ankles; she had been threatened with guns. Not on television, not in New York. In Lugano, in Switzerland. Incredible!

If she had gone to Marc's apartment during her lunch hour, perhaps nothing would have happened. But Cain's work and Doppler's balances had precluded that. Even though she was leaving, she had worked through lunch, wanting to be remembered favourably. Employers, especially bankers, asked around, and progress for a woman was difficult enough without references that damned with faint praise.

There had been no movement from Dominic Cain since they'd left Lugano. Presumably he was still there, huddled on the floor of the car, cradling his gun. A strange man, Dominic Cain. Such suppressed violence about him. He reminded her of a panther stalking restlessly in a cage. He was so determined, too, the kind of person who would go through or over or underneath an avalanche. She recalled the way he'd come into Marc's study that first time, gun drawn, shouting, ready to kill. Not so the second time. He'd been bluffing, then. Intuition told her that, even though he'd thumbed back the safety catch. She felt there was a rationale to Cain's violence, totally unlike the crudeness of

77

those louts who had ransacked the flat. She felt he wouldn't have hurt her unless he had to, which was a strange conclusion when she knew he'd killed before.

It was ridiculous, Dominic thought, incredible. Chartered accountants wore dark suits and bowler hats, muttered soothing incantations about discounted cash flow and inflation accounting. They didn't crouch between the seats of a tiny car, threaten bank officials with guns, or evade the police. The Institute would be outraged at that. Pulling a gun on a woman, forcing her to break the law, that was the behaviour of a swine and a cad. But then the Institute didn't have to cope with Midas or have gunmen stuffing Lugers against their collective spine. With his knees touching his chin, Dominic reached out and unrolled the print Claire had taken from Marc's apartment.

It was of a medieval engraving 'Melancholia' by Dürer, a cloaked figure seated amongst scattered implements symbolizing the indecision that besets talent. Dürer himself had spent a few years in Italy at the time Michaelangelo was working for Lorenzo the Magnificent. But that didn't explain why Claire had been so anxious to get the print out of Marc's apartment without showing it to the police.

They were travelling smoothly and at speed. Dominic sat up, and saw they were on an autoroute, which meant they were heading north towards Bellinzona and Zurich, or south towards Milan. The light was going rapidly and cars rushed by with headlamps fighting the dusk.

Claire saw his head in the driving mirror and said, 'Ah, the brave Mr Cain arises. You can relax now. There are no big, bad policemen to frighten you.' Humour, her salvation lay in that, and in keeping a clear head. They couldn't drive on forever, and she had to get out of this ludicrous situation somehow. Not with a melodramatic swerve across the autoroute with lights and horn going. The way her luck was running today she'd probably hit an oncoming truck head on, or Cain would panic and let loose with the gun.

No, all she could do was watch and wait and not panic. All she could do was keep a clear head.

'Sarcasm will get you nowhere,' Dominic said.

'Nowhere – is that where we're going?' Bad joke, but still the right note of lightness, of balanced neutrality. She hoped he would understand that, while she wasn't for him, she was very definitely not against him.

Dominic climbed onto the front passenger seat. Claire saw with relief that he had pocketed the gun.

'What the hell were you doing in Marc's apartment?' he demanded.

His anger was for show, Claire decided, compensation for the humiliation of hiding and running away. After all, she told herself, men were only little boys grown bigger. 'I was looking for something to remember him by,' she said. 'We were good friends.'

A blue and white sign flashed past. They were twenty kilometres from Bellinzona. Attractive profile, firm jaw, and brown hair streaking in the breeze from the open window. She drove a car well, too, without the hesitation between clutch and gear typical of so many women drivers. A brave girl, with the resilience of steel. Most girls would have screamed or fainted their way through the last hour. But not her. She could keep going, and even make bad jokes. Dominic liked that. 'Why the Dürer?' he asked. 'Why not something else?'

'Why anything?'

That wasn't clever, but she wasn't an experienced liar. Dominic wondered whether she too was part of Midas. 'What were those others looking for?'

'I don't know. Whatever it was, they didn't find it. How about you? What were you looking for?'

'Something that would tell me why Marc was killed.'

'Marc *killed*!'

The reaction was genuine enough. Surprise, horror, a feeling that her world was going crazy. 'Someone took a wheel off his Lotus. He crashed because someone wanted him to.'

'But that's ridiculous!'

'About as ridiculous as those men in the apartment. About as ridiculous as that little man who got too close to me with a gun.'

She rummaged one-handed in her bag, took out a cigarette and lit it. Hers was the world of modest, respectable, hardworking people who came home at night, enjoyed their families, took a holiday every year and watched Kojak on the box. In her world, people didn't go around pointing guns at each other. 'But why?' – blowing smoke at the windscreen, trying to understand. 'Why?'

'Thirty-four million quid,' Dominic said. 'That's why. Marc was involved with an organization called Midas. Midas wants to smash the Banco Lattoria.'

Claire asked, 'Why would anyone want to smash a bank?'

'Armed revolution is not the only way to win the people's war,' Dominic quoted. 'Sabotage, jam the computer, smash every lethal machine in the land. That's the message. Taking out a bank is more effective than hijacking a Boeing, or laying bits of plastic in Piccadilly Circus.'

'Midas, or whatever you call them, had nothing to do with the bank's losses,' Claire said. 'They couldn't have. The losses were caused by Charles bloody Edgar.'

'Tell me,' Dominic said.

Claire asked, 'How long have you worked for Edgar?'

'Twenty-four hours.'

She shrugged. 'Then you wouldn't know that Edgar is turned on by success. Money is his thing. He is all get up and go, the original take-the-ball-and-run man. Edgar should never have started Marc at the top.

'Marc used to say if you're big enough you'll fill the job. That was pure Edgar. But Marc was no Edgar, and it didn't help that right at the beginning he was lucky. At the beginning, Marc made money. A lot of money. Then he started to push it, to take risks, because he had to be bigger and better and make more profit, which is what big daddy Edgar wanted. A few months ago, he started to lose money. With his lack of experience and the system working against him, that was inevitable.'

'Why inevitable?' Dominic asked.

'In the old days,' Claire said, 'when exchange rates were fixed, if there was a run on any currency, the Central Bank of that country would come into the market and maintain the currency at its agreed level, come hell or high water. So a dealer knew that there was a limit below which the currency could not fall, and therefore a limit to his risk. With floating exchange rates, all the Central Bank will do is slow the trend, try to stop the value of its currency dropping too quickly. No one knows when a Central Bank will come onto the market, how long it will stay, or when it will pull out. Under those circumstances, there is no limit to the dealer's risk.'

'And that's what happened to Marc?'

'Marc miscalculated the bottom of the market. He was left with losses building up while the Bank of England allowed the pound to float down and the Federal Reserve Bank did the same with the dollar. Marc did not allow Edgar to know the size of those losses, and like all gamblers he doubled his bets, hoping to average out his losses so it wouldn't look too bad. With a lot of luck or a lot of time, he might have come out even, or made a small profit. He simply wasn't lucky.'

'How come you know so much about foreign exchange?'

Claire laughed. 'I spent a year with Eddie Machin. He was the best. And he wasn't a gambler. He limited the down-side risks and with him it was ninety-eight per cent analysis, two per cent luck, and a lot of bloody hard graft.'

'Was Marc depressed about these losses?'

'If you're talking about the last three months, I would

say he was pretty depressed. But not the last time I saw him. Not last Friday. Last Friday he was happier than I've seen him for a long time. He told me his troubles were over.'

'And on Saturday night, a wheel came off his Lotus and he crashed into a tree.'

'He always drove fast. In London he had a Lancia and he was always being stopped by the gestapo for speeding.'

London. Dominic remembered that, before he'd joined Edgar, Marc had worked in London for the Union Banque Suisse. 'You knew Marc in London?'

'Yes, five years ago.'

'What was he like?'

'Well, different.'

In London, Marc had had a flat in Bayswater which he'd shared with a young American who was writing the ultimate Hunter Thompson piece for *Rolling Stone* magazine. In those days, Marc had played poker a lot, thrown parties full of heads and musicians. He'd been involved in politics too, seeking a different society where people could fulfil themselves as individuals, without being fucked up by parents, or the establishment, or the fuzz. Yes, Marc had been a true flower child. At least in London.

'But he was different when you met him again in Switzerland?'

'He was older, yes. Quieter. Less involved. We're never the people we were.'

'And you still fancied him?'

That question was totally irrelevant. She really should refuse to answer it, but if she was being honest with herself, she'd be unhappy if he hadn't asked. 'I still liked him,' she said. 'It's something you wouldn't understand.'

'Like you were just good friends.'

Claire laughed. 'Marc, my darling, was queer as a three-speed roller skate.'

So his death wouldn't break her heart, Dominic thought. He could sleep with her and not raise ghosts. Then he wondered if Marc had been blackmailed. Homosexuality was an accepted fact in Switzerland, but it wasn't flaunted, admitted to in public, or considered a qualification for high office. After Marc had returned to Switzerland, he had wanted high office. Otherwise why would he have moved from the Union Banque Suisse to an aggressive, youth-oriented outfit like Edgar's.

'What's so special about the Dürer?' Dominic asked.

Claire hesitated. It was Marc's last request, not exactly a question of trust. She had not promised secrecy, and if it was true that he had been killed . . . She lit another cigarette and said, 'Two weeks ago, Marc told me that if anything happened to him, I should give that print to a friend of his, Gabriel Marchetti. He's an architect, and lives in Bellinzona.'

They were only five kilometres from Bellinzona. 'Let's do that,' Dominic said.

Bellinzona was an ugly town sitting astride the junction of roads that lead to Locarno and Lugano. Marchetti lived in a three-storey apartment block to the north-east of the town on the way to Roveredo. When they got there, blue light was bouncing off the walls and shooting along the street. A small crowd stood before the apartment block, kept back by the parked police Volvos.

Dominic parked and, taking Claire's hand, cleared a way for them through the crowd. Part of the pavement had been roped off and on it there were chalk marks that could have been the outline of a huddled body, and a splotch of something dark and liquid that might have been blood.

'What happened?' Dominic asked a lantern-jawed man, whose pale uniform made Dominic think he was a porter.

'It is Signor Gabriel, the architect. He has suicided.'

Dominic heard Claire's startled breath, tightened his grip

on her hand, crushing the fingers, creating a physical pain to distract the sense of shock. Marchetti had died leaping out of a third-floor window. Now it was a police matter, and Dominic wondered if they would ever discover whether Marchetti had fallen by accident or someone else's design.

CHAPTER THIRTEEN

'Dominic, I think we should go to the police.' Claire spoke with the assurance of one accustomed from childhood to a fire brigade which rescued kittens and policemen who helped old ladies across the street.

They were in a restaurant on the Monte Ceneri, a modern place, surrounded by glass and artificially aged wood, with a bar in one corner, an espresso machine and a tiled kitchen, clean as an operating theatre. They drank Dole, tangy and Burgundian, made from *pinot* and *gamay* grapes. A buxom Yugoslav waitress brought them *costoletta alla milanese*, which they picked at without appetite, neither of them hungry, and Dominic's stomach still hurting from the kick in Marc's apartment.

'No way,' Dominic said. 'There are two police forces involved and I have no proof. By the time they get things straight with each other, the bank would have collapsed and Midas done a runners.'

'So what are you going to do? Go after them yourself?' She was leaning across the table, looking concerned, eyes bright, the colour of backlit amber. For the first time Dominic noticed the laughter lines surrounding the eyes, the vestige of dimples in bronzed cheek and chin.

'Something like that,' Dominic admitted.

'Just like you went after Gavin Thirstone?'

Dominic put his glass down slowly, feeling his body tense in a slow explosion of shock. His eyes went flat and expressionless as buttons. 'What the hell do you know about Gavin Thirstone?' he asked.

She stared back at him, fingers curling away from her glass to the stick lighter and pack of Viceroy, her jaw jutting forwards. 'Don't you look at me like that,' she said, dropping her head as she lit a cigarette. 'Don't you bloody look at me like that.'

Dominic stopped looking at her like that. 'What do you know about Gavin Thirstone?' he repeated.

Claire leaned away, exhaling smoke through lips and nostrils. 'I only knew him to speak to. He was two years senior to me at college. He was one of those flamboyant characters you find at every university, apparently wealthy, surrounded by girls, with a reputation that was exciting. I had a crush on him in my first year, which was how I came to be interested in how he died.' She'd heard of the death from a college friend, followed the story in the newspapers, and she'd remembered the name, Dominic Cain. At the time she had thought how biblically ironical, a killer called Cain. She remembered also that three other people had died with Thirstone that day.

That day Dominic and Martin had tailed the four men in the white Pontiac all the way from Marseilles, and Martin had known Dominic was going to waste Thirstone. The men had holed up in a farmhouse, splitting the scag, making ready to take off in different directions. Martin decided to go in, to talk. As he walked up to the front door, Thirstone had shot him, and Dominic had had to let Martin lie there until the light went and he could make his way round to the back of the farmhouse.

He'd gone in through an upstairs window. He'd come down the stairway and found them seated round a table. Thirstone had reached for the Sturm-Ruger Blackhawk lying by the neatly packeted parcels, and Dominic had fired. Dominic knew guns, was used to them. He was accurate and they weren't. He had got three of them before they were able to loose off the first shot. And then he'd killed the youngest, as the boy was trying to get to his feet, raising his hands. Dominic hadn't known if it actually had been a gesture of surrender or if the boy had been reaching for the shotgun suspended on the wall above his head.

86

Dominic said, 'So you know I killed Thirstone. He was the only one I wanted to kill. He was responsible for my sister's death. Had she lived, she would have been about your age. You didn't know her, did you?'

Claire remembered, surprised she hadn't made the connection. No, she hadn't known Sarah. But she'd known what had happened to her. 'How terrible for you,' she said, thinking of the pain that had driven him to murder, thinking of the horrible emptiness afterwards. 'There were three others.' She'd read that one of them had been only nineteen.

'It was necessary,' Dominic said. He'd had two years to think about what he had done and why he had done it. Of course he'd have preferred an alternative, but he'd had no choice. He thought bitterly, it had been kill or be killed. That was the lesson he had learned, not in the farmhouse at Chagny, but long ago. Peace and love didn't work, not if the other side had the artillery.

Claire drew her hand away from his. 'I don't understand,' she said.

'You can't,' Dominic said, 'not unless you were there with me that day in Chagny.'

Claire looked down at her plate, toyed with her food. Behind her, Dominic could see the northern end of Lake Maggiore in a canopy of dappled light. It looked peaceful.

In a low voice, Claire asked, 'And is that what you will do with Midas? Trap them in a farmhouse and kill them?'

'If I have to, yes.'

'Why, Dominic? Because they are a threat to your way of life? Because they are trying to change this sick, money-worshipping society of ours?'

Dominic took his eyes away from the lake, to look at her. '*They* need labour camps, barbed wire and armed guards, they need man-killing dogs and minefields to keep their people *in* – and *we* are the ones who are sick?'

'Dominic, you can't go around killing people because you think differently from them.'

'I don't give a damn what they think,' Dominic said. 'I don't give a damn if their childhoods were disturbed or their heads are full of acid. But when they start saying they represent the people, when they believe that so strongly they think it gives them the right to kill, then I do care. And I'll tell you something else. Those people in Chagny didn't give a damn about the people. The Midas gang don't care about the people. All they're concerned about is one thing, their own private ego trip, their own power. The people, you and I, are expendable.'

'You're not an accountant,' Claire said. 'You're some kind of a policeman.'

'Yes,' Dominic said. 'I'm a fascist pig, the kind they believe they have a sacred duty to kill. Except, I'm going to get them first.'

'That won't stop others.'

'I'm not concerned about others. I'm concerned about Midas. They have killed three people already. Someone has to stop them.'

'*Three* people?'

'Marc, Marchetti and Lew Carmody. You must have read about Carmody in your evening paper.'

'I did,' Claire said, suddenly fearful. 'Dominic, you can't do this thing alone.'

Dominic grinned. 'I'm the only one here.'

'But Carmody has friends. They'll help you.'

'What do you know about Carmody?'

Gushing with relief, she told him about the Interstellar Textiles account, about Tom Haden and Tony de Marco, about her two hundred and fifty francs a month, everything, just so he would agree not to do it alone. Then she went and called Tony de Marco and they arranged to meet in a pull-off ten kilometres from the Monte Ceneri, because de Marco felt that he should not be seen in public with Dominic Cain.

CHAPTER FOURTEEN

Dominic drove counting the pull-offs. Assistance was what he needed, access to information, a new cover, people amongst whom to spread the risk.

The threats he had made in the restaurant, though real, were partly to assuage his loneliness and fear. Take on an organization like Midas and there was a very good chance of being killed. Fight them alone and the risk increased a thousandfold. He knew that when it came it would be a secret kind of death – a runaway car, a sniper with a target-rifle and long-range sights, a parcel that exploded in his face. With Midas, death was everywhere, all the time, and the all-pervading presence of death only made life more sweet. Everything was fresh and beautiful and exciting, so that the hardest thing in life was the leaving of it, leaving this cool and velvet night, the sense of motion, the sound of tyres on tarmac, the wind whipping through the open window, the awareness of a woman huddled beside him, sensuous, half mysterious, and slightly withdrawn.

'Dominic, what do you really do?' She sat huddled in the passenger seat, hands hugging her knees, voice tinged with lassitude or sleep.

'I work for the government.'

'And that was Carmody's job too?'

'Yes.'

'How long have you been doing this?'

'A few years.'

'Why this job?'

'Partly because of Sarah, partly because my father wanted to be a cop, partly because I'm good at it.'

'That's a lot of partly's.'

Dominic laughed. 'Mostly because I like it,' he said. 'Not

the killing. Not even the violence, though that's another partly. It's being responsible for your own fate, knowing that you win or lose on your own judgements. It's being aware all the time, knowing things, seeing things, feeling things. It's what hunting is all about.' He reached out casually and took her hand. She let it lie there, soft and pliable, thinking again that men were just boys grown bigger.

She asked, 'You make your work sound so solitary. Will you work with de Marco?'

'Oh sure,' Dominic said. 'We're on the same side.'

He saw the sign for the pull-off and slowed, braking gently, changing lanes early, moving the car easily into the black and yawning entrance. The pull-off was dark and empty, a semi-circular swathe of road separated from the autoroute by a clump of trees, a raised pavement and a flat-roofed building with an entrance marked *Damen* and another marked *Herren*, and on which the signs were extinguished.

That and the silence worried Dominic. He went on to parking lights. At the far end of the pull-off he made out the shape of a car parked to the left of the exit road, facing him. As he looked, the car flashed its headlights twice, half blinding him.

Dominic braked by the kerb and waited for his vision to return. Between the flashing lamps had been the silver grille of a Mercedes with white saloon bodywork, an open driver's door, a glimpse of a man standing sideways behind it.

'Is that de Marco?' he asked.

Claire peered through the windscreen. She'd met de Marco once at the bank, a stocky, bull-necked individual in a double-breasted suit, a squarish solid-looking head, bulbous eyes and the kind of moustache that went with two-toned shoes.

Dominic flicked his headlamps once.

'That's him,' she said.

90

What the fuck was he doing standing sideways behind the car? Dominic had his hand on the headlamp flasher, de Marco's image dying on his retina. The agreed signal was two flashes each, but he felt something was wrong. A feeling, not an actuality. The Mercedes was facing them, covering the exit road. They couldn't reverse out of the pull-off. With only one entrance the Mercedes should have been parked with its rear to them, facing the exit. Which meant de Marco had deliberately turned it round. An unnecessary manoeuvre. Dominic worried about unnecessary manoeuvres.

'Is that you, Mr Cain?' De Marco's voice carried through the night air. A car rushed by on the autoroute with a great thwacking of tyres and patchwork of headlights through the trees. Dominic eased the Renault into gear, allowed it to trickle forward. Then he flashed its headlamps the second time.

Brilliant white Mercedes with open door, dark shadow of a head crouching behind it, shiny black tubular reflection across the bottom of the window pointing towards them. Dominic gunned the Renault into a screeching arc, aiming it at the side of the Mercedes. Five yards from the shadowy hulk, he blazed the headlamps, saw de Marco jump up in white-lit brilliance, the gun with its long silencer drop over the door. De Marco came erect, but couldn't move, raised a hand in front of his eyes, opened his mouth in the beginning of a scream. He was petrified, unable to force his legs to move. He stood there a whole second that seemed like eternity.

Claire screamed. The squat front of the Renault crashed into the door, slamming it against de Marco's body, trapping him. A tinkle of glass, the whump of bending metal, a thousand-pound hammer smashing metal against de Marco, crushing collar and shin bone like matchsticks. For an instant, de Marco towered above them, dreadfully elongated. Then blood burst out of the nostrils and ears, erupted from the mouth, as a shot caromed off the metal skin of the Renault and screeched into the night.

He'd kept the engine going. Thank God he'd kept the engine going. Dominic picked reverse and tyre-screeched backwards, stopping halfway beside the flat-roofed toilets. A single headlight cast a drunken beam towards the exit road.

There had been two of them. De Marco by the car, the other in front of the toilets, trapping him in perfectly angled crossfire. 'Down,' Dominic said, opening the door, hitting the tarmac on all fours, pulling out the Luger. Paving and shallow concrete steps leading to the toilets. No one to be seen in the skew glaze of the headlamp. There was no cover beside the building and de Marco's friend had gone inside. One entrance on each side of the building, a division between, and no way to flush him out except with a grenade.

'Let's get away,' Claire whispered.

'No.' Dominic had to know who the other man was. 'Take your shoes off,' he said to Claire.

'Why?'

'Do it.' He heard the rustle as she eased them off her feet. He handed her the Luger. 'Go round the back of the toilet,' he whispered. 'There'll be windows at the back. Push the gun through the third window from the end and fire into the gents.'

'But Dominic—'

'Don't worry, you won't hit anything.'

She crawled out on his side of the car, ran silently across the pavement and disappeared behind the ladies. Dominic crawled slowly behind the car, crouched and took a good look at the building. If the gunman was in the gents, the side of the building would prevent him seeing the car. Or Dominic. *If* he was in the gents.

Dominic raced quickly across the pavement in a

crouched run, flattened his back against the roughened walls of the front of the building. The only sound was that of engines straining along the autoroute. He sidled crab-wise hurriedly along the front of the building, till he reached the edge of the wall. No one crouching down the side of the building. If the gunman came out now, there was nothing he could do. 'Hurry up Claire,' he mouthed silently. 'Hurry up.'

A clatter from the back of the building, then gunshots. One, two, three, puncturing the night in rapid succession. Then the pounding of feet against paving, the jingle of coins and snapping flutter of clothing, the sound of harsh breathing, a heavy body running.

As the gunman reached the end of the wall Dominic stepped round and hit him. His fist jarred into solid muscle somewhere about the man's chest. Dominic realized that the gunman was big, taller than him, wider, stronger. The gunman slowed, moved aside, swung a roundhouse right with the gun, trying to get distance enough to use it.

Dominic grabbed the flailing wrist with his left hand, held it above his head, tried to swing a right, felt his own wrist taken in an iron grip. He was an ugly man, with a long face, close-set piggy eyes, large teeth, crew-cut blond hair. Arms locked and widespread, they moved in a heaving circle and Dominic concentrated on the gun, avoiding thought of the man's superior strength, or the sweat breaking out over his body, the rippling tension of his back and arms. Dominic tried to swing the man round and kick his ankles away, but couldn't get the man moving fast enough. He must have weighed over two hundred pounds and the cost of speed was strength.

Dominic pulled his right hand backwards, pushed it for-ward rapidly, back again, stamped on the man's foot. A gasp, nails clawing at his wrist as it tore free. He punched at the man's face, fingers outstretched, going for the eyes.

The man had expected that. He leant his head and body backwards, pulling Dominic to him. Then a fist like a cannonball smashed into Dominic's stomach; a hard tearing ball of pain folded him in two. He felt the sweaty gun wrist wrench out of his grasp, then the vicious left cross to the side of his jaw. His legs straightened, lifted, he couldn't feel himself breathe, then the sharp jar of pain across his shoulders as it took the weight of his body crashing onto the concrete.

Dominic's feet scraped helplessly. Rubbery hands pressed down trying to give lift. The man was standing five feet away, upright, gun hand outstretched, pointing at Dominic in the classic stance, as if he was at a shooting range. At that distance, he wasn't going to miss.

'No,' Claire screamed. 'No!'

Dominic gasped voluntarily. There was a shot and he felt no pain. He felt nothing, as the man's head exploded like an orange dropped from fifty feet. First time lucky, Dominic thought mechanically, first time and she got the almost impossible, lethal head shot. The gunman folded at the knees and fell across the steps.

Dominic struggled to his feet. Claire was standing beside the entrance to the toilet, head bowed over the gun, gun trembling in both hands, sobbing. He put his arms round her, pulled her to him. 'It's all over, love,' he said. 'It's all over.'

Over for her, but there were still things to do. He took her back to the car, took the gun away from her. The gunman's name was Lee Grady. Both he and de Marco had ID's showing they were employees of Interstellar Textiles. Dominic thrust the Luger into de Marco's hand, took away his ·38. Then he drove the crumpled Renault onto the autoroute in the direction of Lugano, hoping it wouldn't be seen before he could hide it away.

'Why?' Claire asked in a low voice. 'De Marco and Grady were with Carmody in Interstellar.'

Dominic remembered that Carmody had come to Martin, had told him that Sunday morning over breakfast that his organization had been penetrated.

'Looks like they were working the other side of the street,' he said.

She crossed her arms about her shoulders, huddling into the seat. 'What do we do?' she asked. 'Dominic, what do we do?'

'We go on,' he said. 'Life goes on.'

'The police?'

'Not now. Not till we get absolution.'

CHAPTER FIFTEEN

They collected Claire's VW from outside Marc's apartment and drove twenty kilometres or so in convoy to the north of Lugano, to the valley where she had a farmworker's cottage stuck at the end of a rutted track. The development company that had bought the farm had been affected by the credit squeeze, and all redevelopment had stopped soon after the interior of the cottage had been modernized. The three-foot thick irregular stone walls were still intact, the roof was sloped and slatted, the gables still exposed to the elements. They were miles from anywhere, and Dominic was able to hide the Renault in a ramshackle barn.

Claire preceded Dominic into the house, turning on lights, revealing the architect-designed open-plan living area that combined lounge, kitchen and dining room. It was all wood and scattered carpets, low leather sofas to match the low ceilings, shields and pikes and a disused musket on the uneven walls. A door from the lounge led from the living area to a large bedroom, with an unmade bed.

Claire went to a pine cabinet, poured herself a slug of scotch. She gulped it down, replenished the glass and walked towards him, colour flooding her cheeks, gripping the glass in both hands, tightly controlled.

He had to stop her thinking about it. He had to make her think of why. 'What did you tell them?' he asked.

She walked past him, sat on the leather sofa and lit a cigarette, staring at the empty fireplace. 'I didn't tell them anything,' she said. 'All I told them was that you were an auditor sent from London and were a friend of Carmody's.'

And they had tried to kill him for that!

'They would have killed you too, you know that?'

She looked at him blankly.

'Tell me about Interstellar Textiles.'

'I've told you all I know.'

'In that case, could you analyse their account for me, tomorrow? Tell me if you find anything unusual.'

Claire nodded. 'I want to go home,' she said.

Dominic considered that. London was the obvious place to be when there were killings in Lugano. But they would use it against her afterwards, and her sudden departure might give the police a lead. No, it was better to carry on as if nothing had happened. Their only hope lay in buying time.

When he told her this, she said, 'I suppose you're right.' She knew the damnable intrigue would spread and spread. There was no end to the contamination of pressing a trigger. She hadn't wanted to kill the man. She'd only wanted to frighten, to prevent him hurting Dominic. Surely any judge would understand that.

'No,' Dominic said. 'Not here in Switzerland. Not because you were with me.' He paused and added kindly, 'Brooding over it won't help.'

Brooding wouldn't bring back the dead. By now some horrified motorist would have discovered the bodies. The police would be out there, with meatwagons and analysts, search lights and dogs, and Wolweber would be getting some idea of what Chicago had been like during prohibition.

The Luger in de Marco's hand would make them think, confuse them, but not for long. They would realize soon enough that the Luger was a plant, that there were others involved. They would start to look for another car, but they wouldn't know what model until they had analysed the paint samples, or were lucky enough to find a witness. In time, however, they would get round to everything. In time they'd put the pieces together and know what had happened. Before that Dominic had to find Midas – Midas and absolution.

He booked a call to Martin Pelham and picked up the Dürer. Claire sat opposite, staring wide-eyed into space, drinking the whisky with a slurping noise. There was nothing he could do right now, to take away the pain or the horror. Re-living his own horror was not going to help so he concentrated on the Dürer, and thought it was a bloody depressing picture.

He stared at the massive, despondent figure in the right foreground, with the clutter of useless implements scattered around it. Was it a memento of undying love to Marc's boyfriend or a kind of aesthetic revenge? It was even more depressing that he didn't know why Marc had picked this picture and not another. The picture was melancholy all right, with the calf's head and the globe, the carpenter's plane and the calendar. Dominic wouldn't want it in his Christmas stocking at any price. He could understand the symbolism of the tools, but the calendar? A symbol of the effluxion of time? A reminder of mortality? There were no dates on it, no months. He peered closer. It was not a calendar. It was a row of figures. To be precise: four rows of figures, forming a square of sixteen numbers. Automatically he added them up, and slowly it started to make sense.

That square of sixteen numbers was popularly known as a magic square, a mathematical novelty in which the figures added vertically, horizontally or diagonally all gave the same result. When Dominic was a child, his *amah* had given him a magic charm of his own. It was called the *lo shu* and its numbers always added up to fifteen. When he grew older, he'd learnt that the charm had been a third-order magic square; that is to say, it consisted of nine numbers arranged in rows of three, and gave a constant result of fifteen. The Dürer square was of the fourth order, sixteen numbers in rows of four, the columns all adding up to a constant 34. Dominic remembered that fourth-order magic squares were linked to Jupiter by Renaissance astrologers and were believed to combat melancholy. Which accounted for its place in the Dürer print. But not Marc's use of it.

Waiting for the phone to ring, Dominic took out his notebook, scribbled permutations on a piece of paper. He extrapolated the square with its mirror image, moved its duplicate on all four sides of it. He remembered the anstalts which had profited from the bank's losses. Intra, Kastel and Sulden. Dominic also remembered that Marc had introduced these anstalts to the bank, had probably run them. Perhaps the magic square was a mnemonic by which he could remember various account numbers.

One problem though. Since computerization, most banks favoured account numbers of eight digits. Those in the square were no more than six. Unless of course one added the constant magic 34 at the beginning or the end of the digits. That could just make sense. Marc couldn't have run a system that was too complicated. A complicated system of clandestine accounting was perilous; in the end serious mistakes were made and much time was lost. Ripping out a sheet of notepaper from his notebook, Dominic wrote out the twelve possible eight digit combinations and handed it over to Claire.

'Could you check if any of these numbers correspond with any accounts at the bank?' he asked.

She listened dumbly as Dominic told her about the square and looked at the figures.

'All right,' she said and thrust the paper on the sofa beside her.

The phone rang. 'Martin,' Dominic said. 'I'm still in Switzerland.' He told Martin what had happened.

'Boy oh boy,' Martin said. 'When you drop 'em, you

really drop 'em. You've killed two of Carmody's people, you say.'

'That's right.'

'You'd better come back,' Martin said. 'You should have listened to me when I told you that this afternoon.'

'What about the girl?' Dominic asked.

'Bring her out with you,' Martin said.

'Won't that mean unnecessary questions?'

'Believe me, dear boy, with the number of questions you're going to have to answer, you wouldn't know the difference. Get the first plane back, both of you. Meanwhile, I'll try to call Tom Haden and see if I can't square things with him this end. But it will be tough, Dominic. No one's going to let me whitewash the death of two operatives.'

'I realize that,' Dominic said and suddenly thought: what a lot of shit. The deaths would be squared away on an inter-departmental baisis. Haden, whoever he was, would persuade Wolweber that the matter should be dropped. Everyone would forget about it, and one day, somewhere, someone Dominic didn't know would walk up to him, stick a gun against his ribs and pull the trigger.

'Why?' Dominic asked. 'Why should Carmody's people want to kill me?'

'I don't know,' Martin said. 'It isn't our operation.'

'Ask Haden that,' Dominic said. 'Ask him loud and clear. Tell him that until I find out, I'm staying. Tell him that until I find out, I know there is no place to run to.'

'Don't be silly, Dominic. Take the first plane back. Bring the girl with you.'

'They know about Lew,' Dominic said quietly. 'They wouldn't stop just because we were in London. I have to find out what they were worried about. If Haden knows, call me.' He gave Martin Claire's number.

'Come back, Dominic,' Martin said. 'Come back.'

'In time,' Dominic said. 'Take care, old friend,' and he put the phone down.

Claire looked at him. The brown eyes were feverish, there was a strained look about her mouth, and her lips were dry. 'So you've fixed everything,' she said quietly, almost bitterly. 'You've spoken to your influential friend and two murders will be forgotten.'

'Not forgotten,' Dominic said. 'Not yet.'

'Killing is easy for you, isn't it,' she said. 'You kill, and someone else washes away the blood.'

'What do you want?' Dominic asked. 'Punishment?'

She shook her head, mouth trembling over the glass, eyes brimming with tears. 'I don't know,' she said, 'My God, I don't know.'

Dominic watched her sit crouched on the sofa, sobbing, with shoulders heaving. Crying was better than sitting there, all uptight and worried. He took her glass and re-filled it.

After a while she stopped crying and asked tearfully, 'It's real, isn't it, Dominic. It's true. I did kill that man. It's not a nightmare. I did kill him.'

'It's true,' Dominic said. 'It happened.'

'My God! Is that all you can say – "it happened"? Of course I know it bloody well happened! I did it, didn't I?'

Dominic went across to her, took her by the elbows and drew her to her feet. 'It happened,' he said. 'You did it. Nothing can undo it.'

'You lousy bastard!' she cried, broke free from him and flung the whisky in his face.

Dominic reeled back, his face ice cool, his eyes stinging from the spirit.

'Is that all you can say? You made me a murderer and all you can say is you can't undo it. You dirty, corrupt creep! I'm not a professional killer. I'm a bloody bank clerk. I can't kill somebody and forget about it. I never wanted to be mixed up in your filthy games!'

Dominic said quietly, 'He would have killed you Claire. If he killed me, he couldn't afford a witness. It was kill or be killed, I promise you, there was nothing else you could do.'

She sighed, walked with the empty glass to the pine cabinet, filled it, drank.

Dominic said, 'Now we have to find out why. When we've done that, we can see about the police. We can see about assuaging your guilt.'

She came back to the centre of the lounge and stood in front of him. 'You'd better go, Dominic,' she said. 'You'd better go. Take your murderous little car and go.' She gave a mocking laugh. 'I kill for you and now I can't stand you. I can't stand your righteous dedication, your switch-blade morality. I can't stand the way you attract death.'

'Sooner them than me,' Dominic said.

She came up to him, eyes blazing, pushing at his shoulders feebly. 'Go, for God's sake, go. Go and leave me be. Go Dominic, get out, get out! I hate you!'

Dominic moved her pattering fists away from his shoulders, folded his arms round her, trapping her hands by her sides. He knew too well that the reaction to murder was always unpredictable. He knew that she shouldn't be alone. She began to cry again, sobbing gently against his chest with a high-pitched trilling noise each time she drew breath. Dominic pressed his lips to her ear. Her hair was damp with sweat. 'I'm staying,' he whispered. 'I'm going to look after you,' filled with a crazy tenderness.

She put her arms around his body, the fingers twisting convulsively in the back of his jacket.

'You'll forget,' Dominic said. 'In time, you will forget. I promise, it will be better.'

'Kill or be killed. It's like the jungle,' she said. 'There's no morality. We're no better than animals.'

'The jungle is out there, not here, not with us.'

She pressed against him, twisting her body against his. 'Dominic,' she said, 'fuck me.'

Dominic understood that too. In the presence of death, there was always a need to affirm life.

CHAPTER SIXTEEN

It was eleven-thirty in the evening Washington-time when the TWA 747 landed at Kloten. At Kloten it was six o'clock in the morning. The sky was just turning silver and there was a stillness in the air that presaged a hot day.

Tom Haden hurried down the gangway, moved with long strides across the tarmac, past the passengers spreading out in a wide, ambling line. He was a lean man and very tall, with the wide shoulders and loose walk of a basketball player. He was about fifty, with a long, sensitive face, strong chin, smoke-grey eyes and a mouth that women considered pretty. His hair was thick and brown, touched with grey, worn collar-length, parted from the side and very much in place. He'd freshened up half an hour before they landed.

He'd spent all morning – all last morning – tabling evidence before a Congressional Committee. No, Senator, I had no knowledge of any attempt to, nor did I at any time myself poison Fidel Castro's cigars. Kidnapping Moishe Tshombe likewise. I have not knowingly employed or caused to be employed anyone known to me to be a member of the Cosa Nostra or Mafia or any similar organization for any purpose and that includes the assassination of Rafael Trujillo. I have not directly or otherwise placed a bug in the President's electric toothbrush, golf cart or football. Senators! Representatives of the people! Never having had open government, they were now trying to divert the people's attention by trying to run an open secret service. What a bunch of horses' asses they were!

For the last three years, Haden had run an organization that was code-named Octopus. Octopus was the most modern and efficient counter-terrorist organization operating outside the United States. They had a comprehensive system of files, names, fingerprints, aliases, numbers of passports both fake and genuine, names of mistresses, lists of contacts and friends, sources of funds, safe houses and sympathizers, even which side of the bed certain people preferred to sleep on. In the past year they had prevented seventeen aeroplane hijackings, two assassinations, four robberies, seized an illegal shipment of arms, 220 kilos of morphine base and 500 pounds of hashish. They had helped trace a theft of nuclear weapons from a NATO armoury, wiped out a hired gunman carrying a hit list of prominent businessmen and entertainers, resolved two kidnappings and prevented four others. But not one of those jerks had asked him about these things. Disasters averted and lives saved didn't make the headlines in the same way. And without headlines there were no reputations. Good news might have told the people the truth, but it was easier to be a bleeding heart, to get indignant about wire taps and the illegal opening of mail. It was much easier to be sanctimonious about that. Politicians, Tom Haden thought, thrusting his diplomatic passport through the grille. Give me used-car salesmen anytime!

He threw himself into the back of the waiting Opel Diplomat, told Rayner, who had woken at some ungodly hour in order to meet him, that it had been a lousy trip and that certain people whose names he wouldn't mention would be more usefully employed shovelling shit. Rayner laughed politely, and the car sped along the deserted autoroute to Zurich, told him that Lew Carmody was dead.

Haden didn't say anything to that. He simply looked out of the window and listened. Once he took out a cigarette, remembered Lew, and put it away again. He and Lew had started together. They'd been in the business twenty-eight years. Lew was retiring this fall. Lew Carmody had been the best operative he'd ever known. Haden made a mental note to contact Hilda, and see if she required any help with transportation or the funeral arrangements. Then he asked the driver to take him to his office, and Rayner to use the car telephone and tell everybody to get their asses over there, like it was yesterday.

'What the fuck was Lew doing in Lugano?' Haden asked. 'What the fuck job was he on?'

The answer to that was simple. No one knew. Situation reports, operation reports, back files, notebooks, all drew a blank. The only facts they knew were that Carmody had gone to Lugano on Saturday, then flown to London, returned to Lugano on the Sunday and died. And what the hell did those two clowns de Marco and Grady think they were doing, wrecking a company car and getting themselves killed in a pull-off between Bellinzona and Lugano. Jesus wept! You left the shop for one week, and everybody goofed!

Haden got rid of everyone, sat in his room alone, thinking. It was very unlike Lew not to make reports, very unlike Lew not to touch base. And altogether, there was too much goddam Lugano in this business. All Haden could surmise was that Lew had been on something big, something big and too dangerous to tell his own people about. So he had gone to London. London . . . It was only seven-thirty in the morning, but Haden decided he would return Martin Pelham's call.

By the time he'd finished talking to Pelham, things were a whole lot clearer. Haden knew what he had to do. First he had Rayner arrange a meeting with Chief Inspector Wolweber of the Lugano *Kriminalpolizei*. Then he sent for Abraham Stone.

Stone came in, sleepy-eyed, tousle-haired, the blond stubble hardly showing on his boyish face. Stone had worked for three months with Lew. Lew had thought he was very good. Haden gave him a file and said, 'Read that.'

Stone rubbed his eyes, took the file, read it. 'What do I have to do?' he asked.

'One simple thing,' Haden said. 'Find me Dominic Cain.'

About the time Tom Haden's plane was landing at Kloten, Dominic Cain woke up. Smoky-grey morning light filtered into the room. He could just make out the old Valentino poster beside the door.

Claire lay on her side with her back to him, one shoulder upraised, head cradled on her arm, brown hair spread over the pillow, breathing slurpily through her mouth.

Last night she had wanted a kind of release. 'I don't want to,' she had said going with him to the bedroom. 'It isn't right. It shouldn't be like this,' when he'd unfastened the jangling buckle on her jeans, and peeled them down her legs. She had lain on the bed naked and unprotesting, gazing blankly at the ceiling, seeing him without emotion. It had taken a long time for her to feel anything but indifference to the pounding of her flesh, a long time before she whispered, 'That's nice,' and begun to move with him, taking his mouth with hers, holding him with her arms and her body.

Last night Dominic had needed a woman too, he'd needed arms and breasts, a mouth and entwined limbs to take away the loneliness and fear and horror.

But now, looking at her in the grey morning light, it was different. He wanted her. Claire. He wanted the bank clerk with guts enough to kill, he wanted the woman who'd drunk whisky and cried in his arms, he wanted her brightness and her ambition, even the greed that made her take two-fifty a month in backhanders from Interstellar.

She came awake quietly, brown eyes wide and smiling, hands unbelievingly stroking his body. He eased her gently

108

with tips of fingers and tip of tongue, fondling her nipples into round, hard buttons, entering her gently, reaching for the furthest parts of her, stroking her, loving her from the inside, holding back till she choked and came with tiny strangled screams that racked on and on through the grey, translucent dawn.

And again – they spent themselves again – flooding away nightmares. Again, more abandoned, touching, exploring, tasting salty surfaces in happy lubricious confusion.

Afterwards she asked, 'Are you always like this in the morning?'

'Yes,' he said. 'I've seen a doctor about it. She thought it was super too.'

They both would have liked to stay, to lie there watching each other and the day fulfil itself. But Claire had to go to work, and Dominic to Zurich.

Standing by the VW in the bright morning sunlight, listening to the rustle of the wind in the unkempt grass, Dominic asked her why she had chosen to live there. It was cheap, Claire said, and here she had peace and quiet. Peace and love, peace and quiet. Dominic thought of Midas and said it was the wrong place to be in during the middle of a shooting war.

'Why should Midas want to do anything to me?' she asked, bouncing the VW carelessly down the rutted lane.

'For the same reason as they killed Marchetti and Marc.'

'But I know nothing.'

'The problem is, will they believe that? You'd better check into an hotel in Lugano.'

She protested, but agreed.

She left him in the Via Caccia, to hire another car and go to Zurich.

'I'll call you as soon as I get there,' he said. 'You'd better have some information for me, girl.'

'Is that the only reason why you'll call?' she smiled.

'What other reasons are there?' he asked and kissed her very hard, before he walked away. He did not turn and wave as he hurried along the pavement to the arcade of the Via Nassa, and he had to admit he wasn't observing very closely, either. He felt as if he had been breakfasting on champagne, that he was about to explode, and even when he went into the car rental office and spoke to the pretty, trimly uniformed girl behind the counter, he was still full of her, feeling her in the sweet pain in his loins, but not yet admitting even to himself what had happened to him.

CHAPTER SEVENTEEN

Dominic reached Zurich just on eleven o'clock, made straight for the airport at Kloten. Modern air terminals were fantastic places. They provided car rental services, money-changing facilities, meals, an extensive coin box telephone service, and the ability to wait around without attracting attention.

Dominic collected fifty francs in change from the bank, and phoned Claire. She came on the line out of breath and sounding puzzled.

'Johann Winthrop?'

'It's me, Dominic.'

'Oh darling! I've—' Her voice was a paean of gladness.

Dominic felt that way too, but he said, 'This is not Mr Darling. It's nasty old Johann Winthrop wanting his account numbers.'

'Well, nasty old Mr Winthrop must wait, because nasty old Mr Doppler wants some work done first.'

Dominic tried to imagine her behind the desk in Doppler's office, wondered whether the wisp of hair had strayed over her cheek as yet, imagined too vividly, and forced himself to listen.

'There's a flap on after yesterday's newspaper story.' No laughter in her voice now, her tone low-pitched and urgent. 'Edgar's flying out. They are worried he might be arrested.'

A very salutary experience for Mr Edgar, Dominic thought. He said, 'The numbers, girl. When are you going to check those numbers?'

'Give me twenty minutes. I have to give Doppler his estimates first.'

'Fine.'

'Is that all you have to say?'

'That's all Mr Winthrop has to say,' Dominic said. 'I love you.'

'Then you should—'

'How's it going? Have you heard from Midas yet? How are you feeling?'

'Better, but—'

'It'll soon be over,' Dominic said. 'I'll call you back in half an hour' – and he put down the phone.

Dominic inserted more coins and called the Fieldhaus Bank. Yes, a director would be pleased to meet with Mr Cain, even if Mr Cain would not tell the gruff male voice at the other end of the line Mr Cain's business. The voice took pains to imply that at the Fieldhaus they were most discreet. Herr Wiedermayer, however, would not be free till half past two this afternoon. Dominic said half past two was just fine, and wandered over to the Air Quick Restaurant for breakfast.

He had time to kill, though 'kill' was not a word he favoured that morning. At that hour the restaurant wasn't busy. The proper breakfast eaters had eaten proper breakfasts at proper breakfast time, three hours ago. The restaurant was now peopled by a few stragglers like himself and the odd member of the brandy-before-take-off brigade.

While he ate, Dominic amused himself watching them park the incoming planes so that all the aircraft of each airline were kept close together, like a sales display. The sight of the armoured personnel carrier and the soldiers wearing mountain camouflage reminded him that it was not all neatness and order. That even here automatic rifles could start chattering and bombs explode.

On that sobering thought he pulled out his notebook and checked through the account numbers again. By adding 34 to the beginning and end he'd come up with a combination of twenty-four 8-digit groups, and four 7-digit groups. He'd discounted the 7-digit groups as being too conspicuous for Marc to have used them. He hoped that Marc had stuck the 34 at the beginning or end of the group. If he had inserted it on a random basis, Dominic was lost.

Partly to amuse himself, partly to see if he could discover something new, he set about constructing a fourth-order magic square. It was simple enough to do. First he wrote the numbers 1 to 16 in blocks of four.

1	2	3	4
5	6	7	8
9	10	11	12
13	14	15	16

Then he wrote out the diagonals and reversed them.

16			13
	11	10	
	7	6	
4			1

Finally he entered the remaining figures in their original positions.

16	2	3	13
5	11	10	8
9	7	6	12
4	14	15	1

And presto, a magic square! But not the square Dürer had used.

Dürer had transposed the second and third columns, so that his square looked like this:

16	3	2	13
5	10	11	8
9	6	7	12
4	15	14	1

That made no difference to the square's magic properties, and Dominic tried to recall what he knew about these mathematicians' playthings. In 1838 someone in France had published three volumes on the subject, but then they didn't have television in those days. There was a square of greater magic properties that had been found on the wall of an eleventh century temple in India. Nothing to do with Dürer – and then, staring at the two sets of figures, Dominic saw why the columns had been transposed.

For Dürer the square had not only been a charm against melancholy. It had also been a calendar. The middle figures of the fourth row showed the year in which the engraving had been made: 1514. Cunning Dürer. Dominic hoped Marc was less devious, and went to phone Claire.

'You have problems, Mr Winthrop,' she said. 'None of the figures match up.'

'You mean the computer threw them all out?'

'All except three groups. It wanted those re-keyed.'

Which meant there was a digit missing or transposed. 'Give me the numbers.'

Claire took a deep breath then began. 'Sixteen, three, two, thirteen, thirty-four. Five, ten, eleven, eight, thirty-four. Four, fifteen, fourteen, one, thirty-four.'

Those groups were made from the horizontal numbers on the Dürer square. Dominic felt a surge of elation. He had been right. They were the account numbers made up to eight digits by the addition of the figure 34 at the end. But the computer had thrown them out. Correction: the computer had wanted the numbers re-keyed, which meant he was getting warm. He took out the square he had made and said, 'Try these. Sixteen, two, three, thirteen, thirty-four. Five, eleven, ten, eight, thirty-four. Four, fourteen, fifteen, one, thirty-four.'

'I'll try,' she said. Then she lowered her voice. 'But Doppler's put an embargo on the use of the computer.'

'Try,' Dominic said. 'For God's sake, try. A lot depends on it.'

'As if I didn't know,' she replied. 'Call me back in an hour, Mr Winthrop.' And this time it was she who put the phone down first.

If it were done at all it were best done quickly, Claire mused, went over to the teletype and dialled the time-sharing computer's number, and heard the familiar beep-beep of the computer's affirmative reply. Rapidly she typed in 'HELLO' and waited. The teletype chattered back, 'USER NUMBER'.

She typed in the number. Immediately the computer came back: 'SYSTEM'.

Claire typed in, 'BASIC'.

Computer time was measured in seconds. For all she knew alarm bells would be ringing in Doppler's office. She wished she could get the formalities over and the business begun.

The teletype went, 'NEW OR OLD'.

Claire typed in, 'OLD', grateful she could use the same program she had used that morning.

The teletype asked, 'OLD PROGRAM NAME'.

Claire typed, 'MIDAS'.

At last the computer said, 'READY'.

It was at least forty-five seconds before the computer finished scanning all the bank's accounts and matched the numbers. Forty-five heart-stopping seconds and it began to type. '16231334 INTRA ANSTALT, 51110834 KASTEL ANSTALT, 41415134 SULDEN ANSTALT'.

In her excitement, Claire typed in 'THANK YOU' and added two crosses before tapping out the customary 'BYE'.

Leaving the printout in the carriage, she went over to the filing cabinet where the contract files were kept and took out copies of the last payment orders made to each of the anstalts. All the payments had been made to the Fieldhaus Bank in Zurich. The account numbers there were Intra 21171434, Kastel 31061534, and Sulden 13812134, the vertical colums of Dominic's transposed magic square.

She put the documents back and shut the drawer, smiling in triumph. If this is what the chase was like, no wonder Dominic loved it so. She could hardly wait for him to call.

She was still standing there with a dreamy smile on her face when Herr Doppler walked in. Without even pausing for breath or shutting the door, he shouted, 'I have told you before, the computer is not to be used. It must not be used without my direct authority.'

Claire shuffled her feet and looked shamefacedly at the floor. 'I'm sorry, Herr Doppler, there was something—'

'It does not matter if it was anything. When I give you an order you must obey it. I tell you not to use the computer and you do not use the computer.' His voice carrying through the open door must have filled the bank. He was red-faced and quite helpless with rage. 'And what is this important thing that you have to use the computer for?'

Panic-stricken, Claire looked at the teletype with the incriminating evidence still in the carriage.

'You are a foolish, frivolous young woman who is disobeying my orders and causing trouble. You must be punished. I will have—'

Brian Keith appeared in the doorway. 'I hope this isn't a private party,' he said, smiling. 'Claire, my girl's gone sick, and I was wondering—'

The pause had only given Doppler time to get his breath. 'You are using the computer and making criminal offences. We are busy having meetings and have accounts to prepare, and enough troubles without your foolishness.'

Brian looked from Doppler to her and then to the teletype. Then to Claire's horror he walked over to it and ripped off the printout. Claire could feel her heart thudding

116

with dreadful slowness, the blood rushing from her face. She thought she was going to faint.

Then Brian looked up from the printout and over Doppler's shoulder, and winked. 'Herr Doppler, I have some urgent work for Miss Denton.'

Doppler controlled himself with an effort, and protested that a reprimand was necessary.

'If she is with me, Herr Doppler, she cannot use the computer.'

Doppler hesitated. Then he said, 'All right. But we will have to discuss this later.' And, turning smartly on his heel, he left the room.

Brian Keith walked over and put the printout on her desk. 'I thought someone was being murdered in here,' he said. 'We could hear him at the other end of the building.' He smiled at her. 'You obviously needed rescuing. I also have a couple of urgent letters to do.'

Her legs were trembling and she could barely get the words out. 'I'll come over right away,' she heard herself say, 'After I've tidied up here.'

It was only much later when she was sitting in Brian's office, taking down a complicated market report addressed to the Handls Bank, that she remembered that Dominic would ring. And prayed he wouldn't.

But there was radar interference under heaven that day. She was still taking down the report when the switchboard announced a call for her from Mr Winthrop. Brian stopped dictating and indicated that she could take the call.

'Oh Mr Winthrop, thank you for returning my call. That second set of figures you gave me are the right ones.' Dominic was trying to say something, but she couldn't let him ask any questions.

'You'll find everything matches up. Everything. And if you check with Zurich, you'll find the verticals match up too.' She put the phone down quickly and looked up at a quizzical Brian Keith.

'Obviously someone you don't like,' Brian said. 'You didn't even say goodbye.'

'Johann Winthrop is a drip,' Claire said. 'He's always double-checking his settlements.'

'And what on earth are verticals?'

Claire shook her head: *what on earth were verticals?*

'Did I say that? I must have meant columns.'

Brian Keith laughed. 'No wonder Winthrop double-checks his statements. I'll never understand you foreign-exchange people. Maybe that's why I'll never go any higher in the bank,' and he resumed dictating, continuing for the next fifteen minutes.

Afterwards he showed her into the ante-room which his secretary normally used. 'You'll be better off sitting up here,' he said, 'where you can't get into trouble with computers.'

Claire took the typewriter cover off and sat down, hoping he would leave her alone.

'Claire,' Brian asked. 'What were those accounts you were checking this morning?'

'I misplaced some account numbers,' Claire said. 'It was quicker to check them on the computer than look.'

'Intra, Kastel and Sulden – why those?'

'I wasn't sure if their outstandings had been cleared,' Claire said.

'Wouldn't it have been easier to check the settlement lists?'

Claire felt her face grow hot, angry with herself for being thought stupid, for being caught lying. 'I didn't think of that,' she said.

Brian rested a well-rounded haunch on the desk. Claire fidgeted, lit a cigarette, mechanically offered him one. She was surprised he took it. When they were both smoking, he asked, 'Who is this Johann Winthrop? I don't know any Johann Winthrop.'

'It's a new account,' Claire said.

Brian looked at her keenly. 'Johann Winthrop or Dominic Cain?'

'Dominic – no!'

'I was in the Via Caccia this morning,' Brian said. 'I saw you two together. It is my business, Claire. What is your relationship with Cain?'

Claire said, 'My personal life is nothing to do with the bank.'

'In this case, I'm afraid it is. I don't trust Cain. I don't know who he works for and why. I don't know what made Charles Edgar send him out here. But I do know that he leaked the story of our problems to the papers. That he helped start a run on the bank, and that if I'm out of a job next week, it's going to be because of him.'

Claire remembered Brian was nearly forty. He'd spent most of his working life abroad and would not want to go back to England, even if he could find a job there at his age in the present depressed economic climate.

'I've got two kiddies still at school,' Brian said. 'I wouldn't want anything to happen to them.'

As the only two foreigners at the Banco Lattoria, Brian and Claire had met socially through the past year. She knew his marriage had broken down soon after he'd begun working for Edgar. That he lived alone in a large apartment on the Corso Pestalozzi, but this was the first she knew of any children.

'I didn't know you had any children, Brian.'

'Two boys,' Brian said. 'And I'm not going to let someone like Cain bugger them around. I can't allow an incompetent like him to ruin Charles, this bank, or me.' He looked at his cigarette as if surprised to find it between his fingers. 'There's nothing I wouldn't do to prevent that, even if it means giving you your marching orders, my girl.'

119

Marching orders would suit neither her career prospects nor Dominic's investigation. Marching orders meant facing a murder charge too. 'Dominic doesn't want to ruin the bank,' Claire said. 'He wants to save it.'

Brian pulled awkwardly at the cigarette, wrinkled his face up against the smoke. 'No,' he said. 'We've got enough trouble without his help.'

'Dominic believes that Marc helped Intra, Kastel and Sulden to defraud the bank.'

'Marc!' Brian cried. 'That isn't true!'

Claire thought rapidly. She couldn't tell Brian about last night, about Marchetti and the men in Marc's flat.

'You knew Marc,' Brian went on. 'He wouldn't do a thing like that.'

Claire chose her words carefully. 'Marc was in trouble,' she said. 'He took up some very risky positions. And those three anstalts had no reason to make so much money.'

'They were gambling, Claire. They won and we lost.'

'That's only one possibility,' Claire replied. 'If they were working in collusion with Marc, if we can get the money back...'

Brian ground out his cigarette and stared at the floor. Please, Claire thought, please give Dominic a chance. We all need to give him a chance. She could feel the fear coming back again, the tears at the back of her eyes and the lumpiness in her throat. For the sake of something to do, she lit another cigarette.

'Why doesn't he come to us?' Brian asked. 'Or tell the police about it? I mean if it is a question of fraud—'

'He needs proof,' Claire said. 'No one will believe him without that.'

Brian stood up, stretching thoughtfully. 'What information does he want?' he asked.

Claire hesitated. 'Just – just information on those three accounts.'

'I hope to hell he's right,' Brian said. 'Okay, tell him

what he wants to know about the anstalts. If he wants any other information, clear it with me first.'

'All right,' Claire said.

'You promise?'

She nodded, unable to bring herself to say the words.

Brian walked to the door. 'I hope he pulls it off,' he said. 'Tell him I said that. Tell him we would like to help and that he should come to us.' He smiled at Claire. 'He should come to Charles and me.'

Claire watched him go and wondered how the hell she was going to get at the Interstellar accounts.

CHAPTER EIGHTEEN

Herr Wiedermeyer was square and rugged, with flat cheek-bones, clear brown eyes and a nose that looked as if it had once hit bedrock at the end of a long and steep piste. He wore a light brown suit and a dark brown tie. He moved with the exaggerated athleticism that betrayed a man who did weight training in his lunch hour. He welcomed Dominic with heavy joviality as if he were determined to prove that banking was fun.

The fun aspect became somewhat less obvious when Dominic told him he hadn't come to open an account at the Fieldhaus Bank, but to seek information. Dominic produced Charles Edgar's letter. Wiedermeyer read it warily, and asked, 'What can we do for you?' accompanied by an expression that hoped it would be very little.

Dominic gave him a summary of the Banco Lattoria's problems, ending with, 'We want to trace the owners of certain bank accounts.'

Wiedermeyer looked more uncomfortable, started to murmur about Article 47 B of the law of 8 November 1934. Dominic knew all about Article 47 B. It imposed a fine of twenty thousand francs and/or six months' imprisonment for violation of bank secrecy by a bank employee.

'But we suspect a criminal offence has been committed,' Dominic said, the only way around 47 B.

'In that case, you should go to the police.'

And the police would take six days to get their paperwork right, and then they could all go before a judge and get an order, and by then it would be much too late. Meanwhile, if Wiedermeyer felt so inclined, he could have a nice heart to heart with his customers.

'By the time we complete the formalities,' Dominic said,

'the Banco Lattoria may have collapsed, the suspects may have flown, and the Federal Banking Commission will be wanting to know who helped these rogues.'

Herr Wiedermeyer got very thoughtful about that. A bank failure meant disgrace, a severe denting of Switzerland's financial reputation. The Banking Commission wouldn't be overfond of other banks who had helped criminals to escape. But still, the law was the law.

Dominic could see Wiedermeyer deciding to go to the Banking Commission himself. 'Never mind who owns the accounts,' he said. 'All we're interested in is if the money is still with you, so that we can decide if the investigation is worth continuing with. There's no use in throwing good money after bad.'

That was a sentiment any banker would agree with. 'Do you have the account numbers?' Wiedermeyer asked.

Dominic hoped he'd understood Claire's message. '21171434, 31061534, 13812134. Names Intra, Kastel and Sulden.'

Wiedermeyer gave him a broad smile. 'I can tell you about that without any breach of confidence. We have no money for those accounts here. No money at all.'

'But we paid sixty to seventy million francs into those accounts at your bank.'

'And the money was taken out of those accounts.'

'Taken where?'

'You know I couldn't tell you, even if I knew. But in fact I don't. The money was taken out in cash.'

Less the bank's commission, of course, Dominic thought grimly. 'Did you not think cash transfers in these amounts somewhat extraordinary?'

'No.'

There was no sense in antagonizing Wiedermeyer. Dominic smiled. 'It's not our concern how other people run their businesses. How was the money drawn out?'

'By single signature. Number only. Every week or so, a

young man would come in, write out a requisition, sign it with the correct number and take out all the money in the account.'

'The same young man?'

'Not always the same young man.'

'And do you have a record of who these people were?'

'No. On that our instructions were specific. We were to pay the money without question to anyone who signed the correct number.'

'A right set-up for a fraud.'

'We hold indemnities against that. I warned them about it when I accepted the account.'

'Who?'

'Our correspondents in Vaduz.' Herr Wiedermeyer stood up. 'In fact I was wondering if that was the reason why you came. You see, only last week someone took eighteen million francs from the account. And yesterday there was someone else, demanding the same amount.'

Dominic resisted the urge to grin. It looked as if someone had taken Midas for near six million quid. Someone – probably Marc.

Dominic reached Vaduz two hours later and checked in at the Hotel Engel. He had a room at the front of the hotel, overlooking the two streets which looped together to form the centre of Vaduz and the smallest one-way traffic system in the world. Below him, cars stretched in an orderly queue all the way to the Postage Stamp Museum, a dull ochre building at the head of the sweeping curve. The cars moved slowly past the café and the two banks, the souvenir shop and the post office. Directly opposite him, across the large parking area was the other half of the loop, a gas station, more cafés and souvenir shops. Vaduz was compact, clean, orderly and industrious, and from its centre you could still see fields and cows.

Dominic watched the people in the café below, ran his eyes along the cars parked by the kerb, looking for a black Mercedes or something else unusual, he wasn't sure what. He'd driven the Peugeot hard from Zurich, keeping it flat out on the stretches of autoroute and the sporadically lonely fast traffic route past Hohenems. He had deliberately ignored speed limits. A Porsche and a big Datsun had got past him, but nothing had stayed with him. He felt reasonably sure he hadn't been followed.

He shut the door to the balcony and drew the net curtains. It was too early to eat, too early to call Claire. He took out his notebook and played with his magic square. Of the twelve groups of eight-digit numbers available, Marc had used six, those made up from the square's horizontals and verticals. Dominic wrote these down in two groups of three, marking the first group 'Banco Lattoria' and the second 'Fieldhaus'. Which left him with two diagonal groupings, three groupings made up from converting the magic square into smaller, two-sided squares, and one made up from the central four numbers. If Marc had been logical, he would have three accounts at a bank in Vaduz, and, eliminating the groupings progressively, used the diagonals and the first of the two-by-two squares to record the account numbers. Marc might have been both a fool and a thief, but at least so far he had been logical.

It seemed to Dominic that Marc had lost money on his dealings, while at the same time altering his records so that whatever profits were available were shared between his friends and himself. But that was too simple, too obvious a theory. It didn't entirely make sense. Marc appeared more fool than knave and there had been no evidence of the vast amounts of money he must have made; not in his bank accounts, not in his spending. And the Fieldhaus Bank had gone eighteen million francs light. Was that why Marc had been killed? Had he tried to rob them? Or stop them?

Dominic showered, changed and ate in his room. For the

present, the fewer people who saw him in Vaduz the better. Afterwards, he called Claire, succeeding in locating her hotel two hours later, at the thirty-first attempt. There were a lot of hotels in Lugano. She'd waited in for his call. Where was he, and was he all right?

Dominic told her he was in Vaduz, on the trail of the money. He told her that he was well, and that he hadn't been followed. Hearing her voice made him want to touch her. It would have been good to have slept in the same bed tonight, not making love, just touching and talking, providing the same intimacy of personality that their bodies had already relished.

She was telling him that Brian Keith had found out she was helping him, that consequently she had not been able to get the latest figures. Dominic felt the tenseness return. He wasn't sure of Keith. Keith seemed an honest, hardworking banker, a fraction too old to be a political guerrilla, but as with friends like Martin, there were ambivalences, and no one could be trusted.

Dominic felt bitter that she had endangered him. But reason supervened. Claire wasn't as used to intrigue as he was, hadn't lived with the suspicion and fear, the paranoia that came to easily to the agent in the field. What else could he say but tell her to reveal as little as she'd have to, thinking at the same time that if Edgar and Keith were allies, something might turn out good.

She wanted him to tell her he missed her, but that sounded artificial when their voices were wired through space, and the sound of the words in an empty room would sound banal. So he said he'd be back soon, tomorrow or the day after that.

It was then, wanting to prolong contact however insubstantial, that Claire told him about the takeover bid. A lawyer, acting for an un-named principal had made an offer to bail out the bank, in exchange for Edgar's controlling shares. The offer was for seventy million Swiss francs,

127

sixty million of which would be made available right away, to meet the bank's immediate needs.

Dominic couldn't help it. He had to look for reasons, for possibilities. An anonymous principal sounded like Midas. But then in small financial communities like Lugano, or even Switzerland, people often preferred anonymity, so that bad relationships in one sphere of business did not affect good relationships in others.

Claire didn't know the name of the lawyer. Her source of information was an overheard conversation between Keith and Doppler, and afterwards Keith had called Edgar.

It was food for thought, something to mull over and keep away nightmares. If Midas had ruined the bank, why would they now want to take it over?

Dominic said goodnight, promised to call again to-morrow and prepared for bed. For a while he lay awake in the darkness, listening to the accordions pumping in the restaurant below, thinking about Midas and Carmody and Marc, of living and dying, and why he was doing what he was doing. Finally he drifted into sleep, reaching across empty sheets, his last waking thoughts of Claire.

CHAPTER NINETEEN

The next morning Dominic went to the Companies Office, paid his fifteen francs and obtained neatly typed sheets which told him that Intra, Kastel and Sulden had been formed a year ago, that each of them had an original capital of fifty thousand francs, and that the directors of all three were a Swiss gentleman in Berne and a lawyer called Eugene Beck who lived in Vaduz.

Beck's offices were just outside the town boundary, part of a new complex that was only partly let and most of that to a property development company. Dominic walked up highly polished stairs to the first floor. Tall windows on one side of the building let him look over fields and trees to the dark green hulk of the Churfirstern. Beck's office had the same view, from a slightly different angle.

The offices were sparse, neat and unrevealing. A polite young secretary sat in the outer office, and there was a young man in an inner room, looking over account books, glancing up from time to time at Dominic and smiling shyly, as Dominic thumbed idly through last week's *Time*.

Ten minutes later, the young secretary ushered him into Beck's presence, and gave him coffee. Beck was a big-boned man in his mid fifties, with the clear-eyed, fresh-complexioned look of someone who spent a lot of time breathing mountain air. He was soberly suited in dark blue. His head was square with a crown of silvery brown hair and he wore gold-framed glasses. His hands were unusually small and freshly scrubbed, and there was a dryness about them as he shook hands and waved Dominic to a seat.

The office like the rest of the building was sparkling, furnished in a tasteful combination of antique and modern furniture. Beck's desk was of Scandinavian design, polished wood, black leather and chrome, the chairs were Trafalgar rope-back and there was a carved chest by a door that led onto a sunbaked terrace. The pictures on the roughened walls were modern originals, and behind Beck was a calendar issued by a gasoline company, with pictures of scenery that would have looked treacly on chocolate boxes. It was all neat, ordered, businesslike and very remote from evil.

'Mr Cain, you say you are here on urgent business from the Banco Lattoria in Lugano.' Beck's voice was guttural, very German.

'That's correct. I am investigating a fraud. Intra, Kastel and Sulden, three companies you represent, may be involved.'

Beck listened to the names impassively. Then he said, 'Impossible.'

'You are aware that the Banco Lattoria has paid these companies something like seventy million francs?'

'Yes. It was money due to them from the bank.'

'We feel they were working in collusion with the head of our foreign-exchange department and that together they defrauded the bank.'

'I read only yesterday,' Beck remarked, 'that the Banco Lattoria is having difficulty honouring its obligations. I wonder if you are not trying to make my clients scapegoats for the bank.'

'We suspect fraud,' Dominic said, refusing to go on the defensive.

'Then without doubt you will have your employee arrested and have the police talk to me.'

'The employee was killed in a car accident on Saturday night.'

'That is unlucky for you,' Beck said and leaned back in his chair, steepling his fingers. 'You have no evidence. I am sorry I cannot help you.'

130

'Who is the real owner of these companies?'

'That also I cannot tell you.'

'I am staying at the Engel. Can you ask the owner to meet me there?'

'I will give him your message. He will meet you if he wants to. How long are you staying in Vaduz, Mr Cain?'

'As long as necessary.'

Somehow Dominic had expected a younger person, someone more in keeping with the image of Midas. But of Beck's obstinacy and discretion there was no doubt. He hadn't given anything away, except that he represented someone. Who? Some megalomaniac or some genius, taking a lunatic revenge on society?

'Ever hear of anyone called Midas, Mr Beck?'

'That is a fairytale.' That was what Claire had said. Beck made a heavy joke. 'You have the Midas touch, I think?'

'You're too nice to be involved with Midas,' Dominic said. 'They're murderers.'

'My business is company work,' Beck said. 'I do not know anything about murderers.'

Didn't know, or didn't want to know, Dominic wondered. 'We know about Midas,' Dominic said. 'Our foreign-exchange dealer left enough clues before he died.'

'You are telling me this for some purpose?'

Yes, Dominic thought, I'm trying to stop you acting like a slab of Swiss mountain rock. 'You tell your client what I have said.'

'If and when I see him, Mr Cain, and if he wants to listen.' He unsteepled his fingers and sat upright, his gaze as blank as the snow on the Churfirstern.

Dominic said, 'Your client wouldn't be interested in taking over the Banco Lattoria, would he?'

'That is my client's business. Do you have an interest in the matter?'

'Yes,' Dominic said and stood up, smiling. 'I know your

client happens to be eighteen million francs short, and I know where to find it. Please tell him that. If and when you see him.'

After that there was nothing to do but wait. Dominic ordered lunch on the terrace of the Engel and watched the traffic grind by. There was a blond young man in blue denim who kept eyeing him curiously, but Dominic wasn't worried. If Beck had made contact with Midas, Midas would know Dominic was too valuable to be killed.

Claire phoned, hoping to leave a message, surprised to find him there. Because of the other work she'd had to do, and because Doppler and Brian seemed to be watching her, she hadn't been able to check all the Interstellar accounts. What she had checked, however, were the transactions authorized by de Marco over the last three years. Except for four transfers of one hundred thousand dollars each, made just over two years ago, it all looked normal. Two of the transfers had been made to someone called Garnham, and two to Kevin Cormack. What she had found intriguing about these four transactions was that in every case the money had been repaid seven to ten days later.

Kit Garnham and Kevin Cormack, Dominic thought, members of the Movement, of Midas, part of Duval's cell. Interesting!

Claire asked if that information was helpful.

'Terrific,' Dominic said. 'Terrific.'

She wanted to know when he was coming back.

'Soon,' Dominic promised. 'Very soon,' and then she had to go because she could hear Doppler coming into the room, and Dominic went back to the terrace for his lunch.

For the first time in three days, Dominic ate with relish. He ate slowly, took care to refuse the traditionally copious second helping and to drink sparingly of a small carafe of Fleurie. Yet, however slowly he ate and however parsimoniously he drank, the meal had to end, and an hour after coffee time hung heavy.

Out of boredom and drowsiness came an idea, not of great importance in itself, but cheeky, the equivalent of a two-fingered gesture at Midas. Dominic walked over to the nearest bank and said his name was Johann Winthrop. He was expecting a transfer of funds from the Fieldhaus Bank in Zurich. Had he come to the right bank?

The clerk said unfortunately he had not. But as there were only three banks in Vaduz, he should try the other two.

The girl who served him in the next bank looked puzzled. She left him, went into a back room and came back saying they were correspondents for the Fieldhaus Bank, but they had no remittance for Mr Winthrop. Would he like her to phone the Fieldhaus Bank, or could he come back to-morrow morning, when it may have arrived in the post.

Dominic said she was very kind, but no thanks. Could he now deposit some money into the accounts of three friends. The girl, already tainted with a banker's avarice for deposits, said of course he could. Dominic took the deposit slips, wrote out the account numbers made up from the diagonals and the first square, and gave them to the girl with three hundred francs. She looked at the papers, frowned and said okay and then asked to see his passport. She frowned even more when she saw it and said, 'But you are not Mr Winthrop?'

'That is correct. Mr Winthrop is sick. He is in his room at the Engel.'

'Ah,' the girl said and recorded his name and passport number on the slips. Dominic thanked her and turned away from the counter, pulling out his notebook and almost bumping into the blue-denimed young man he had seen at the Engel. What the hell difference did it make if the young man was from Midas? After all, Dominic wanted them to know how much he knew.

He came into the street and went for a walk around the loop. When he had completed the circuit, there was no sign of the denimed young man. But there was a red Ferrari Berlinetta Boxer with Italian plates, parked outside the bank.

Whatever anyone else thought, Dominic felt that Ferrari built the most exciting cars in the world. There was something about their uncompromising styling, the howl of their twelve-cylinder engines, their total dedication to producing drivers' cars instead of good-looking boulevard cruisers, that had endeared Ferrari to Dominic ever since he was old enough to tell the difference between makes of cars. Now he stopped and drooled over this one. It was low and chunky and functional, pretty near the ultimate in road performance, with a five-speed gearbox and road-holding that had something to teach leeches. Even parked it was stirringly beautiful.

A vaguely familiar voice said, 'You like the car?'

'It's lovely,' Dominic said, unable to take his eyes away.

'Perhaps you would like to go for a drive, Mr Cain?'

Dominic turned and looked into the plumply smiling face of Gianni Siccoli.

'Do not look so surprised, Mr Cain. It is my car. I came from Lugano in one and a half hours. It seems you frightened the good Doctor Beck very much.'

'Are you Midas?' Dominic asked.

'No,' Siccoli said. 'I am to arrange a meeting between you and Midas. Also, I want to engage your services.'

'For what?'

'You will meet Midas later on this evening,' Siccoli said. 'I will arrange that he will come alone. I will pay you one hundred thousand dollars if you will kill him.'

CHAPTER TWENTY

Such an outrageous proposition required both coffee and brandy. The terrace café at the Engel provided both.

Before he would take the job, Dominic said he wanted evidence that Siccoli's offer was genuine. Money alone wouldn't convince him of that. There weren't any pockets in a shroud, and dollars weren't legal tender in heaven. The only way Dominic could assess the credibility of the offer was if Siccoli told Dominic everything about his involvement with Midas. He should start, Dominic suggested, at the beginning.

The beginning was sordid and predictable, the story of a man of wealth seeking to preserve that wealth. Siccoli said that Dominic, being an educated man, would understand that right back to the time of Garibaldi, Italy had been a mess. Garibaldi had united provinces, not formed a nation, and a Milanese was still a Milanese, different from and better than any Neapolitan. Italy was chaos and confusion, the poor prize of a struggle amongst the Church, the Communists and those ignorant southerners in Rome who deluded themselves that they controlled things. Under these circumstances what was a sane and sober businessman to do?

Inflation was rampant, taxes were penal, the value of the lira continued to fall, and the country had a strike record surpassed only by that of Dominic's own. So being prudent, as well as sane and sober, Siccoli had thought to make provision in case, and may all the saints prevent it, the worst happened. He had followed the example of those millions of others who since the Reformation had sought financial solace in Switzerland. It was, after all, his duty to make sure that he and his family had a pittance on which to survive. That too was traditional.

The difficulty was that as time went on the authorities got tougher, the problems of getting money out increased, and the cost of bribes took all the profit out of the transactions. Eight months ago, Midas had been referred to him by a close business friend, an aristocrat. At first Siccoli had been suspicious. Midas were young men whose ways he did not even pretend to understand. But their rates were absurdly cheap.

He had started off with small transactions, five thousand dollars worth of lire, that kind of thing – pocket money. As his trust increased, the amounts became more substantial, and always, always Midas delivered. No shipment ever went astray, they never took more than the agreed figure, and any extraneous expenditure was scrupulously accounted for. He imagined that Midas had such a large turnover that they could afford to work for so little, and had even got to quite like his way-out band of couriers.

Until a year ago. A year ago someone from Midas had come to talk to him, someone slightly older, less carefree. He was an Irishman named Kevin Cormack. He came with a proposition. Midas were expanding into other businesses and, knowing how useful they had been to Siccoli, Midas was sure he would like to invest with them. The first payment was only twenty-five thousand dollars, and now Siccoli realized how foolish he had been to pay it. It would have been cheaper to bribe someone high up in the Foreign Exchange Department, or, in the last resort, to have paid a fine or gone to jail. But having paid once, he had to pay again. And again. The hundred thousand dollars Duval had been smuggling had been another instalment off Siccoli's 'investment'. Over the last year, he must have 'invested' nearly three-quarters of a million dollars, and he knew of at least one other person who had done the same.

Rich as he was, he could not afford it, so paying a hundred thousand dollars to end it was really quite cheap.

The story sounded probable, could even be true. It certainly fitted Dominic's theories, and what little evidence he had. 'Who is Midas?' Dominic asked. 'Who is the man who runs the group?'

'I do not know. I only know of him as Midas. All my contacts have been with the young men and this Kevin Cormack. Beck maybe knows, because after your visit I received instructions to contact you in Vaduz and arrange for you to meet with Midas at my lodge in Malbun. You have information about eighteen million francs that has gone missing.'

'But why choose me to kill Midas? For the kind of money you are paying, you can buy the best hit men in the business.'

'I chose you because you are good, and because you want to kill Midas. I know how good you are. Ellis will never shoot a gun again. It serves him right. His instructions were to follow you, nothing more. But what can you do with employees nowadays? They do what they like.'

'What other reasons?' Dominic asked.

'Ah, the most important one. Midas wants to talk to you. You will have the chance to get close to him. So you have the desire, the skill and the opportunity.' Siccoli seemed to think that settled the matter.

Dominic said, 'It takes a lot to kill a man the first time. How do you know I will do it well?'

'Because for you it is not the first time. Midas knows that. I was warned to be careful of you.'

Dominic looked at the street and immersed himself in thought. He saw the blond young man in blue denim walk by, looking at them with studied curiosity. Then he caught Dominic's eye and looked away. Perhaps he was Siccoli's bodyguard, Dominic thought and said, 'How will you pay the money?'

'Half when you start the job, half when Midas is dead. You prefer Swiss francs or US dollars?'

'Swiss francs,' Dominic said. 'They keep better. How many bodyguards will he have?'

'I've been told to arrange food and accommodation for three. So two bodyguards.'

'Do I have to kill them as well?'

'Not unless it becomes necessary. I have a plan to keep them out of it.'

To explain his plan, Siccoli had first to tell Dominic about the location of his hunting lodge. It was on a peak beyond Malbun, reached by a tortuous road which was part tank track. The most rugged vehicle took over three hours to get there. Rather than build a more practicable road, Siccoli had installed a tele-cabin lift – some of his visitors were quite susceptible to the weather – which ran from Malbun lift station. His lift was private, though in the winter he allowed skiers to use it.

There were only two tele-cabins in use in the summer and they ran at intervals of twenty-four yards. Dominic and Siccoli would go early and wait for Midas at Malbun station. At eight-thirty in the evening, the station would be deserted. When Midas came they would be cordial and welcoming, and naturally, wanting to discuss the missing eighteen million francs, Midas would ride in the first tele-cabin with them. He could not possibly suspect anything. Siccoli would be there and his guards in the tele-cabin immediately following. He could not know of the twenty-four yard gap.

Once they were in the cabin, Dominic would kill Midas. The question of how was Dominic's problem. They would reach the lift station at the top, twenty-four yards ahead of the guards, who would not think it unusual if Siccoli got out first and walked to the control room. Once Siccoli was

138

in the control room he would stop the lift, leaving the guards suspended in mid air until they had thrown away their weapons. The possibility was that having lost their leader, they would be malleable. If they weren't, they could easily be taken care of.

'Will there not be revenge?' Dominic asked.

'With Midas dead, they will not be able to organize revenge.'

'What happens,' Dominic inquired, 'if Midas is armed?'

'You'll find a way,' Siccoli said. 'If I knew all the answers, I would do it myself.'

'Okay,' Dominic said, 'I'll do it.' And he agreed that Siccoli should meet him at the Engel at seven. They would go and inspect the tele-cabins and work out the details before Midas arrived at eight-thirty.

'And don't forget to bring the money,' Dominic added.

There were three possibilities. Siccoli was lying. Siccoli was telling part of the truth. Or Siccoli was telling the whole truth and nothing but.

If Siccoli was lying, Midas's men would set about Dominic in Malbun and try to persuade him to talk about the missing eighteen million francs. After his excellent bluff, they wouldn't believe that he didn't know and the effect of that would be to prolong the torture. In the end, whether he talked or not, they would kill him.

The second possibility was that everything would go according to plan, until Midas was killed. Then either Siccoli would let the bodyguards get Dominic, or Siccoli's own men would grab him. That way, Siccoli would save his hundred thousand dollars and the scenario would revert to that in the first possibility, with the exception that they would be even more vicious, having the moral justification of dealing with the man who had just killed their leader.

It was also possible that Siccoli was telling the truth.

Possible, but slightly incredible. But Dominic had little alternative but to go with Siccoli. The only thing he was sure of was that Midas wanted to see him. And for that it was worth taking a risk.

Dominic's counter plan was absurdly simple. He could go to Malbun with Siccoli, using Siccoli's car. Once there he would inspect the tele-cabins, discuss methods of killing. Half an hour before Midas was due to come. Dominic would attack Siccoli, knock him out. Then Dominic would hide in the station building.

When Midas arrived with his two bodyguards, he would see Siccoli's Ferrari parked outside the station and assume that everything was all right. The three of them would get out of the car and walk up to the steps. Every lift station has steps, and when a group of people come to narrow steps there are always problems of precedence. Before a natural and safe order of ascent emerged, Dominic would start shooting. He intended to wound, but if necessary to kill the bodyguards. Which would leave Midas.

If Midas was really going to be there.

CHAPTER TWENTY-ONE

Dominic badly needed his own gun. The bodyguards would be armed and he would be shooting in tricky light. A familiar gun would have made all the difference, but a familiar gun wasn't to be had. So he bought himself a Grisbi diver's knife, with a four-inch blade and one serrated edge. The rubber grip felt comfortably lethal in his hand, and he had the edge below the serrations honed to razor sharpness. The knife came with a rubber sheath and straps for fastening around a diver's calf.

Dominic strapped it as high as possible to the inside of his right thigh, adjusting it so that he could sit down without having the hilt stick him in the testicles. The top strap wasn't designed to go round a thigh, and he had to stretch it near to snapping point to make it fit. Conversely, the lower strap wasn't designed to go around the top of a knee, and he had to cut a hole in the rubber to make it fit reasonably well. When he looked at himself in the mirror, a small bulge showed. Never mind, he would wear his trousers a little lower on the hip, and he bought himself a black leather coat that came down to his knees. A black leather coat might look unusually warm for a summer evening, but Dominic could always explain that he'd thought evening air in the mountains was chill.

Siccoli arrived at the hotel shortly before seven, carrying a canvas bag. Dominic had him come up to the room.

'Open it,' Dominic said, pointing to the bag. He'd heard of booby-trapped money caches before.

Siccoli shrugged and did so.

'Put the money on the table.'

Siccol had brought the Swiss franc equivalent of one hundred thousand dollars, all in 1,000 franc notes. Dominic counted them, put them back in the canvas bag and threw it into a drawer. Siccoli looked concerned.

'It's only money,' Dominic said. 'And there's more to come.'

He allowed Siccoli to precede him to the door, then took out de Marco's gun and jabbed Siccoli so hard with it that he fell forward against the door, spreading his arms out against the frame to stop himself.

'Stay like that,' Dominic said, still jabbing. Siccoli stood still while Dominic searched him. All he had on him was a small Biretta which Dominic threw into the drawer with the money. 'I'm the one who's being paid to do the shooting,' he said. 'Let's go.'

It took them twenty-five minutes to get to Malbun, along a narrow, winding road. Siccoli didn't hurry the Ferrari unduly, and it was a smooth ride, with the Ferrari exhaust snarling angrily at the mountains.

Malbun station was a single building supported on a raised concrete platform. Skeins of wire stretched up the mountainsides like giant cobwebs, rising high over the valleys. Everything in Malbun was still, and the car park was deserted.

Siccoli parked the Ferrari and Dominic noticed with relief that there were narrow concrete steps leading up to the station. The building seemed to be divided into two areas. The larger area housed the lift machinery and control room. The remainder consisted of a small room, with windows on three sides, and was presumably used as an office. One of the windows overlooked the car park, and another the steps. If he could get into the office Dominic could cover Midas's approach with no difficulty at all.

Except that now a swarthy young man was strolling down the steps to greet them. He was a stocky, solid-looking figure, with tight black curly hair and a moustache, wearing a blue and white striped T-shirt and pale blue

142

slacks. The muscles under the T-shirt were tight too. And big.

He greeted them with a broad smile and Siccoli introduced him as Pietro. Pietro looked after the lift machinery and Siccoli had asked him along in case Dominic had any questions. He would return to the lodge well before Midas arrived. Which suited Dominic fine.

The three of them went up to the steps, and Dominic noted how Pietro shuffled and hesitated, trying to decide if he should show his master the way or follow deferentially. They walked onto the platform. Below them the land fell away steeply to the valley and then rose to a series of tree-dotted, rock-strewn peaks, the twin brown wires stretching out above them, swaying slightly between the pylons.

Pietro led them into one of the control rooms, a large circular area with a coiled drum in the centre and two tele-cabins standing around it, painted blue and grey. To one side was a yellow-painted, glass-fronted control box and there was a constant hum from the electric motor. Dominic couldn't make out that the cabins were twenty-four yards apart, but Pietro said that was because they were standing in a circle and the cable was coiled. He showed Dominic the 'start', 'stop' and 'hold' switches in the control room, and the switch for the motor. Dominic didn't have any more questions.

They went across to the tele-cabins, tiny compartments like attenuated railway carriages, with metal racks on the outside for skis. They had large windows fore and aft, so that the head and shoulders of anyone seated inside could clearly be seen. That would have been a problem if Dominic had intended to kill Midas. Even at half past eight in the evening there would be enough light to see twenty-four yards, and certainly enough light to shoot that distance. On either side of the tele-cabins were spring-back doors, going nearly the full height and width of the carriage.

Pietro opened a set of doors and stooped into the first cabin. Still stooping he pressed a catch, opened the doors on the other side and got out. With both sets of doors open, the whole contraption looked too fragile to support the weight of four human beings, 1,500 metres above the trees. Siccoli was standing close behind Dominic, as if he wanted to look at the inside of the cabin too. Dominic bent forward and got in.

The next moment Siccoli pushed him. Hard. Dominic shot forward, spreading his hands onto the seats to brace himself and stop the forward impulsion. For a split second he stopped there, palms flat on the seats, body stooped, head thrust forward, then the edge of Pietro's hand chopped across the back of his neatly offered neck and his knees went.

He fell forward onto his arms, felt them go, felt his face pulled against Pietro's T-shirt, even smelt the acrid tang of Pietro's body, mingled with aftershave. Then an arm grasped him round the waist and he felt the pocket of his leather coat become weightless. That was the last thing he remembered.

CHAPTER TWENTY-TWO

A rod of pain across the back of his neck, and a gentle, swaying, rhythmic motion like the swing he rode as a child. The swing used to be under the breadfruit tree, a contraption of rope and wood, and he could still remember the fruit, thick and green and swollen. Slow, soft swinging – why was *amah* pushing him sideways? She had no business pushing him sideways when he wanted to go up and up, and if she wouldn't push him higher, he'd tell his father. His father! No! That thing sitting in the chair with its head lolling and tongue protruding was not his father, not that thing with blood on its shirt and those horrible dripping stumps of hands...

Dominic came awake sweating, ready to spring, his hand gripping the knife between his legs. He opened his eyes and lay panting across the seat of the tele-cabin. It was still light. He could see the sky darkening outside the window. He looked at his watch. It was five past eight. He'd been unconscious hardly twenty minutes. He waited.

He waited while the pain surged and throbbed, the nausea rose to the back of his throat. He breathed slowly and deeply, emptying his mind, concentrating on an ultimate blackness. Later, when he sat up, the pain had almost gone and it was almost dark.

But not so dark that they couldn't see him. A metallic voice opposite crackled, 'I'm pleased you've woken up Mr Cain.'

On the seat opposite was a walkie-talkie radio. Dominic reached out for it. Despite the static he could recognize Siccoli's voice. He sat up and looked around. He was alone in the tele-cabin, suspended exactly halfway between Malbun and the station at the top. In front of him a light glowed in Malbun station. Behind him was a rapidly growing darkness and a hell of a lot of space. The cabin was at least a thousand metres above the darkening tree tops and deepening shadows of rock.

'Mr Cain, why don't you tell us about the eighteen million francs?'

Good question. The only problem was all he knew about the eighteen million francs was that it was missing. Even if he knew where it was, it wouldn't make any difference. They still meant to kill him.

'We intend to keep you there till you tell us,' Siccoli said.

It seemed his only choice was the manner of his death. He could leap over the side and end it quickly, or he could die slowly, from heat, thirst and starvation. On a hot summer's day, he would roast like a turkey in an oven, sweat out pints of precious water. Maybe he would last forty-eight hours. For want of something to do, he took the knife out of his trousers and strapped it to his calf. The knife hadn't proved any good. He looked out of the windows again. The same amount of space between him and the valley. Only darker.

He hurled himself to the floor as a bullet shattered the glass of the fore and aft windows. The cabin bucked and swayed at the sudden transfer of weight and he pressed himself to the floor, trembling. Siccoli had only wanted to frighten him, but in that light he could so easily have missed.

'Relax, Mr Cain,' the radio squawked. 'I am a very good shot. I even hunt bear.'

Piss-artist, thought Dominic and, switching the radio to transmit, said so.

'It would be wiser to talk about the eighteen million francs,' Siccoli said.

'Altitude makes me forget.' Dominic was sure that only Siccoli and Pietro were at the Malbun station. Any more

146

people and they would have kept him there, where they could see him suffer. 'Let me talk to Midas.'

'He isn't here. He went away when he found you were so high.' Siccoli seemed to think he'd made a joke.

So Midas hadn't come. 'Siccoli, tell me, are you Midas? If you are, I'll talk to you.'

A long silence before the radio crackled again. 'I am not Midas. But you can talk to me. Everything you say will be faithfully reported to Midas.'

I bet. Midas must be very powerful if someone like Siccoli would not take his name in vain, even to gain an advantage. Dominic stared down the twin strands of wire running down the pylons to the light at the far end. How the hell was he to get out of this?

'I will not talk to you. I will only talk to Midas.'

'That will take too long. You will be dead by the time he gets here.'

'Not if you bring me down.'

They didn't know he had the knife, and if they pulled him back to the station, perhaps the surprise of his attack would give him the advantage.

'My instructions are that you stay up there till you talk.'

'You'll have a bloody long wait, my friend.'

'You too,' Siccoli replied.

Dominic sat and watched the sky grow dark. Below him sparks of light dotted the valleys and the sides of the peaks. Behind him the station was in total darkness, the cables hardly visible now, swinging up from pylon to pylon, all the way to the top. He had to get down, Dominic thought, he had to get down. He wondered if there was some way he could loose the tele-cabin from the cable. No, even if he had the tools it would be dangerous. Either he and the cabin would fall into the valley below, or run back down the cable and smash into the solid walls of Malbun station. Dominic tried to imagine how the lifts worked. The cables

147

weren't electrified; he'd never seen a lift that sparked. No, the system was based on drums at each end, powered by electric motors, coiling the cables round and round. He could get out of the cabin, grab hold of the cable and slide down it to the station.

That wouldn't work. Getting hold of the cable was difficult enough, but sliding down it would flay his palms to shreds. Besides, it was a long drop and he knew his arms and shoulders could not take the strain of his weight for the length of time it would take to slide down so far. That idea was a hairsbreadth from suicide. What else could he do?

'Cain, it's getting late. Don't be foolish. Tell me where the money is.'

'When you've brought Midas to me, not before.' If he held out long enough, Siccoli might do it. But that wouldn't do Dominic much good, unless he wanted to die looking into Midas's face.

The darkness was spreading, and Dominic was surrounded by a growing blackness. He knew he could last the night – but what about the next day, and the day after that? Seventy-two hours without water and he would certainly be dead. And then, an idea. Dominic opened the door, heard the rustle of the wind as it rushed into the cabin. Gripping the edge of the door he leaned out into the blackness and looked up. Then he turned and looked up the hillside towards the top station. He sat down and closed the door.

'Siccoli, bring me down and I'll talk.'

'I can't do that.'

'Bring me down or bring me Midas.'

'No, Mr Cain.'

His plan was wild and dangerous, but it was the only plan he had. 'All right then, I'm breaking off communication. In five seconds I am throwing your radio out of the window.'

'Don't be silly—'

Siccoli's words were abruptly cut off by the smashing of glass as Dominic hurled the radio through the remnants of the aft window. They wouldn't see it fall, but he hoped they'd hear the glass breaking.

Dominic sat and waited in silence. The cabin swayed in the breeze, but didn't move down, not then, not an hour later. Whatever else they did, they were going to leave him there all night.

Dominic waited ten minutes more and opened the door. The breeze wafted in, and he stood in the doorway gripping its sides, frighteningly aware of the yawning blackness below. There was no ledge below the door, nothing on which he could get a foothold. He turned sideways in the doorway and put a foot into space. The door began to bend as it took his weight and he slid his foot along the side of the cabin until it reached the ski rack. There was a foothold there, but it had been designed to take skis, not the weight of a man, and in any case he could not get the rest of his body out to join his foot. It was also at the back of the car, which was the side he didn't want to be. Not as long as Siccoli had a rifle.

He came back into the cabin, trembling, his palms covered with sweat. The only way out was through the front window. He took out the knife and picked out what was left of the glass. Then, sitting on the back of the seat and gripping the top of the window, he leaned out backwards and looked. The roof of the cabin curved above him, and above that a few tiny stars in the sky. He dared not look down. Slowly he inched himself further and further upwards and outwards. His fingers closed around the guttering. It was too narrow and brittle to take more than the weight of rainwater. He moved his hand away from it, upwards, edging his body after it. His hand ran along the roof. It felt as smooth as ice.

There was still two feet between his outstretched hand and the first of the two steel rods that fastened the cabin to

149

the cable. His hand was sweating again, and beginning to slip. Hurriedly Dominic thrust his legs inside and transferred his weight to the interior of the cabin. Then he pulled his body through, and sat, sweating.

The only way to do it would be to crouch in the window, facing into the cabin. Then a quiet straightening up and a lunge for the steel rod. He tried not to think of his body wheeling into the blackness below, told himself that the pinpoints of light were just that, and the trees no more than ski sticks. When the sweating of his palms had ceased, he decided to go.

Once again he sat on the back of the seat, thrust his body out of the gap. The cabin was tilted upwards, so that he had to fight its angle. But once he got out it would help him to fall forward onto the cabin.

He gripped the top of the window and thrust his neck out, drew his legs up till he was wedged in the window. The wind tugged at him and the cabin swayed. Now came the difficult bit, when he had to straighten his body, keeping the tilt of his body in alignment with the cabin, so that he was always pressed against it. A little too much pressure, another gust of wind, a shot from Siccoli, and he would tip backwards and hurtle into space.

He concentrated on his calves and knees and thighs. The movement must come from below, a gradual straightening, pressing the upper part of his body to the roof, hoping to keep some hold on the cabin by friction. Slowly his body came up, his head drew level with the roof, the muscles of his legs bulging, protesting, feeling as if they had run five miles. He kept on raising himself, and slowly, very slowly, brought his arms up stretched out above his head, pushing the palms flat against the metal roof. He must not try to pull with them. Leave it all to the legs, straightening ever so slowly, feeling like firebrands.

And he did it. He was standing on the window ledge, his

face and palms flat on the roof. But he was still a foot from the rod.

There was no help for it. He would have to lunge. He could not keep this position for more than a minute. First the palms would start to slip, then the legs would go, and he would tumble helplessly downward.

Now, he thought, *now* – he pressed down with his legs, jumped, felt an arm slip, fingers curl, grab the rod, slip, grab it again, hold, hold it like that, drag his other arm to it. His palms locked round the rough metal and then he forced his arms to pull, dragging his body onto the roof. As his stomach came over he began to slide the other way and he pivoted his body round the axis of the shaft, so that he ended up lying diagonally across the roof, his hands still locked round the rod.

No time to think now, no time to rest, and he must not think of the yawning emptiness below. He dragged himself against the rod and, holding the rod, stood up. The wind was snatching at him, and far below him he cold see the tiny glow that was Malbun station. He wondered if his body was silhouetted against the mountains peaks, if Siccoli would start shooting. But he had to rest, his body was dripping with sweat and fear, and his breathing was as loud as that of a running dog.

He looked up at the top station, then reached up and took hold of the cable with one hand. For a while he stood there, tilting backwards, one hand on the shaft, the other on the cable. Then he let go of the rod, grabbed the cable with both hands and walked up the inclined roof to its edge.

He kept his eyes fixed on the top station. He had to keep looking up. To look down would have been disaster. He leaned forward with his arm as far as he could, and then kicked his body away from the roof, gasping as the arms took the shock of his weight and left him dangling in space.

This was to be the most exhausting bit. Moving up the

cable, hand over hand, each movement sending a violent shock of pain all the way down his arms into his shoulders. Hand over hand he inched upward, each movement jarring his body, bouncing him as the cable swayed. Sometimes he thought he was slipping back, and his palms began to burn. Despite the night breeze, his body was bathed in hot sweat.

Once more, he had to do it once more. And then again. Once more, once more, getting more difficult as the cable looped upwards to the pylon. He could feel his fingers growing rigid, the first dull pain of cramp. But he had to go on, he could not allow himself the luxury of even a second's rest.

The pain in his hands subsided; they were like distant, metal things, and he knew it would not be long before he lost control of them, before they unhooked and allowed him to plunge into the valley below. He must not think of that, he must keep going on. Out of the darkness he could see the lattice work of the pylon loom in front of him, and he swung furiously, harder, faster, it was only feet now, inches.

And then his foot scraped metal. With a surge of relief he reached upwards, harder, faster, and then he was able to lock his feet against the pylon, have them take the weight from his straining arms.

The pain was incredible. He felt his muscles knotting convulsively, but he had made it. He hung there panting and when the pain had gone, he moved the last few inches, easier now, with his body's weight shared between feet and hands. He reached out and grasped the pylon. Then, and only then, did he dare to look down.

After that all he had to do was climb down the pylon and five minutes later he was standing on rough grass, and earth had never felt so sweet.

CHAPTER TWENTY-THREE

Dominic walked down the valley, moving quickly from one row of pylons to the next. It was a moonless night, and his presence was hardly more than a shadow. He felt sure he could not be seen from the station. He swung his arms as he walked, feeling a delightful sense of freedom, a refreshing tingling of the blood. He went up a small rise and down again. The valley was mostly scrub and once or twice he stumbled against a rock. It took him over an hour to get within sighting distance of Malbun station.

Two pylons from the station Dominic broke away to the right. He walked parallel to the station till he was well past the extreme edge of the platform, then turned left and flung himself to the ground. He decided to crawl the rest of the way, and as he smelt grass and earth, he felt no fatigue, only a great awareness, his mind concentrated wonderfully on its task.

Hugging the ground, sometimes rising into a crouching run, he made the escarpment, ten foot of crumbling brick separating the station and the road from the valley. Again he walked away from the station, looking for a place far enough away where the brick had crumbled enough to leave footholds. When he found it, he went up quickly and without effort, rolled himself over the top and lay flat on the road.

He paused there, getting his breath back, his eyes fixed on the station. The lift area and control room were in total darkness. There was a faint glimmer of light from the office beyond. He hoped Siccoli and Pietro were comfortable and warm. Apart from the light, there were no signs of life. There was also no cover. Reaching downwards, he eased off his shoes and stuffed them into his pockets. Reaching down again, he rolled back the rubber strip that held the knife in its sheath. Then in a series of crouching runs he made the edge of the platform and leapt onto it.

He landed crouching, and stood still for a moment, knife drawn and extended in the classic fighting pose. He stood still, smelling the air, every sense attuned to the slightest movement. Nothing moved. Still crouching, he hurried across the platform into the lift area. The electric motor was still humming, and a row of red and green bulbs shone from the control panel. He went into the control room and studied the lay out carefully, before he turned the switch that illuminated the console. Then he studied the layout carefully again, and flicked the switch that brought the tele-cabin back down.

Immediately the humming in the control room increased. There was a harsh grinding as the drum began to turn. Dominic turned and saw the tele-cabin sway and start to move downwards. He watched it move and then pressed himself into a corner of the control room, away from the light, the drawn knife pressed hilt downwards against his thigh.

Seconds later he heard a shout, followed by the patter of running feet. Pietro heeled into view, trotting fast through the lift area. He paused and looked and then charged into the control room. He had eyes only for the illuminated console and the switches on the panel. He moved the lift switch to 'hold', and Dominic thrust the knife at the splayed out palm.

Pietro only heard a rustling movement, saw a bright flash of steel, then felt the searing pain as the knife ripped between the fragile bones of his outstretched palm and transfixed it to the wood of the console. Blood spurted round the silver blade. He was opening his mouth to scream when Dominic moved forward and hit him across the throat.

154

Pietro choked, reeled, felt the knife saw at his hand and moved forward again.

'Not a word,' Dominic said. 'I've come back from the dead.'

Pietro stared at him, eyes protruding with pain, mouth writhing with suppressed cries.

'Now you'll know better than to hit me again,' Dominic said. He leaned his weight on the knife and Pietro winced.

Dominic asked, 'Where's Siccoli?'

'In the office.'

'Would you like to die?'

A rhetorical question. Pietro didn't want to die. 'Keep silent when I take the knife away. Keep silent till after I've gone.'

Pietro nodded vehemently.

Dominic wrenched out the knife, allowing the blood to spurt after it hungrily. Some of it spattered on the desk, and splashed over his trousers. 'Remember,' Dominic said. 'Not a word. Or I will come back and it will be worse.'

Pietro clasped his hand and sank into a chair. Dominic found a safety harness, stripped it and roped Pietro loosely into the chair. There was a first-aid box in the control room, and Dominic wadded Pietro's wound, telling him that as long as he didn't move he wouldn't bleed to death.

Afterwards Dominic went out of the control room, across the lift area and onto the platform. He hurried down the platform to the office. The door was open, just as Pietro had left it. Siccoli was eating spaghetti and tunny fish at a wooden table that doubled as a desk. A half empty plate opposite him showed that Dominic's descent had interrupted a late meal. There was wine on the table and beer, the smell of coffee from a Calorgas stove in the corner.

Dominic slipped silently through the open door, placed the point of the knife in the back of Siccoli's neck.

'Pietro,' Siccoli said, hearing the slurp of that last

stealthy footstep, then feeling the cold sharpness of the blade against his skin and going very still.

'It's Dominic Cain, back from the dead,' thinking it was too late at night to be original. 'Take my gun out of your pocket and put it on the table.'

Siccoli did so, moving like an automaton, twisting his body to the left to get the weapon out of his pocket. Dominic leaned over, picked up the gun, checked there was one ready to go, then walked over to the stove and poured himself a large mug of coffee. The arduous climb along the cable and the long walk afterwards had made him thirsty.

Siccoli saw the blood-stained knife and asked, 'Pietro?' in a voice that managed to mix resignation with fear.

Dominic nodded and sat down opposite him. He placed the gun and the knife on the table where he could get at them easily, lifted the mug of coffee and drank.

'How did you—?'

'I also walk on water,' Dominic said, and picked up the gun thoughtfully. Now that he was here, the problem was how to make Siccoli talk. Dominic had no cover, no assistance, no protection and not much time. Siccoli was an intelligent man with a devious mind, a man used to shadowy nuances and half truths, a man who had taken great risks to fulfil the ends of Midas. Now, as he sat opposite Dominic, round-shouldered, palms face down on the table, snapping turtle-head erupting out of the silken shirt collar, he gave an impression of great watchfulness. Dominic thought Siccoli had brought Pietro to do his musclework for him. That day in Menaggio he'd sent Morrie Ellis after Dominic with a gun. Siccoli wasn't used to physical violence and, with all that surplus weight, probably not used to physical pain either. Pain, Dominic decided, that was the technique to use, or rather the threat of pain. Sometimes crude was best.

Dominic levelled the gun at Siccoli, eased off the safety

156

catch. 'I'm as good with this as you are at shooting bear,' he said. 'The first time you lie to me, I shall shoot your ear off. If you keep very still, I won't miss.'

Siccoli said, 'There is no need for violence. I will tell you what you want to know.'

That was too co-operative, Dominic decided. No one could be *that* frightened of pain. Besides, Siccoli was smart enough to realize that if Dominic killed him he wouldn't get any information at all.

'Midas,' Dominic said, deciding there was no help for it and beginning with what he already knew. 'Tell me about Midas. Tell me how they're organized and what they do.'

Siccoli's answer was prompt and tallied with what Dominic knew or surmised already. Midas was a movement composed of young, educated people seeking to change society. They were disillusioned with the lack of results shown by the more orthodox revolutionary groups, and had embarked upon a campaign of sabotaging the system from the inside. Currency smuggling not only gave them finance, but gave them power over certain influential people. It also weakened certain currencies. Company frauds gave them finance, but also meant that other people lost money, and faith.

'What about drugs?' Dominic asked. 'What is their connection with the Movement?'

Siccoli looked back at him uncomprehendingly. 'Drugs?' he said. 'I know nothing of drugs. These people are businessmen.' Quickly he explained that Midas was organized into cells. Apart from the couriers, the only people Siccoli knew were Kit Garnham, Kevin Cormack and Jacques Duval. He swore he did not know who the head of Midas was. All he knew about him was that he was someone very clever, very powerful and very ruthless.

So far Siccoli's story checked out with what Dominic already knew. He wondered if Siccoli knew the game Dominic was playing, and was simply keeping to the rules.

He wondered if the lying would come later, and if he would be able to recognize it.

'Why does Midas want the Banco Lattoria?'

'They need a financial base. Switzerland is the best place for such a base. With a bank they can control many things. They can get much financial information and they can also make money.'

Not a word about access to the Interstellar account, though it was possible Siccoli did not know anything about that.

'Why was Carmody killed?'

Siccoli did not know anything about that either. Though, if Carmody had been a policeman of some kind, the order for the killing would have come from Midas himself. The organization had strict instructions that law enforcement agencies were to be left alone.

'What about Marc Landi?'

Siccoli explained away Marc Landi's life quite easily. Landi had worked for Midas, advised them on investments, arranged the Swiss end of the currency smuggling operation. Midas's own investments were held through Intra, Kastel and Sulden. There had been no fraud on the Banco Lattoria, and the one hundred thousand dollars that Duval had been taking to Landi had been payment for services rendered.

That didn't make sense, Dominic said. If Midas had wanted to pay off Landi, it would have been simpler to do so through one of the anstalts than to smuggle money across the Italian border.

Siccoli looked at Dominic mournfully and agreed. He was only making a judgement. He was not a party to the decisions taken by Midas. He simply carried out their instructions. And his instructions had been to give Duval one hundred thousand dollars to take to Landi. Cormack had given him those instructions, just as Cormack had asked him to invite Landi for dinner the night he died.

Landi had eaten well and drunk heavily. The accident was unfortunate, but not surprising.

'His car was fixed,' Dominic snapped. 'A wheel was made to come off.'

Siccoli turned his palms upwards in a gesture of helplessness. 'I know nothing about that,' he said. 'I did not do it. I know nothing about cars.'

Now Dominic was sure Siccoli was lying. But it was too soon to do anything about it. There were more important questions to be asked. 'Who asked you to get at me today?' Dominic asked. 'Whose idea was that?'

'Cormack's,' Siccoli replied readily. 'Beck called Cormack as soon as you left him. Then Cormack called me.'

'Where is Cormack?'

'I don't—'

Dominic fired the gun. The explosion in that cluttered room was deafening. Siccoli bounced in his chair, nearly fell off it.

'The number, Gianni,' Dominic said tightly. 'He must have wanted you to call him back.'

Siccoli gave him a phone number in Zurich. There was a phone in the office and it was obvious Dominic could check the number, so, this time at least, Siccoli wasn't lying. It would be interesting, Dominic thought, to talk to Cormack. But there was something else he wanted Siccoli to do first.

Every Liechtenstein-based company had a founders certificate, without which no alterations in the company's structure could be made, and which normally, unless the owners were exceedingly foolish or trusting, stated exactly who the true owners were. If Beck had formed the anstalts for Midas, he would know who Midas was. In any case, the real name of Midas would be on the founders certificate.

'I want you to call Beck,' Dominic said. 'Tell him I will be at his office in half an hour. He is to give me photocopies

159

of the founders certificates of Intra, Kastel and Sulden.'

'I can't do that,' Siccoli said quietly. 'Beck is no longer in Vaduz. He is in Lugano.'

Of course. Beck was fronting for the takeover of the Banco Lattoria.

'Beck has an assistant. Call him.' Dominic moved the knife with its crust of blackish blood in front of Siccoli's face. The olive skin lightened. Siccoli took in a rapid breath. More people are frightened by knives than guns. It has to do with experience. Everyone has been cut some time or another, whereas few people have knowledge of what a bullet wound is like. It is easier to imagine the severing of skin and blood vessels than the shock of an exploding bullet.

'I don't—'

'Don't fuck about, Siccoli. Call him.'

Siccoli called him. Beck's assistant was only too glad to help. He would meet Signor Cain at the office in half an hour.

Dominic severed the telephone cables with the knife, showing Siccoli how easily it could have been his throat. Then he said, 'Give me your car keys, Gianni. I've always wanted to drive a Ferrari.'

'You can't,' Siccoli said. 'It is a very difficult car to drive. Let me take you to Beck's.'

Dominic waved the knife in his face again. Siccoli gave him the keys. Dominic put them in his pocket and said, 'Now, let's take a little walk.'

Siccoli looked at him in great alarm. In his experience, little walks were always precursors to something nasty happening. 'I will stay here,' he said quickly. 'You have cut the phone, and if you take the car, there is nothing I can do.'

'I agree,' Dominic said. 'But let's go walkies.'

Covering him with knife and gun, Dominic made Siccoli precede him along the platform to the control room. Pietro, clutching his wounded hand, was dozing, and gazed dully at their arrival. Dominic turned on the power and brought the tele-cabin down. Then he marched Siccoli to it.

'Inside,' Dominic said.

'But this is unnecessary. I do not want to do anything to you. I can't.'

'Gianni,' Dominic said softly, 'you tried to kill me.'

'No,' Siccoli said. 'I wouldn't have allowed you to die. We were going to bring you down as soon as we'd finished eating.'

'I believe you, sunshine,' Dominic said, 'but I have to do something about it. A life for a life, you see, and an eye for an eye. You know how it is.' Dominic stepped back quickly and slashed the point of the knife across Siccoli's forehead, twisted, dragged it down his cheek. He pulled the knife away before Siccoli felt the pain and screamed, wheeling backwards into the tele-cabin.

'Show Midas your face, Gianni,' Dominic said. 'Tell Midas he owes me.'

Dominic slammed the door on the cowering Siccoli, ran to the control cabin and sent the tele-cabin on its way up the mountain. When it was halfway up, he cut the power and left it suspended between the station and the hunting lodge. Pietro avoided looking at Dominic as he went out. In the end, Midas would get the message, Dominic thought. In the end, there was nothing as fulfilling as revenge.

Dominic went onto the platform and down the narrow steps to the Ferrari. It was a pig to start, but he finally got it running on ten and drove quickly down the mountain road. By the time he got to Beck's office, his assistant was already there. He met Dominic at the head of the stairs, still wearing his shy smile and holding a large envelope. He lived near the office, he explained, and had got there soon after Signor Siccoli had telephoned. Was this what Signor Cain wanted?

Dominic opened the envelope and looked. Inside were

photocopies of the founders certificates all right. And the owner of each of the anstalts was none other than John Charles Edgar.

Dominic left the Ferrari outside Vaduz and walked the few hundred yards into the town. Edgar, he thought – impossible! But possible! Edgar was an ambitious man. The money thing was only a symptom of that ambition. And now that he had achieved the ultimate in the financial world, what was there left to do? He was a man hungry for power, and what greater power was there than controlling the destinies of nations?

It was past eleven o'clock and Vaduz was closing down. Dominic went straight to the hotel, picked up his key and went up to his room, thinking longingly of the Chivas Regal he'd bought at Heathrow. He fumbled with his key, opened the door and went rigid as a post.

The blond young man in the blue denims was seated in his room, sipping his Chivas Regal. In one hand he held the canvas bag with 125,000 Swiss francs and in the other a Colt Python, Dominic's favourite gun. The only problem was it was being pointed straight at him.

CHAPTER TWENTY-FOUR

He'd shut the door behind him automatically. No way to open it now and get out before the man fired. The man was seated in the little passageway between the end of the two single beds and the dressing table, about twelve feet away, diagonally across the room from Dominic. There was no way Dominic could take the man, and with that realization came the conclusion that he was going to die. There was never a right time for dying but now was especially bad, because it was now, and because of Claire.

'Dominic Cain?' the man asked. His accent was American, his tone soft, but cold as a dead fish.

'Yes,' Dominic replied, waiting for the hammerhead punch of the bullet and the gouting of warm blood that would be his last memory.

'Blood,' the man said. 'You've got blood on your trousers and a knife strapped to your calf. You look goddam weird.'

'Does it matter what I look like?' There was even time for regret. Dominic should have known they'd send someone for the money. Dominic should have planned for that. But that was how this game was played. You fucked up one tiny detail and you got smashed. It was a hell of a way to go, though, and he wondered whether that was what Steiner and Thirstone and young Patrick Kennedy had thought that day in Chagny, when they'd seen him come down the stairs.

The man raised the canvas bag with his left hand. 'This money yours?'

'In a manner of speaking, yes.'

'In a manner of speaking, how?'

The gun was still pointing at Dominic, but vaguely. The

man's grip was loose and the barrel wavered, as if the man had realized there was now nothing to do but squeeze the trigger. Keep him talking, Dominic thought, keep him asking damn fool questions. Make him interested enough, and Dominic could take him. 'Siccoli gave me the money,' Dominic said. 'I was supposed to kill Midas.'

No horrified reaction from the man. 'Did you?' he asked.

'Midas didn't show.'

'How come the blood on the trousers then?'

'Siccoli's and his friend's. We had a difference of opinion.'

The gun was pointing way over towards the bed now. Dominic took one long, careful stride into the room.

'You killed them?' Again the same absence of reaction.

'Worse. Humiliated them. Do you want me to tell you how?'

The man grinned and dropped the bag on the table. Dominic tensed himself to spring.

The man said, 'What the fuck happened to Carmody?'

'He was killed,' Dominic replied. 'He was killed by Midas.'

'You'll have to tell me about Midas.' The man put the gun away into a belly holster. 'I'm Carmody's replacement,' he said. 'Name's Abraham Stone. You can call me Abe.'

Dominic let out a breath he didn't know he had been holding, walked right into the room and picked up the bottle of Chivas. He raised it to his mouth and gulped it down quickly, feeling the burn as it hit his stomach and made his eyes water. 'You got – glot' – through a throat on fire – 'you got identity?'

'None that would convince you. But don't worry, I'm the sucker in the cat bird seat. If you want to check, call Martin Pelham.'

Dominic sat down on the bed and held the bottle out to

Stone. Stone sipped politely and put it away on the table beside him.

'You know Martin Pelham?' Dominic asked.

'I've talked with him. This job moved too fast for Carmody. He hadn't time to file a report or get clearances. So when he got himself killed we didn't know what was happening. We traced him to Pelham, about the same time the Italians contacted us about lifting Duval. Pelham said you'd been handling all this on your own and suggested we touch base with you.'

Dominic remembered that de Marco had worked with Carmody too. He considered whipping out de Marco's .38, decided that if he did Stone would start shooting too, and that a Colt Python stuffed full of .357 Magnum was too much firepower.

'You could have made contact this afternoon,' he said.

Abe Stone shook his blond head. 'No, baby, no. You had friends, and the first rule is never walk into a situation blind. That way you keep living. Not like the way you came into this room. I could have cancelled you.'

'And why didn't you?'

'I needed to talk to you first. Before you came in I wasn't sure whose side you were on, especially when I got in here and found the money.'

'And what made you change your mind?'

'You. The look on your face when you walked in, and the way you made up your mind to take me. You thought I was from Midas, didn't you?'

'Right,' Dominic said. 'You play dangerous games.'

'Had to play it that way,' Stone said. 'Had to check you out. Had to check your reaction.'

And some people had to check if timebombs were ticking by holding them up to their ears.

Stone took another delicate sip of Chivas and handed the bottle over. 'Pelham said for you to brief me and then get your ass back home.'

'Fuck Pelham!'

Abe Stone grinned. 'He said you'd say that.'

'I'm not leaving.'

'It's your decision, man. You do what you have to do. Only fill us in about Carmody and Midas.'

'Why?' Dominic asked. 'Midas is my baby.' Damn it all, Midas *was* his. He'd searched for them, he'd set them up, he was holding himself out as live bait, and now some kid without even enough balls to grow a beard was trying to take it away from him. Dominic knew there was no turning back. If he didn't stop Midas, Midas would stop him. Midas thought he knew too much to live, and after what he'd done to Siccoli they would have to exact some retribution. There was no way he was going to trust his future to the pubescent care of a snotty little kid like Abe Stone.

Stone said, 'Wrong. Midas is our case. We handle it how we like.'

Dominic flung his palms open. 'Go ahead and handle it then, but keep out of the crossfire.'

Stone said softly, 'We might decide to eliminate you, Cain. We have our ways.'

'Screw your ways!' Dominic's hand darted to his pocket. He didn't waste time pulling out the gun. He just lifted his arm so Stone could see the barrel protruding through the leather.

Stone went very still, the pale eyes resting contemplatively on the projectile shape of the pocket.

'If you're going to eliminate me,' Dominic said softly, 'you'd better be good. You'll have to be a whole lot better than de Marco or Grady.'

Stone looked away and almost absent-mindedly sipped at the Chivas. 'Tom Haden wants to see you,' he said and then whipped out the Colt Python. It was fast, so fast that he had it out of the belly holster and reversed before Dominic could react. 'Pelham said you were a pig-headed son of a bitch,' Stone said, holding the gun out to Dominic. 'He said you liked these.'

Dominic took the gun. It wasn't his Colt Python, but it was good enough. He hefted it in his hand and placed it gently beside him on the bed. Stone giving him the gun was a gesture of acceptance and trust, but before he would agree to meet with Tom Haden, before he would share the information he had, Dominic wanted more. He wanted to be sure they would share their information with him.

'What's this about lifting Duval?' he asked.

Abe told him. Duval had got too hot for the Italians. When Duval had heard of Carmody's death, he'd talked. Loudly, lengthily and all too freely, anything to avoid ten years in jail. He'd described previous smuggling operations, and named names. Some of the names were politically explosive, members of the government and other leading politicians, and true or not, the last thing the government wanted was an 'affaire Duval', especially so soon after the Communists had made such stupendous gains in the regional elections. For the moment, the Italians wanted nothing better than to be able to forget about Duval, and knowing that he was wanted in the States on a narcotics rap, they had offered him to the Americans.

The only problem with their offer was extradition. If Duval didn't want to return to the States, there would have to be proceedings. Duval would talk, and once he did that, the whole purpose of the exercise would have been lost.

'So we lift him,' Abe said, 'with the passive co-operation of the Eyeties. We'll bring him across the border to Switzerland, hole up somewhere and make him talk to us like we were his long lost buddies. When he's finished talking, we send him on a one-way trip to the good old US of A.'

'We?' Dominic asked.

Stone said, 'If Haden okays you, you're in.'

167

'Thanks a million,' Dominic said. 'Hasn't anyone told you that what you're trying to do is illegal?'

'So's that blood-stained knife you're carrying.' He passed the bottle to Dominic. 'If you want to, we can lift Duval tomorrow.'

Dominic grinned. 'I want to,' he said.

'Right. Let's get our asses in gear and go talk to Tom Haden in Zurich.'

Dominic arranged with the hotel to return his car and travelled in Abe's dusty white BMW. Dominic wasn't surprised to learn that this was Abe's first foreign posting. He'd come out three months ago as an understudy to Carmody, and now found himself, as he described it, in the hot seat. He was only twenty-six and must have had an excellent record for them to let him handle this on his own. The question was whether he was paper good or action good. The question was how he would react under fire.

While Abe drove they talked about how they would take Duval. Fact: Duval was being transferred from Menaggio to Milan at eleven o'clock the next morning. Fact: the transfer would be by police van which would take the lake road to Como and then the autostrada to Milan. Fact: the lake road was slow, and after noon would be reasonably empty. If the Italians were co-operative, Dominic felt they should be able to stop the police van at the southern end of Lake Como, somewhere after Argegno. They would then whisk Duval along the autostrada across the Swiss border and into Lugano. There, rather than waste time transporting him to Zurich airport, they would find a safe house. That night, speeding along the autoroute to St Gallen, it looked almost too easy.

They reached Zurich a little over the hour, drove quickly past the university complex and down the Ramistrasse to the Quai Bridge. Traffic was light and Abe picked his way through the one-way systems with surprising ease for one who had been in Europe for only three months. They crossed the Sihl and went up the Stauffacherstrasse. Somewhere past the modern church that was dedicated to Saints Felix and Regula – a brother and sister who had been scourged, plunged into boiling oil, forced to drink molten lead and then been beheaded, Abe turned into a narrow driveway. He bounced the BMW up a small ramp and down into an underground car park.

Abe slotted the BMW between an Opel and a Chrysler, its front to the wall. From beyond the Chrysler a lift door opened; a yellow rectangle of light seeped across the floor. A big man stepped out of the lift, slid between the Chrysler and the wall towards them.

'Hello, Willie,' Abe said, already out of the car.

Dominic eased the door open gently to avoid hitting Willie. 'Hello,' he said, got out and turned to walk round the car. The lift door slid shut, plunging the car park into darkness. Something swished in front of Dominic's face, wrapped itself round his throat and tightened, cutting into his windpipe, lifting him onto tiptoe.

'Don't go for the gun,' he heard Willie whisper in his ear, 'or I'll wrench your head off.'

Tears started from Dominic's eyes, his chest felt tight as a drum, his mouth opened sucking dry air. 'Hands wide,' Willie said. Dominic spread his hands apart, feeling the pulse thudding in his head, choking for air, anything to breathe again.

Abe came round in front of him, whipped the guns out of his pockets. Then they cuffed his hands behind him, and led him in darkness to the lift.

CHAPTER TWENTY-FIVE

They hustled him from the lift and across a small corridor into a squarish, low-ceilinged room. The room was an office of some kind, with filing cabinets, a calendar and crossed football pennants on the wall, a desk with a battery of telephones and a photograph of a smiling President stepping off Air Force One to a welcoming semicircle of high-ranking military officers and watchful civilians.

Standing near the desk were two men. The tall one with the cat-like eyes and the leisurely look of a ranch hand assessing the weather was one of the watchful civilians in the photograph. The other man was smaller, with thinning silvery hair, scholarly-looking, with a firm, kind face and pale polished skin.

Willie made Dominic sit on a straight-back chair before the desk and fastened his arms to the chair back.

The taller man nodded to Willie and Abe. 'Thanks boys,' he said and waited for them to leave. Dominic heard the door slam, the sound of their footsteps receding down the corridor.

The taller man walked up to Dominic. 'My name is Tom Haden,' he said. 'Let's take your protests as read. I want to know why you killed de Marco and Grady. I want to find out how we have been penetrated and I want to know all about Midas. There isn't time to evaluate what you have to tell me. So I have asked Doctor Brunner to assist me. In a moment he will give you an injection of a specially developed compound of sodium amytal. It will cause you no permanent harm and there will be no after effects. All it will do is relax you, make it easier for you to say what you want to say.'

All the bastard hadn't done was thank him for his cooperation. Dominic tensed as Haden leaned forward and unbuttoned his jacket and shirt. Escape was impossible. Hitting Haden with the chair was impracticable and futile. Dominic had not been trained to undergo this type of interrogation and he had a morbid fear of drugs. He tried to remember all he'd ever heard about sodium amytal. Truth drugs are ordinary anaesthetics. Administered in sub-anaesthetic doses, they produce the same effect as drunkenness, in that they release conscious control and lower the discretion barrier. If he was determined not to talk, the drug couldn't make him do it. He forced his mind into blankness.

Brunner stood in front of him now, looking at his pupils with a pen torch, placing a stethoscope against his bare chest and checking his respiration and pulse. He took a syringe and two phials out of a black bag and Dominic forced his mind away. This wasn't happening. It wasn't happening to him. Saints Felix and Regula had had the better deal. Haden pulled his head forward slightly and Brunner returned, carrying a swab of spirit and squirting the syringe to check for air bubbles.

'This won't hurt a bit, Mr Cain,' Brunner said gently, and to Dominic's surprise it didn't. There was only the chill of the spirit as Brunner swabbed his arm, followed by the sensation of something warm trickling down his arm. It wasn't molten lead, and he was able to enjoy the blankness.

It took ten minutes before his vision started to go. Haden and Brunner shimmered as if he was seeing them through a wall of water. The room became blurred with corners that floated and shimmied. There was music too, soft and measured, a Bach fugue. He recognized that. And the words of a poem. *'When the lamp is shattered the light in the dusk lies dead.'* Shelley. Too late Dominic realized that he shouldn't have concentrated on blankness. He should have fixed his mind on something, anything, but not blankness. Claire? No, she was too recent, too associated with what had gone on. Martin? Chagny?

Haden was speaking to him now, gently, his smoke-burred voice warm and sympathetic and reassuring. He was asking simple questions. Where was Dominic born? Did he still see his parents? In which part of London did he live? How long had he taken to write his book on computers? Did that take much research? He couldn't believe Dominic had really had a problem with binary numbers. He hadn't read the book of course, but everyone he knew spoke highly of it. Very highly. What was his favourite food? Haden liked steak too. You got good steak in Zurich, in fact anywhere in Switzerland. And of course there was wine. Haden liked a good fruity wine, but he knew more about Californian wines than European.

His voice was relaxing, gentle, reminding Dominic of his father's voice. Dominic told himself he mustn't relax, he must think of something else. But that was his father's voice. . . He hadn't thought of his father in a long time. He remembered him though. He could still smell the sun-baked leather of the Ford V8 sinking softly into the hollows along the red earth road. His mother had said the car had bulletproof glass and was built like a tank, so that the terrorists wouldn't get him. His father would never let the terrorists get him, Ford V8 or no.

It was dark and the crows were cawing noisily in the short twilight, the rubbertrees spreading their shadows eerily. The house with its white walls and red-tiled roof looked silent and menacing in the half light. The front door was open and he heard his mother gasp. As they went up the steps onto the verandah, a metal shutter banged.

'Dominic, go and wait in the car.' There was a frightened note in his mother's voice. But the car surrounded by evening shadow looked menacing too. He stood hesitating on the verandah, and then went in through the front door. There was a smell like rotting fruit and the angry buzzing

173

of flies. A policeman in khaki shorts lay on his back by the door, oblivious of the flies which were swarming over his face. The two other policemen were blood-stained khaki hulks sprawling at the back of the room, and in the centre of the room, sitting with lolling head, was his father.

There was blood on the matted hair of his chest and his tongue protruded. His eyes looked at Dominic so strangely. He was wearing only his shorts and was trussed upright to the chair, and as his mother went up to him, Dominic saw the flies rise from the stumps that had been his hands. Once more he felt the fear that he had felt then, the anger, and the helplessness. 'I'll kill you bastards,' he heard himself shouting with the high treble voice of a child. 'I'll kill you bastards!'

After that there was a succession of faces. There was Aunt Emma saying, 'There, there, you poor child. What will become of you.' There were masters and heads of schools, impersonal and pitying; there was Sarah saying, 'As soon as term ends, I'll come and stay with you in Beirut.'

'I'll kill you bastards!' Dominic was shouting but this time his voice was level, and this time he meant it.

Dominic felt a hand on his shoulder, firm and reassuring, the smoke-burred voice saying, 'It's all right, Dominic. We will help you. . . Dominic, is that why you killed de Marco and Grady?'

His father wanted to know. 'I killed them because. . .' No, de Marco and Grady had nothing to do with that. 'They wanted to kill me. Claire and me. We killed the bastards.'

'Why did they want to kill you?'

'Because they wanted to prevent me finding out about the Interstellar accounts. They had been manipulating the account, using it for private purposes.' He could see de Marco in the headlights of the car now. 'The bastards tried

174

to set us up. They set up an ambush in a pull-off near Bellinzona.'

'Dominic, what happened to Lew? He was my friend. He shouldn't have died like that.'

'He was my friend, too. Midas got him.' Dominic heard his voice go on and on, reliving everything that had happened in the last seventy-two hours. He felt compelled to tell, and he told Haden everything, even Cormack's telephone number.

He was lying on a bed surrounded by the warm aroma of coffee. Haden was sitting beside him, looking concerned. Dominic tried to get up but Haden placed a hand on his shoulder and restrained him. 'Have some coffee,' he said. 'I'm afraid we miscalculated slightly. We didn't know how strenuous a day you'd had.'

Dominic's mouth was dry, but his head felt very clear, his body lithe and relaxed as if he had been asleep for fifteen hours. 'What time is it?' he asked.

'A little after three in the morning. You haven't been out long.'

Haden gave him the coffee. Dominic was in a small bedroom, and the only light came from a shaded reading lamp beside which Haden was sitting. Dominic sipped the coffee.

'How do you feel, Dominic?'

'I feel fine.'

'Fine enough to accept an apology from a suspicious old man?'

'You didn't have to do it,' Dominic said angrily.

'I agree. That's what Abe said, too. But old habits die hard, and after Pelham told me we'd been penetrated I couldn't take any chances.'

'Pelham should have told you I was clear,' Dominic said.

Haden smiled contritely. 'I was wrong. I am sorry.'

Dominic sipped more coffee. There was a slight taste of brandy in it, and it felt good and black and warm.

Haden said, 'I'd like you to work with Abe and me. I'd like you to carry on just as you have been doing. I want you to find Midas.'

'Edgar is Midas,' Dominic said.

'If he is, we'll need more than the founders certificates to prove it.'

'Like Duval?' Dominic said, thinking carefully.

Haden nodded. 'Like Duval.'

'If I stay too long in Switzerland, I'll end up facing a murder rap,' Dominic said.

'De Marco and Grady,' Haden said. 'I'll take care of that, first thing in the morning.'

Dominic sat up, amazed at how easily he could move. 'You've got a deal,' he said.

'I'm glad,' Haden said. He eyed Dominic carefully. 'Lew Carmody was a friend of mine,' he said. 'I very much want you to get Midas, whoever he is.'

'I knew Lew, too.'

Haden smiled. 'My regards to Claire, when you see her. Now if you feel up to it, let's go and see Abe before he bursts a gut wanting to know if you will still work with him.'

CHAPTER TWENTY-SIX

'A right fuck-up, that's what it was,' Abe said. They were speeding down the autoroute to Lugano. Haden had given them steak and Gevrey Chambertin, listened gravely and approved their plan. He had instructed Abe about what vehicles to use, where to make contact with the others, and given them both a phone number in case of trouble.

'I told Haden you were okay,' Abe said, 'but that son of a bitch has to walk into a puddle to find out if it's wet.'

'It's all right,' Dominic said, vaguely embarrassed by the length and intensity of Abe's protestations. He felt quite at peace, lulled by the speed of their passage through the night. He felt no animosity towards Abe or Haden. He felt as if he had been exorcised of a hidden pain that he had suffered from but never located.

'I traced Cormack's number and went round to see him,' Abe said. 'He'd blown. So had your friend Siccoli. Got down from the tele-cabin and flown away.'

'That must have been Pietro,' Dominic said. 'Pietro must have got free and decided to help his master.' He didn't think it was that bad – Cormack and Siccoli on the run and Midas knowing they were hitting back.

'I'm going to have to fix the scheduling for tomorrow,' Abe said. 'You want me to find you somewhere to sleep?'

'I know somewhere,' Dominic answered and when they got to Lugano, he had Abe drop him outside the Hotel Walter.

The clerk behind the desk inquired if he had a reservation.

'Better than that,' Dominic said. 'I have a friend.'

He called Claire from the lobby and took the stairs two at a time. She opened the door to his knock, wearing a white towelling bathrobe and nothing else, pulled him into her arms, kissing him fast and furiously on the cheek and neck and eyes. 'Oh Dominic, Dominic, I was so worried when you didn't call.'

Dominic placed his arms under the bathrobe, on her naked flesh. 'I was hung up,' he said. His hands came up along her spine and tugged at her hair, forced her head back till she was looking up at him. 'I am here,' he said. 'I am glad to be here,' and kissed her on the mouth, very long and very slowly.

She leaned back and closed her eyes and let him take her mouth, let him absorb her lips with his, search her with his tongue. When he took his head away, she murmured, 'I'm glad you're here, too.'

Dominic eased her away and put his case at the foot of the bed.

'You've got blood on your trousers. Dominic are you hurt?'

'No. It isn't my blood.'

'You haven't – haven't—'

'No, I haven't killed anybody.'

The joke was awkward. She crossed her hands in front of her chest, pulling the white towelling robe tight around her. 'How can you joke about something like that? How can you come near me covered in someone else's blood?' Her mouth trembled. 'Dominic, when does all this killing stop?'

Dominic told her about the founders certificates.

'It's impossible,' Claire said. 'Edgar owns the bank. If the bank collapses, it's the end for him. He's personally guaranteed a loan of three million pounds to an Italian property company. If the bank goes under, that loan will be called in, and neither Edgar nor the company can pay. That's why he's coming out to Lugano tomorrow for the take-over meeting, even though it means he might be arrested.'

It was a serious offence in Switzerland to run a bank without funds. If Edgar had in fact diddled the bank it was unlikely that he would risk arrest in an attempt to save it. But Dominic couldn't give up the idea of Edgar being Midas. In all other respects it fitted so well. 'Maybe he knew he was in trouble and decided to nick the petty cash.'

'You don't know Charles Edgar,' Claire said. 'He's a game-player. Making money is secondary. The game is the important thing, and stealing isn't a game. It's too easy for someone like Edgar.'

They could talk for the rest of the night, but she wasn't going to be convinced. 'Okay,' Dominic said. 'I give in.' He went into the bathroom and stripped. He washed the knife and watched the blood disappear down the sink like molten rust. After that he showered and went back into the bedroom. Claire was lying in bed, smoking.

'I saw Tom Haden in Zurich,' he said. 'He believes that de Marco and Grady tried to kill us. He's going to arrange things tomorrow. You won't even have to make a statement.'

He climbed into bed beside her, put an arm around her shoulders. 'It will be all right,' he said. 'I promise you.'

She lay still, looking at the ceiling, not responding to his touch. 'Afterwards, when all this is over, will you go on doing this job?'

He turned on his side, ran a finger over her lips and kissed her chin. 'You mean will I keep working for the Department?'

'I mean, will you go on doing jobs that make you kill people.'

Dominic took his finger away from her skin and looked at it. 'I don't know,' he said. 'I'm not sure I like this job any more. But then, if it weren't for bastards like me, bastards like them would win. And that would be much worse.'

'You can't save the world, darling,' she said and sud-

179

denly pulled his head down and kissed him on the mouth.

'No,' he said when she released him. He kissed her lightly on the cheek, where there was a vestige of a dimple. 'Can I use your cottage tomorrow?'

'Of course.' A moment's silence. 'The keys are on the table by the bed. Why do you want to use it?'

'I have to talk to someone.'

'What's wrong with this place?'

'It's too public,' he said.

She went still again, unresponsive. 'I don't know,' she said at last and she wasn't talking about the cottage. 'I really don't know.'

'You aren't going to change anything, Claire,' Dominic said. 'Your place or someone else's, what's going to happen will happen.'

'I hate you when you talk like that,' she said.

They lay a long while together, side by side, staring at the ceiling. Outside a boat on the lake hooted, a car roared down the Via Caccia, footsteps beat on the pavement. Claire reached to turn off the reading light and Dominic caught her hand and stopped her. 'Don't,' he said. 'I want to be able to see you.'

She laughed, with a hint of embarrassment, then came easily into his arms. For a while they lay on their sides, face to face, while Dominic kissed her forehead and nose and lips and chin, let his hands explore her, run up her slim flank and across the flat of her belly, knead the insides of her thighs. Then he buried his head on the firm cushion of her breasts and kissed the flatness in between. Gently, he inflamed her nipples with his fingers and mouth and tongue, and when she began to sigh softly, moved her onto her back and entered her.

All of her seemed to be clinging to him, moulding her flesh to his. He moved inside her, slowly.

'Look at me,' Dominic said.

She opened her eyes.

180

'This is me and you.'

'You and me,' she said. 'I love you.'

Dominic would have liked to say it too, but he couldn't. Love was both now and far away, and he kissed her, moving inside her very slowly, almost too gently, fixing his eyes and mind on her face, on her, expelling all that had to do with today and tomorrow, everything but now and him and her: her eyes opened wide against his, her mouth soft and pliable and warm, their tongues touching vibrantly, till he was aware of her and her only, aware that all of her was soft, pliable, warm and moist, smelling of sleep and musk, feeling her now move with him, her splayed out legs clasping him to her as he thrust and thrust and thrust, eroding away the pain and the hurt. Now there was time for loving and only that, loving and loving and Claire, seeing her head going back, and despite herself, her eyes closing, her mouth writhing against his, feeling the faraway sting of her nails on his back, and then her mouth breaking away and she was moaning into the night, her body melting into his and when he came it was like a cascade of stars.

Afterwards he lay on his back, spent, feeling her against him.

'I love you and know nothing about you,' Claire said. 'Is that wise?'

'Perhaps it's for the best,' Dominic said, remembering his father again, wondering if he should tell her how he had been murdered by the terrorists.

'What do you have to hide?' A note of alarm. 'Are you married?'

'I'm not married. I once thought I'd be a priest.'

'I'm glad you're not a priest,' she said. 'I hope you never become a priest.'

'Who knows,' Dominic said and, wrapping her in his arms, fell asleep.

CHAPTER TWENTY-SEVEN

Dominic came down to the lobby next morning twenty minutes early. Abe, he thought, would have difficulty parking outside the hotel, and a few minutes saved now could become vital later. Abe must have had the same thought, because he came in five minutes afterwards. He'd left a van stolen from a charcuterie butchers on a meter outside the hotel. His BMW was already in the hotel car park. There was time for coffee and a final run-through of the plans.

Dominic would take the BMW to Menaggio, from where he would discreetly follow the police van. Abe would take the charcuterie truck south along the autoroute and double back along the Italian side of the border, after Como. Dominic couldn't mistake the truck. It was covered with pictures of romping little piggies. A stolen green Alfetta was already on its way into Italy. Dominic would meet up with it soon after Argegno. It would be parked facing him, and the signal would be a single flash of the headlamps.

Dominic would change cars and keep following the police van. When the charcuterie truck came into view, he would allow it to get between him and the police van, and stay reasonably close. One kilometre before the hit, Abe would turn on his hazard warning lights briefly. Dominic would then close right up, tailgate him till he pulled out and took the police van. When Abe had stopped the police van, Dominic was to box it in with the Alfetta. It sounded fine, Dominic said, and he felt sure it would work, especially if the police were co-operative.

He reached Menaggio surprisingly quickly, and with surprising punctuality the blue Fiat police van left the station right on the stroke of eleven o'clock. Dominic had no trouble following it. The road wasn't busy and there were no turn-offs before Argegno. Dominic was content to keep well back and admire the luxuriant sub-tropical vegetation and the peaceful sheen of the lake.

Cadennabia came and went, as did warm Tremezzo. The Sasso soaring above the road became the Monte Crocine which soared even higher. They went through Lenno and past the strange tower with a Gothic belfry outside Campo. It was like taking *fetuccini* from a baby. Near Argegno, he closed up so as not to lose the van during the changeover.

The green wedge-shaped Alfetta was parked facing him, just after Argegno. The police van had to pull to the centre of the road to pass it. For a moment it slowed, and Dominic wondered if they would stop and book the driver of the Alfetta. But it must have been a too casual gear change, because the van speeded up and Dominic brought the BMW to a stop in front of the Alfetta's radiator.

He left the engine running and got out. The Alfetta had been driven by a big negro, wearing full tribal smock and pantaloons, necklaces and a wild Afro hairstyle. If he'd brought his drums they could have sent Abe a message.

'Mr Cain,' black hands and pearl-white fingernails extending keys to him. 'It's all yours.' The negro came back with him to the Alfetta. 'Your hardwear is in the glove compartment.'

Dominic looked. Abe had left him Siccoli's Biretta. Useful, if there was going to be any shooting. But there wasn't going to be any shooting. The Italians were going to cooperate.

'You're to take out the lock at the back of the van.'

'I'll remember,' Dominic said, and whirled the Alfetta into life.

The negro gave him a clenched fist salute. 'Good luck,' he said. 'I'll see you later.'

You and Wolweber, Dominic thought, and whisked the car round in a tight U turn and set off after the van.

They would have to make their play fairly soon. A few

kilometres after Brienno it became built up, getting more and more crowded until the buildings merged with the outskirts of Como. The van with its pictures of gambolling piglets was waiting in Brienno, pulling sharply between Dominic's rapidly closing Alfetta and the police van. Dominic braked hard and tucked in behind. They were hardly out of Brienno when the hazard warning flashers started to go.

It's too soon, Dominic thought. They were too close to Brienno. *Abe you idiot, it's too soon.* Also there was a red Alfa Giulia exploding in his mirror, and nothing Dominic could do about it. The hazard warning flashers died and the nearside trafficators came determinedly on. Abe pulled out to pass the police van.

Dominic threw the Alfetta into second, hardly aware of the smoothness of the gear change, as the piggy van drew half a length ahead. After that it all happened quickly.

Abe threw the piggy van sideways, slamming it into the police van, throwing both vehicles into the wheel-high stone barrier that bordered the road. Locked together in a death-like embrace, both vehicles mounted the barrier and smashed into the rock wall beyond. Dominic screeched to a stop behind the tilted rear of the police van, picked up the gun and jumped out. As he did so, the Giulia that had been behind him screeched past, locked wheels spuming smoke, a glimpse of huddled figures and the smell of burning rubber, then the wheels freed and the car broadsided across the road and stopped, doors falling open like broken wings. Three men wearing Lone Ranger masks jumped out of the stalled Giulia, with automatic M-16's at the ready.

Dominic glimpsed Abe running up the road towards him as he fired at the van's locks. One of the masked men came towards him and jerked the door open. Inside a dishevelled policeman was reaching for the carbine trapped behind his shoulder.

'Don't touch it!' Dominic yelled. 'Leave it alone,

motherfucker!' The sound of his voice and the gun in his fist persuaded the policeman that it was the wrong time for heroes. Dominic breathed a sigh of relief. From behind the policeman, a lanky long-haired figure appeared and looked at them with surprise.

'Jump, Duval, for Chrissake jump!' It was Abe's voice from behind him, from near the Alfetta.

Duval jumped, Dominic grabbed him, raced with him back to the Alfetta, while the masked man covered their retreat with his rifle. Abe was already in the passenger seat, and Dominic hurled himself behind the wheel. The rear door swung open and even before Duval was in, Dominic had wound the car round the locked vans. He braked hard, swung hard left, feeling the car heel over, seeing the tail of the stalled Giulia sweep past, then he was twisting the wheel to the right. Get the boot right in, water and stone skimming past, the sensation of slipping on gravel, and then the Alfetta was back on the tarmac, and going like hell for Como. Dominic remembered that the oncoming traffic hadn't even time to stop.

The Alfetta rode on, 160, 170 kph, putting as much distance between the hold-up and safety.

Dominic felt a touch on his shoulder. 'You can take it easy now,' Abe said. 'You're only attracting attention.'

Dominic braked, revved through the gears, brought the Alfetta screeching into the long turn for the autoroute. A quick look over his shoulder, and he accelerated again.

'Who were the others?' he asked.

'Reinforcements,' Abe said. 'Just in case the police hadn't been briefed.'

In case the police hadn't been briefed, they would have been killed. His unconscious threw out a vision of the driver of the police van slumped against a shattered windscreen, his companion standing with his face to the door of the truck, arms splayed out above him. Those men weren't merely reinforcements, they were professionals. Their auto-

186

matics had been set on rapid fire and they hadn't been fooling around.

From behind came Duval's whining voice: 'Hey man, that was great! You fucked the fucking pigs. That was simply great. I love you.'

CHAPTER TWENTY-EIGHT

They crossed the border a few minutes later, kept going along the autoroute at a steady 130kph towards Lugano. There were questions Dominic wanted to ask about the hijack, about where the men in the Giulia had come from and why he hadn't been told about them. But questions would have to come later. For the present there was driving, and Duval sprawling across the rear seat, mouthing profound inanities.

Man, those Italian pigs were something else. Real people's enemies. Didn't give a damn about anyone's constitutional rights, not even rights of a human being. They had questioned him for hours, and stolen the chocolate the Embassy had sent him. They hadn't let him get to d'Annunzio or any other lawyer. They were vicious bastards. With their guns and uniforms they thought they were gods.

Duval said he could die laughing remembering the pig's face when Dominic pulled a gun on him. Man, that pig must have been shitting in his pants. That was a real cool operation, real cool. And serve those bastards right. They shouldn't play around with Midas.

Soon after Ponte Digno, Abe asked Dominic to turn off the autoroute and drive towards Melide.

Duval couldn't understand why anybody would *want* to be a policeman. Anyone who actually *wanted* to terrorize other people had to be sick. It wouldn't be so bad if they went after real criminals, you know, like robbers and murderers, but they interfered with everything. They wouldn't let a man be.

The BMW was jammed into a parking space on the lake side. The negro waved them down and Dominic stopped. They changed cars quickly and the negro whipped the

189

Alfetta round in a tight U turn and sped back to the auto-route. Dominic drove the BMW more leisurely to Claire's cottage, relieved that the changeover had made Duval simultaneously aware of his position and less garrulous. He only spoke again when Dominic turned off the main road and bounced the BMW along the rutted track.

'Hey man, what are you doing? Where are you taking me?'

Neither Abe nor Dominic said anything until Dominic had turned up the path and parked the car in the unkempt grass. 'Let's go in,' Abe said.

Dominic led them inside and shut the door after him, watching Abe and Duval walk into the lounge and stand before the fireplace.

'Nice place,' Duval said.

'What the fuck did you tell the police?' Abe asked.

'Nothing man. Nothing, sure.'

Dominic, moving into the lounge, was surprised at the speed of Abe's movement. He hit Duval three times, lightning jabs to the body. Duval folded onto the sofa.

'Hey, you got no call to do that! I didn't tell the—'

A brutal kick to the shin.

'Hey man, leave me alone!'

As if in response to Duval's plea, Abe walked over to the kitchen sink, turned on the hot tap and filled it. Then he came back and took hold of Duval, hoisting him to his feet. Duval struggled ineffectively. 'Leave me alone, man, I didn't tell the police nothing.'

Abe frogmarched him over to the sink, made him stand in front of it, then kneed him in the back. Duval's head whipped back and Abe moved sideways, grabbed him by the hair and thrust his face into the water. Duval screamed and gurgled. Abe kept his face in the water for twenty seconds and then lifted his head, dripping and scalded. 'What did you tell the police?' Abe asked.

Duval's face was already turning red. 'I had to say

something,' he moaned. 'They were going to give me ten years.'

Dominic led him back to the sofa, and Duval talked. Disjointedly, with a lot of 'you've got to understand' and 'they were real pigs, man,' he talked. He had been threatened with ten years inside and he'd told the police everything, the names of the people he'd carried money for, the other operators he knew, the routes they used, the cars they drove, even the bank account numbers.

Dominic was interested in Duval's last run. 'You say you made a run every five or six weeks. Why did you do the last run after only three days?'

Duval looked at Dominic, suspicion crowding out his terror. 'Who the fuck are you? You're not Midas.' The skin of his face looked tender, parts of his cheeks covered with large watery blisters.

Dominic repeated, 'Why the run after only three days?'

Duval said softly, 'You're not Midas. You're pigs.' He looked from Dominic to Abe. 'You too. Oh Jesus! You don't look like pigs, but you are!'

Dominic went up to Duval and flicked the skin of his face, feeling the wetness against his fingers as a blister burst. 'I asked you a question, punk.'

Duval talked. He'd made the run because there was a panic on. Kevin Cormack himself had asked him to do it. Because it was only three days since the last run, he'd taken the route over the d'Intelvi instead of the autostrada. He'd thought it would be safer, less obvious. He was taking the money for Siccoli to the Banque Dürer in Lugano. It was to be paid into account number 11107634 and the account was in the name of Marc Landi.

Dominic took out his notebook and checked. The account number was there all right, the figures of the central square.

Abe said, 'Jackie boy, we're going to ship you Stateside.

191

The BNDD got a couple of charges they want to sling at you.'

'You can't do that, man.' Duval looked from Abe to Dominic, seeking support. 'It's illegal.'

'So?' Dominic shrugged. 'Once you're over there, who's going to worry about how you got there.'

'But . . . but—'

'No buts about it, laddie,' Dominic said. 'This time they're going to lock you up and throw away the key.'

Duval's jaw began to twitch. He blinked rapidly, and the pupils in the beady eyes seemed to dilate. 'What did you bastards spring me for then?'

Dominic said, 'We thought you might have something to tell us.'

Abe said, 'Looks like we made a mistake.'

Duval managed a pitying smile. The pigs always wanted to know, everyone wanted to know, they never left you alone. 'Okay, what do you want me to tell you?'

Dominic got in first. 'Is Midas still into drugs?'

'Look, I don't know that scene, man. Not any more. Not since I got busted in Germany.'

'Garnham and Cormack. They must still be into drugs.'

Abe said warningly, 'You aren't cooperating, Duval. I thought you were going to cooperate.'

'Yeah, man, yeah. They're all into it. Siccoli too. But not me. I've got nothing to do with that shit. Nothing. You've got to believe that.'

'What's Siccoli doing with drugs?' Dominic asked. 'He told me he was a revolutionary, he wanted to change society and love the people.'

'That's shit, man. Siccoli's been snowing you. He's no revolutionary. He's a pimp for Midas. You want to know what Siccoli does? He gets his friends to give him money for Midas to take to Switzerland.'

'What about his own money?'

'He hasn't any. He blew it. He's a friend of Kit's and Kit

192

let him into a couple of dope deals to help him out.'

'When was this?' Dominic asked. 'When was Kit so charitable?'

'A couple of years ago, when Kit took over ... after Thirstone and them were killed.'

'What else did Kit take over? Two guys named Grady and de Marco maybe?'

Duval said, 'If you know the answers why ask the questions? De Marco and Grady were smuggling for the Movement. That's what they were doing. The fucking CIA was shipping dope for Kit Garnham.'

Dominic let out a sigh of relief. Grady and de Marco had funded the deals out of the Interstellar account. That's why they had had to stop him investigating it. He raised two crossed fingers at Abe. 'Your serve, I think,' Dominic said.

Abe grinned. 'Now, Jackie boy, the sixty-four-million-dollar question. Who is Midas?'

Duval looked from Abe to Dominic. 'Man,' he said, 'I don't fucking know.'

There was a grating noise from outside the window, a combination of rasp and squeak, a brake shoe biting into grit. Dominic jumped up and looked. A black Mercedes had drawn across the gateway at the end of the path. A slim man in a brightly checked shirt was getting out. He was carrying an Armalite rifle, and with a quick glance at the house started to run for the clump of bushes ten yards from the gateway. Dominic shouted, 'Midas!' and whipped out the Colt.

The man was carrying the rifle awkwardly, running with a crouch that wasn't low enough. Dominic stood back from the window, braced his weight on his heels, grasped the Colt with both hands, aimed slightly in front of the clumsily running figure. The first shot shattered the glass, made the man leap in surprise. Dominic fired again. The man dived frantically for the bushes, legs flailing as he took flight. Dominic fired. A jet of blood from the hurtling body, barrel-rolling as it sprawled into the bushes. Dominic kept his eyes on the spot where the man had fallen. A square of vivid colour behind the foliage, a protruding boot that did not move.

He stepped away from the window and flattened himself against the wall. The black Mercedes was still there, ghoulish and silent. Still looking, he waved Abe back, his head still ringing with the sound of gunfire, his nose twitching at the acrid smell of cordite. They were lowering the tinted rear window of the Mercedes now, not taking any chances with sending any more men into the bushes. The barrel of an Armalite protruded from the half lowered window.

Suddenly, right behind him, there was a cry, an anguished patter of feet. Duval was racing across the lounge, leaping onto the half landing, going like hell for the front door. Dominic turned the gun towards him, held his fire, deciding bullets were too valuable to waste. Abe lunged after Duval in a blur of blue denim. Dominic jerked the gun upwards and shouted, 'No!'

Duval burst out of the front door, raced up the path. The searching gun barrel froze, locked on him, fired. There was a staccato chatter and Duval seemed to lift off, feet and arms flailing in slow, beautiful movements. Then all of a sudden he collapsed and fell like a rag doll.

Which left Abe running right into the barrel of the Armalite, without any protection or cover. Dominic could see the realization dawn on his face as he stopped, skid-turned, tried to make it back to the house. Dominic fired, loosing off three rapid shots, emptying the Colt into the gap between the glass and the top of the door, while the automatic chattered, spattering bullets off the walls, the door, the bushes and Abe. Abe's body jerked convulsively and then he hurtled face down on the steps. Dominic picked up the Python and fired again. He hit someone, because the

194

Armalite wavered, was snatched away, the window rolled up. The car began to move.

Dominic watched it go and ran out to Abe. Abe was lying on his face, one arm stretched above his head, reaching for the steps. The back of his blue denim jacket was pockmarked with blood-ringed jagged holes. Dominic turned him over. There was a pallor to his face, a rigidity to his body, a curious sense of peace. Cradled in Dominic's arms he looked small, innocent and all of five years old. Dominic could feel the blood wetting his arm and he murmured a ritual act of contrition. Abe had been only twenty-six, on his first foreign posting, and the first time he'd gone into something blind he'd been killed.

Still carrying the ·38 Dominic walked up to Duval. Duval was dead too, eyes staring as if in surprise at the suddenness of his end or the perfidy of Midas. The man in the bushes was Kevin Cormack. Dominic's bullet had caught him on the side of the chest, punched a hole as big as a fist through the ribs and kept on going. With that kind of bullet you expected big game to drop at sixty yards. Cormack at twenty had no chance. His chest had been pulped; he had died before he hit the ground, dying for an ideology he did not fully understand, and carrying a gun he didn't quite know how to use.

Dominic looked over the hedge: there was no one coming down the lane. He lifted Cormack's body and carried it into the house, then did the same with Duval.

Abe he laid gently on the sofa. They had been together for less than twenty-four hours, had hated each other, liked each other, had almost been friends. There was a wetness on his cheeks that had nothing to do with the horrible wetness of his hands. Dominic knelt down and rested his chek on Abe's roughened denim shoulder, and as he wept, he felt the old pain come back again, the old fear, and the old consuming hatred.

After a while he stood up, and arranged Abe's hands

over his chest. They were already cold and beginning to stiffen. Then he went over to the telephone and called Haden. He told him what had happened and asked for a body squad. Haden promised they would be there within the hour.

'The door will be unlocked,' Dominic said.

'Where are you going?'

'To find Midas and kill him,' Dominic said. He took Abe's Colt Python and Siccoli's Biretta and went out. Outside the sun was still shining, hard and bright as a mirror.

CHAPTER TWENTY-NINE

Dominic drove Abe's car, trying to focus his mind. He felt no regret for the man he had killed, no regret for Duval. If he hadn't shot Cormack and hurt the gunman in the Mercedes, Midas would have killed him too. Deliberately he replayed the scene in his mind, Duval running towards the car, the barrel of the automatic rifle steadying on him, the rapid burst of fire. They had meant to kill Duval; they had meant to kill their own.

They had meant to kill Abe, too. He replayed that part of it. The time for weeping was not yet and he would not allow himself the luxury of regret. Abe shouldn't have run back to the house. He should have taken cover behind the BMW. It all came down to experience, Dominic supposed, the ability to make the right split-second decision. But what a hell of a price to pay.

He thought back to Duval. Duval had been taking money from Siccoli to Landi's account at the Banque Dürer. To discover why, Dominic could talk to Siccoli or the Banque Dürer. Dürer – there was altogether to much Dürer in this. Perhaps all Marc's architect friend had to do was present the Dürer print to the Banque Dürer. Dominic liked that thought. He stopped at a call box and checked the bank's address.

The Banque Dürer was over a tobacconist's on a street well away from the lake. It was a very small bank, a single room divided by a wooden counter, with three clerks, and the manager's office at the end. The manager saw Dominic straightaway.

His name was Albergo, a lanky, sad-faced man, more Italian than Swiss, with an expression of furtive conceit that reminded Dominic of a headwaiter with his fingers caught in the till.

'Marc Landi had an account here,' Dominic said. 'Number 11107634,' and gave him the Dürer.

Albergo left Dominic in his office, went out and returned with a bulky sealed envelope. 'My instructions were to give this to anyone who brought me the print and told me the account number,' Albergo said. He made Dominic sign a receipt for one envelope, property of Marc Landi, contents unspecified.

Dominic asked, 'Is this all? Didn't he also leave some money with you? Eighteen million francs to be exact?'

Albergo looked even more furtive.

'Marc Landi is dead,' Dominic said.

Albergo nodded. 'I have news of his car accident, yes.'

Dominic took out his notebook and looked at the list of eight-digit numbers he had extracted from the magic square. So far Landi had used ten, the three horizontal groupings for the accounts at the Banco Lattoria, the three vertical groupings for those at the Fieldhaus. He'd used the two diagonals and the first inner square for the accounts in Vaduz, and the central square for his own account at the Banque Dürer.

Which left two combinations unused. Dominic stared at the figures. 31381034, 61215134. He had to choose one of them!

So far Landi had selected the account numbers in a sort of logical progression. If he'd followed that progression, he would have picked the grouping of the second square, 31381034.

But would Landi have persisted with logic to the end? The *end*! If it was the last account wouldn't he have used the last grouping?

Albergo was waiting for Dominic to say something.

Dominic had to choose. One group or the other. He had

198

to choose now. There was no way, no time to get any more information. *He had to choose now!*

'Six, one, two, one, five, one, three, four.'

Albergo was staring at him as if he had mouthed some horrible oath. Dominic felt his heart sink like a lead weight. He'd picked the wrong number. He'd gambled and lost!

Then Albergo said, 'That is also Landi's account, it was opened last Friday. And you are right, it has eighteen million francs in it.'

'Did you know Landi well?'

'Not well. We met once or twice in the course of business.'

'Why did he bank with you, when he worked at the Banco Lattoria?'

Albergo fiddled with the pens on his desk. 'That is not the kind of question which we like to answer,' he said. 'Not in Switzerland.'

Dominic went back to the Splendide-Royal, found they had kept his room for him. He ordered tea and a club sandwich, went upstairs and opened Landi's envelope.

It contained a letter, written in flowery Italian, full of undying adoration and pleas for understanding, addressed to Gabriel Marchetti, the architect who had died in Bellinzona. The letter had been written the previous Saturday.

The first part was just as Dominic expected. Motivated by a desire to succeed, Landi had gambled and lost. Under pressure to make up his losses, he had gambled more heavily, and lost more. Then he had falsified his records, been discovered and given a week by someone, whose name he wouldn't reveal, to repay the bank. The sum was more than he could earn or borrow. So he had cheated.

He had persuaded Siccoli that he could recover his fortune by speculating on foreign exchange. Following Landi's desperate advice, Siccoli had lost, and worse, turned out to be a bad loser. He threatened to reveal the full extent of Landi's losses to Edgar, unless Landi helped him recover his original investment. The method he suggested was simple and fraudulent, the equivalent of writing out betting slips after the race had been run. Landi cooperated at first.

But Siccoli had not known when to stop. Not after the first million, not after the second, or even the third. While Intra, Kastel and Sulden had raked in the profits, Siccoli had threatened Landi with jail, the loss of his job, disgrace, the exposure of his homosexuality and even the revelation of his political record as a student agitator in Paris. Once more Landi had cooperated, hoping that soon Siccoli would have made enough. Landi had cooperated until he realized that the bank could not sustain such losses and survive.

It was at that point that Siccoli had told Landi about Midas. Midas *wanted* the bank to collapse. They needed a financial base in Switzerland, they needed to sabotage certain other businesses, they needed access to a particular account. Despite Siccoli's reassurances that once Midas had taken over the bank, all would be well, Landi had panicked. Swindling a bank was one thing, ruining it and ruining the society he lived in, was another. Landi felt he had a duty to stop them and he had taken eighteen million francs out of the account and put it in account number 61215134 in the Banque Dürer. That money could be drawn by anyone who produced his letter, the Dürer print and quoted the account number. That money should be returned to the Banco Lattoria.

After he had taken the money, Landi had told Siccoli what he had done. He had told Siccoli that if the bank went into liquidation, he would tell the authorities all. That way, Landi was sure Midas would be defeated. He had never used any of the money personally, and there was nothing they could do to him that he had not already done to himself.

Now Siccoli wanted to meet him again and he was going to the meeting. Landi felt it likely that his meeting with Siccoli would end in disaster, but that was a chance he had to take.

'*If my attempt fails, Gabriel,*' Landi had written, '*you must take this letter to the authorities. The disgrace and shame then will not affect me. I ask you this last favour. Ever yours, Marc.*'

Fastened to the back of the letter was a drawing of the magic square, a list of account numbers and banks that tallied with those in Dominic's notebook, and a bulky accounting of all the foreign-exchange transactions Marc had undertaken on behalf of the anstalts. The genuine transactions were marked with asterisks. There were not many of them.

Dominic put the letter away and looked at his watch. It was a quarter after four. The takeover meeting at the Banco Lattoria must have already begun, and here in his hand was all the evidence necessary to frustrate Midas. But who the hell was Midas? And how could he be drawn out of his hiding place?

Dominic took the letter downstairs and deposited Marc's confession in the hotel safe. Then he had an idea. He drove to the Hotel Walter and booked a room there, next to Claire's. It was an elaborate way of renting a safe deposit, but, if he was staying at the Walter, Midas would never imagine he'd deposited the confession anywhere else, and the advantage of keeping it in a luxury hotel was that he had access to it at any hour of the day or night.

By the time he had completed this charade it was quarter to five. Dominic decided they had had enough time and set out to walk to the bank.

He walked along the narrow and twisting arcades of the Via Nassa, part of the old town, filled with opulent shops

201

and tasteful window displays, watches and cakes and jewellery, the precision of Omega and the discreet opulence of Piaget. He stopped and looked at watches and rings, and mentally bought one of each for Claire.

He reached the Banco Lattoria and went in through the staff entrance, took the lift to the third floor. The board-room was at the front of the building with a view over the lake. It was halfway down a sumptuous corridor, lined with modern paintings of a nautical kind and a portrait of a singularly serious Swiss wearing a frock coat. A notice on the heavy door said the boardroom was '*occupé*'.

Dominic opened the door.

There were six of them there, five seated together at one end of a rectangular mahogany table, each with a notepad and Doppler with a pile of bulky files. Edgar sat at the head of the table with Brian Keith on his right and Doppler on his left. Beside Doppler was Claire, taking notes, and beside Brian Keith, Dr Eugene Beck. At the far end of the table, opposite Edgar, sitting with an inquiring smile on his face, was Martin Pelham.

The stench of Doppler's cigar greeted Dominic, only half as distasteful as Doppler's square-lensed look. Claire looked at him with anxious surprise, Brian Keith with curiosity. Edgar was annoyed and Beck had the expression of a visitor suddenly confronted with his host's tiresome child.

Doppler was the first to speak: number two trying to impress number one. 'You have no business in this bank, Mr Cain. No business in this room. Would you please leave now.'

Dominic said, 'On the contrary, what I have to say is of interest to everyone in this room.'

Edgar said, 'Cain, you've caused enough trouble. Will you get out, or shall I have you thrown out?'

Dominic grinned at him. 'Selling the bank, Edgar?'

'It is nothing to do with you. Pelham, would you get rid

of your friend.'

Dominic said, 'You were discussing the terms on which you will sell this bank to clients of our good friend, Dr Beck. The sum you are haggling about is sixty million francs, though Dr Beck would prefer the figure to be nearer forty-five. Right?'

'Right,' said Brian Keith.

'We will not disuss this—' Doppler cried. 'How do you know all this?'

'Because I am holding, in a bank in Lugano, the difference between Dr Beck's original offer and his present one,'

There were gasps of amazement and Doppler's mouth dropped open.

Dominic advanced into the room. 'I have also got a signed confession from Marc Landi. It sets out in great detail how he conspired with Gianni Siccoli and some of Dr Beck's other clients to defraud the Banco Lattoria of nearly sixty million francs.'

'Do you have this confession with you?' Edgar asked.

Dominic shook his head.

'Then we must continue with our meeting,' Beck said. 'Until this matter is proved—'

'Until this matter is proved, Dr Beck, you should ensure that the monies notionally belonging to your clients remain under your control. If the money were to suddenly disappear, your participation in their offences might appear less than innocent.'

'I have not—'

'Forget the three wise monkeys, Beck. Just hang onto the money. If you like I'll have a court order for you tomorrow.' Dominic turned to Edgar. 'Adjourn the meeting for twenty-four hours, and you'll save your bank.'

'And when do we see this – this confession?' Edgar asked.

'Tomorrow.'

'Why not now?'

'Because,' Dominic said, 'I need it.' He looked round the room. Someone here was Midas. 'Someone called Midas wants to see it too.'

'I do not understand,' Doppler protested.

'You're not expected to. Now, gentlemen, I suggest you adjourn this meeting. At best, you will have saved yourselves sixty million francs. At worst, you'll find that Dr Beck has increased his offer by eighteen million. Now, please let Dr Beck get on his way. He has urgent business to discuss with his clients. If your clients wish to see me, Dr Beck, I am staying at the Hotel Walter.'

Beck looked inquiringly from Doppler to Keith, from Keith to Edgar. Keith nodded.

'We will adjourn this meeting till the same time tomorrow, Dr Beck,' Edgar said. 'That is if you agree.' The look on his face made it clear that he expected Dr Beck to agree.

After Beck left, he asked, 'All right, Cain, what is this nonsense about a confession? As far as we know Landi lost the bank's money. That's all there is to it.'

'There was a conspiracy to defraud. I can prove that. You will have the proof tomorrow.'

'Why the delay, old boy?' That was Martin, from the further end of the table.

'Because the conspiracy was organized by a group called Midas. I want Midas. Landi knew who Midas is. Midas will come to me for the confession.'

Edgar said, 'Cain, you're a mad man or a genius. But I am going to back you. You've got nerve and I like that, but you'd better have that confession here by this time tomorrow or I'll have your guts for garters.'

Martin got to his feet. 'And on that cordial note, Charles, I would suggest Dominic and I adjourn to a nearby hostelry. There's a lot we have to talk about.' He limped up to Dominic and took his arm. 'Congratulations,' he said. 'You've done a splendid job.'

Dominic moved away from him and stood in front of Claire. 'You coming?'

Claire looked hesitantly from Edgar to Doppler. 'Not yet. I have things to do.'

'We all have things to do,' Edgar said. 'For a start I think I'll take a look at Landi's records. I'd be grateful if you would stay and help me, Miss Denton.'

Dominic shrugged and turned to Claire. 'Ring me before you leave the bank. I'll be at the Walter. I'll walk you home.'

'But Dominic—'

'I'll walk you home,' Dominic said firmly, and allowed Martin to lead him out of the room.

'Let's go back to your den of iniquity,' Martin said, 'and get loaded. Then you can tell me all about Midas.'

'Get back we may do, but get loaded we do not. Tonight we dispense iniquity.'

'Fine,' Martin said. 'Give me ten minutes and I'll join you at the Walter.'

Twenty minutes later, Martin came into his room at the Walter and drank Dominic's duty-free Chivas. Martin had come with Edgar, representing the Department. There had been rumours that Edgar would be arrested if he set foot in Switzerland. He told Dominic the Department wanted Midas.

'I thought the Department was being neutral. That they didn't want to be involved.'

'They've changed their principles.'

'Too late,' Dominic said. 'There are other people who want Midas.'

Martin said, 'I hear you lost Abe Stone.'

'That's right,' Dominic admitted.

'What happened?'

'I don't want to talk about it. Not now. I don't want to talk to anyone about Abe or about Midas.'

'You're strange,' Martin said, and for the next forty-five minutes he talked about cricket.

By seven o'clock Claire had neither phoned nor arrived. Dominic called the bank and got no answer.

'I'll come with you,' Martin offered.

'No,' Dominic said, 'I'll be quicker on my own.' Trying not to remember the pain on Martin's face he raced out of the hotel and through the Nassa Arcade. He didn't stop now to look at watches or rings, nor to admire the window displays. He tried to tell himself that the bank's phone was on a night line, ringing in an unoccupied office, that he was behaving like a fussy old hen. Nevertheless, by the time he reached the end of the arcade, he was running.

The Piazza della Riforma was filled with people seated at the pavement cafés under blue and yellow umbrellas. There were lights on in shop windows and on the ground floors of banks. Lights on in the Banco Lattoria too, but the doors were locked and the lights only in the plateglass window, illuminating the day's stockmarket prices and foreign-exchange rates. Cold tentacles of fear gripped Dominic's heart. For a moment he experienced a blind panic, a need for help. Then he saw the black Mercedes travelling quickly on the further side of the square, and through its tinted glass glimpsed the faces of Brian Keith, Kit Garnham and Charles Edgar.

Claire wasn't with them. Claire wasn't at the bank. She hadn't come straight back to the hotel. Edgar, Garnham, Keith, they were all in it together and they'd taken Claire.

Dominic turned and sprinted back to the Hotel Walter and Martin.

CHAPTER THIRTY

Martin said, 'Now, let's take it very, very easy.'

Ten minutes after he'd told Martin about Claire's abduction, Dominic was doing just that. He was stretched out on the bed, breathing in slowly, holding his breath, concentrating on letting it out, all in measured beats, trying to still all emotion, to think of Claire as simply another victim, trying most of all to quiet the screaming panic inside that wanted him to give them the confession and get the hell out. He opened his eyes and looked at Martin.

Martin said, 'It's your decision, old chap. The girl or Midas. If you want to give up Midas, do.'

'That isn't the way it's played,' Dominic said.

'Queen and country will love you for that, old son. Do you want an OBE or the girl?'

'That isn't the choice,' Dominic said. 'The truth is, there is no choice.'

'Rubbish, Dominic. All you have to do to get the girl back is give them the confession. The only thing to watch out for is that you aren't double-crossed.'

'It isn't that simple,' Dominic insisted. 'We both know too much. They cannot allow either of us to walk away free.'

'Then what do we do?' Martin asked.

'We wait.'

Ten minutes later Martin said, 'It might save time if we had the letter with us. They don't know me. Shall I go and collect it?'

Dominic considered that. With the consideration came a horrible realization. Midas might be anybody. Charles Edgar, Brian Keith, Siccoli, Tom Haden, Doppler, even Martin. 'No,' he said. 'I'll do that when the time comes.'

Five minutes passed. Martin said, 'We *have* to jolt them. We *have* to throw them off balance.'

'How?'

'Hit them at their strongest point. Your association with the girl.'

Dominic wished Martin wouldn't refer to Claire as 'the girl', as if she were some inanimate object. Martin explained what he wanted to do.

Dominic said, 'It's risky.'

'But it's the only idea we have.'

The first phone call came through at precisely 8.05. Martin and Dominic eyed each other. Martin nodded. Dominic took a deep breath and picked up the phone.

'Dominic Cain?' The voice was metallic, the accent mid-Atlantic.

'Yes.'

'We have your girl.'

Dominic paused, counting. When he reached ten, he asked, 'Who are you?'

'Don't be fucking stupid man. Who do you think? Midas.'

'You are Midas himself?' he asked disbelievingly.

Martin reached out and wrestled the receiver from Dominic. He lifted it to his ear and said, 'I didn't hear that, my friend.'

'I said we've got the girl and we want the confession. Who the fuck are you?'

'Pelham's the name. Martin Pelham. Cain is my assistant. What is it you want?'

'Cain,' the voice at the other end said. 'I want to talk to Cain.'

'You will have to talk to me, I'm afraid. Because of his association with the girl, Mr Cain cannot play any further part in this. Anything you want to say you can say to me.'

208

'Look, arsehole, tell Cain he talks to us or the girl is dead.'

'How very melodramatic. Cain has been relieved of his duties. He cannot talk to you.'

'We'll kill the girl, man. Now.'

'What happens to the girl is no concern of mine. I have certain documents which I intend to pass over to the Swiss and the Italian police. I should also warn you that the penalties for kidnapping and murder are extremely severe.' Martin put the phone down.

'For Christ's sake!' Dominic blurted. 'You've over-played it.'

'Did I? I'm sorry.'

'You don't know these mothers. They'll kill her just for the hell of it.'

Martin seized hold of Dominic's wrist. 'We'll have to sweat it out,' he said.

The seconds afterwards could be measured in heart beats; each passing minute was a funeral bell. Two minutes. Three. And nothing. Dominic and Martin stared at separate walls, the tick of Martin's Omega a reminder of life passing, of Claire dying... If they killed her, if they had to kill her, Dominic prayed that it would be quick. Let her not suffer, he thought, let her not feel pain – as if that was some compensation for dying. He stared at the wall, stared at the watch. His mind and his emotions were beyond control, his thoughts focused on a terrified Claire, bundled into the back of a car, her head forced between her knees, shot. From somewhere underneath the fear, the anger began to burn. If Claire died, he would spend the rest of his life hunting Midas. He would seek him out from under whichever stone he crawled. He would never relent. Then, he thought, after that, what?

The phone jangled. A hoarse clattering sound that made them both start. Dominic felt his hands tremble. Martin picked up the receiver. 'Pelham here.'

'I want Dominic Cain.'

'Cain's not available. If you want to talk about the girl, you talk to me.'

'All right, motherfucker. Listen, and listen carefully.'

Martin reared a thumb at Dominic and smiled. 'I'm listening.'

Dominic felt the tension rush out of him and sagged across the bed. Claire was still alive: relief flooded his body. She was still alive!

'We have the girl and we will kill her. Cain knows we are capable of doing that.'

'Go on,' Martin said. 'You're repeating yourself.'

'This is what we want in exchange for the girl. One, Cain has eighteen million francs of our money. We want an irrevocable instruction from him to the bank, authorizing that sum to be paid to Intra Anstalt. Two, we want the confession of Marc Landi, all copies that have been taken, and the names of everyone who has seen that confession. Three, we want a letter from Cain addressed to Dr Eugene Beck, stating that he knows of no reason why the monies paid to Intra, Kastel and Sulden Anstalts should be released to them.'

'That's a lot for the life of one girl.'

'Is that how you measure life, pig? In terms of money?'

Martin said, 'Let's not get dialectical. Cain is a government employee, and this is a government matter. We have standing instructions not to accede to demands of this sort. I will have to put your demands to London.'

'You have twenty minutes,' the voice said. 'Call London now.'

'I want to speak to the girl,' Martin said.

'You can't.'

'There's no deal until I speak to the girl. I want to make sure that you have her and that she is alive.'

There was the jar of a receiver being put down on a table,

shuffling and background voices, then a girl's voice, very indistinct. She said something like, 'Dominic?'

'This isn't Dominic, Claire. It's Martin Pelham, a friend of Dominic's.'

Again an unintelligible mutter.

'I can't hear you, my dear.'

More muttering and shuffling. A voice saying, 'Is that better?'

Martin asked, 'What's the matter?'

A girl's voice. 'I'm blindfolded and tied. They're holding the receiver to my face. Can you hear me?'

Martin said, 'I can hear you quite clearly, my dear.'

'Where's Dominic?'

'Dominic is safe. Don't worry, we'll get you out.' Dominic reached a hand for the phone. Martin brushed it away. 'Are they treating you well?'

'Apart from the fact that I can't see, can't move and don't know where I am, yes. Please, I want to speak to Dominic.'

'You can't do that, not just now. But it'll all be over quite soon. Try not to worry. I'm going to ring off now, because I have some phone calls to make so we can arrange your release.' Martin put the phone down. 'She's okay,' he said to Dominic. 'Blindfolded and bound, but okay. Sorry I couldn't let you speak to her. The conversation might have been monitored.' He lit a cigarette and told Dominic of the demands.

'What's all that shit about talking to London?'

'I'm afraid it's true, old boy. Standing instructions. No negotiations with terrorists.'

'Screw that! Claire is my girl. Neither of us is even working for the Department.'

Martin said soothingly, 'Let me talk to London. It will be all right. Besides, I can get some help from the Department. Meanwhile you'd better decide two important questions. Where do we make the exchange? And how do we make sure that you don't get killed?'

'We'll need cover,' Dominic said. 'A place with rooftops, and snipers with night-sights.'

'Risky.'

'There's no other way. They'll want me alone. We've got to get Haden's men or the Swiss police.'

'Haden wouldn't handle a shoot-out in Switzerland, not after what happened this afternoon. And I'm not sure about the Swiss police. They'll either cock it up or raise so many objections that it will be Sunday next week before anything happens.'

'But we need outside help,' Dominic said.

'No, Dominic. Not outside help. Help from our own people. That's what they're there for. That way we will have total control. It will be our operation.'

'When is all this going to happen?'

'Relax old boy,' Martin said. 'I'll do it as soon as I get to the right phone.'

At precisely 8.25 the phone rang. Martin picked it up.

'Well, Pelham, what is your answer?'

'I have no answer yet. London wants time to think.'

There was a rustling at the other end of the phone. Voices as the man discussed Martin's decision with someone else. Then, 'What the fuck is there to think about?'

'That's London,' Martin said. 'They always want time to think.'

'So they want us to kill the girl, right?'

'Let's not prejudge the situation. Let's exercise some patience.'

'You make the exchange now, pig, or the girl gets it.'

'I can't. I need authority from London for that. I promise you everything will be all right.'

'Well, do it then, if you're so sure.'

'Even though I'm sure, I have to wait for word from London. That is how we work.'

There was more background discussion. Then the voice said. 'You have twenty minutes. And that is final. Remember, final.'

Martin turned to Dominic. 'They're getting uptight, but we'll have to spin it out. I'd better go over to the Consulate and call from there. It will leave this phone free and they have a direct line to London.'

Five minutes after Martin left, Dominic decided he had been stupid. What the hell was the point in getting involved with the Department now? What was the sense of exchanging silly bureaucratic bananas when Claire's life was at stake? He should never have let Martin talk him into this. They would take twenty leap years to decide which stationery to use for their memos, and all he had was minutes. No, if he needed help, he should have called Haden. Haden had men right here in Lugano, and Haden owed him recompense.

Dominic called Haden on the panic number and explained the problem. As Martin had predicted, Haden was reluctant to become involved in another shoot-out. He offered to talk to Wolweber and promised to call him right away.

Ten minutes later Wolweber called. Dominic was not to worry, Chief Inspector Wolweber was on his way.

CHAPTER THIRTY-ONE

Dominic sat on the bed, checking the chamber and firing mechanism of the Colt for the fifteenth time since Martin had left. The waiting was getting to him. It would have been different if there had been something positive to do. But there was nothing to do but wait.

Dominic looked at the gun in his hand, lying there black and lethal in the flesh of his palm. The butt fitted comfortably; the whole felt balanced and deadly. He wondered if before the night was over he would use the gun, whether he would use it to kill Midas.

This was not the time for dreams of future action. This was time for thought. There had been two calls so far, made close together. They wouldn't have risked that if they were on the other side of the border. So they were in Switzerland, obviously near Lugano. Lugano was half an hour from Italy, forty-five minutes from Milan. An hour after the exchange, Midas could scatter. So where would they want the exchange to take place? Not in Lugano, surely. Lugano was too public. It would be some desolate road near the Italian border, a lonely farmhouse or an empty villa.

And meanwhile, where were they holding Claire? It could be anywhere. Dominic could of course extend her ordeal while the police searched the most likely places. But that was too dangerous. The police might even find her and Midas might not let himself be taken. He would extract a high price for the end of his dreams, Claire's life for his. There was no other way but to make a deal.

Dominic looked at his watch. Nearly 8.45. Where the hell was Martin? He should be back here by now, not making small talk with London. Dominic's thoughts wandered back to the desolate road. He would have to talk

Midas out of that. He'd have to persuade them to meet him where there was cover. Where? And how?

The phone gave a familiar croak. Dominic stared at it, willing it to stop. Croak, croak. Where the hell was Martin? Croak, croak, with increasing insistence. Dominic picked up the receiver, thinking quickly.

'Cain here.'

'Hello, lover boy. They letting you talk to us, are they?'

'Pelham isn't here. He's over at the Consulate, talking to London.'

'We told him twenty minutes, lover boy. We don't like being screwed around.'

'Nobody's screwing you around. Pelham has to talk to London. The Consulate is the only place he can do it from.'

'What's wrong with the hotel?'

'We have only one phone here.'

'There must be another phone in the hotel.' The man was deeply suspicious.

'It's easier to talk to London from the Consulate,' Dominic said. 'They've got direct lines.'

'What are you trying to pull, Cain?'

'Nothing. Pelham's getting authority for the swop.'

'It's not a government matter,' the voice said. 'Your girl isn't government property.'

'Pelham will be back soon,' Dominic said tightly.

'I told him twenty minutes. What the fuck has he got to talk about for twenty minutes?'

'It's procedure,' Dominic said. 'Bureaucratic red tape.'

'Bureaucratic shit,' the voice replied. 'Cain, I am warning you, don't get smart. We've got your girl, and these guys here have got a hard-on just looking at her. If you don't want her to pull a train, you'd better make the deal, fast.'

Dominic thrust away the vision of hair and lips and flesh and semen, refused to think about that most grotesque of sexual violations. 'Pelham's making the deal,' he said fiercely. 'Anyone touches the girl and the deal's off. Anyone touches the girl, and I kill Midas *first*.'

The cold anger in his voice got through. 'I'll call back,' the voice said. 'Make sure Pelham's there.' The fact of the man's retreat implied that Midas was not there and that he was vulnerable.

Claire lay in enforced darkness, her bound hands forming a hard knot underneath her body, the stiffness moving up her shoulders and the backs of her arms. She could hear voices in the next room, the sound of feet, the scrape of furniture. After she had spoken to Pelham, they had left her utterly alone.

She had no idea of how much time had passed since then. Even less of an idea of how long it had been since they had grabbed her. It could have been as much as ten hours since that telephone call, with that unidentifiable voice crying, 'Claire, something's happened! Meet me in the café across the Piazza!'

Listening to the gurgle of the receiver, she had suspected a trap. She had hesitated and then gone, hoping that the call was genuine, that she was going to Dominic. She remembered reasoning that it was still daylight, that there were crowds of people walking about and sitting in the cafés around the Piazza, that the café itself was hardly thirty yards away. She'd convinced herself that nothing could happen to her, that there was no harm in looking, and she'd left the bank.

Even so, she'd stopped on the steps, looking for Dominic, then walked into the centre of the Piazza. People milled around her. She couldn't see Dominic, but the back of the café was in shadow. She'd stopped, peering, undecided whether to return to the bank, then become aware of a man standing very close behind her, his hand peculiarly angled in the sheepskin vest, of something hard and round pressed into her back.

'Scream, my love, and I'll blow your lovely little spine apart.' His voice had been harsh and excited, its timbre beyond recognition. He'd sniffed in her ear, and she'd looked into his face. He was staring wide-eyed at her, seeing her and not seeing her, living in an internal dream, spaced out.

Two other men were already walking up to her. Young, hard-faced, not particularly anything. They came right up close and took her hands, palm to palm and fingers interlocking, like old friends. Unlike old friends, their grips were purposeful. Together they marched her out of the Piazza.

A red Volvo was waiting in a street nearby. She was made to climb into the rear seat, between two of the men. The third man drove. As the car moved, one of them pulled her head down onto his lap, bruising her mouth against the hardness of his thigh. He held her like that while the other man blindfolded and gagged her, then roped her hands behind her back. They had laid her on the floor of the car and kept her there until the journey ended.

By then she had lost count of time. Without sight she was unable to relate to distance or time; she couldn't say whether the journey had taken two minutes or twenty. When the car stopped, they had tied her legs together and carried her out under a smelly blanket. She couldn't tell how far, how high or where they had taken her. All she knew was that she was lying on a bed, bound and blindfolded, waiting for rescue or death.

When Pelham had wanted to speak to her, they had freed her legs and allowed her to walk to the other room. But the blindfold and the ropes round her hands remained, and afterwards they had brought her back and made her lie in the darkness again. Pelham had sounded firm and confident. She felt she could trust that voice, but wished

218

she had been able to speak to Dominic. It was the not knowing that weakened her, not knowing what these people wanted, what they were going to do, not knowing how Dominic and Pelham would rescue her. Not knowing and darkness. If only they would let her see it wouldn't be so bad.

She heard doors open and voices, the rapid tread of feet. More people had come into the building. There was a voice raised in anger. She recognized that voice. Edgar's. Then the slam of a door, more footsteps, more voices. A long tirade from the room where the telephone was. Claire shivered. Midas himself had arrived.

Martin was the first to arrive, slipping furtively into the room, brushing past Dominic's threatening gun.

'Where the hell were you,' Dominic demanded.

'I was sweetening up London. They're on our side now. They'll come back to us in a moment.'

'I called Haden,' Dominic told him, 'and got the Swiss police involved. Chief Inspector Wolweber will be here soon.'

'He can't come here!' Martin exclaimed. 'They're bound to be watching the place.'

'Wolweber appreciates that. He's got a private entrance.'

As if to prove that, there was a rapid double knock on the door. Martin opened it. Wolweber strode in, grinning heartily at Dominic. 'Now, Mr Cain, we have our hearts-together chat, right?' Behind Wolweber was a scholarly gentleman, wearing metal-framed, circular glasses, sporting a dreary grey moustache and carrying a small case.

'There isn't time to talk,' Dominic said. 'Midas will call back anytime. And they want an answer.'

The small man came into the room, picked up the telephone and started unscrewing the base.

'What the fuck is he doing?'

'We're trying to set up a trace, Mr Cain.'

'And when you've found out where they're hiding, what do you do? Take them out with rockets and napalm?'

'The more we know, the more we can do,' Wolweber said, a hint of reproach in his voice, as if he were remembering secrets that had once been kept from him.

'Sod that. They're going to call any second. And what the hell do you think they'll do if they get a busy signal?'

The little man put the phone down and straightened up. 'Excuse me,' he said. 'I can do this from the hotel switchboard. It will not take long.'

He picked up his bag and went, not quite hearing Dominic's muttered hope that whatever he did, he did quickly.

'I'm having six men made ready,' Wolweber said. 'They will have everything. Flak jackets, walkie-talkies, gas bombs, rifles, infra-red sights. They're members of the police team at the Lugano Rifle Club.'

Dominic didn't inquire whether they had won any cups.

'We must have my men on high ground,' Wolweber said, standing up to emphasize the point. 'So they can look down.' He held his hands before his face in the attitude of a man holding a rifle, and closed one eye. 'And bang, bang.'

Dominic remembered that he and Claire would be amongst the people they were going to bang-bang at, and said, 'Where?'

'The ideal place,' Wolweber said, 'is the Piazza della Riforma.'

'You must be out of your bloody mind,' Dominic snapped. 'You've got six sharp-shooters on a roof picking off a group of terrorists in the middle of a crowded square.'

'Who said the square would be crowded?' Wolweber sat down and gave Dominic a triumphant smile. 'We close off the square at one and make the exchange at two.'

Dominic scratched his chin, thoughtfully. A deserted

Piazza might just work. But would Midas not be suspicious of such emptiness?

'Also, if reinforcements are needed, the police station is close.'

Dominic shuddered. If reinforcements were needed, he was going to be very dead. 'How do we know that Midas will wait that long?'

'He will have to,' Wolweber replied. 'We will tell him that we are still awaiting a decision from London.'

Martin smiled at him warmly.

'That won't work,' Dominic blurted out. 'He'll only—'

The phone croaked.

'—get suspicious. You'll have—'

Martin picked up the phone. 'Pelham here.'

'What's your decision, Pelham?' It was a different voice, more authoritative, more educated. It had a peculiar pitch, familiar, yet distorted, as if the person were speaking through a masking device.

'No decision has been made yet,' Martin said. 'Whitehall needs time to consider this. The Chancellor is being driven down from—'

'Pelham, this is a simple exchange. The girl for the money and the confession.'

'That part is simple enough. But we need Treasury authorization if we are going to deliver Edgar's money.'

From the receiver there broke a long cackle of laughter. 'That's good, Pelham. That's very good. But Cain is here and the money is here. We don't need the Treasury any more.'

'Well, I'll tell London that, and see what they have to say.'

'The exchange, Pelham. When are you going to do the exchange?'

'Now let me see . . . why don't you call me back in an hour.'

'I'm calling you back in fifteen minutes,' Midas said.

'And I promise you this. One of us will have something interesting to hear.'

Claire heard footsteps approaching her room. There were three of them – no, four – walking fast, the sound of their feet growing louder. They were coming for her. They were going to torture her. Didn't the fools realize she had nothing to say? The door opened; feet tramped around the bed. She smelt sweat, heard the sound of strained breathing.

'Get a hard-on just looking at her,' a voice said.

The man on the phone had said that too. She fought back a scream as she realized what they were going to do with her. All four of them. No, they wouldn't, she told herself, suddenly remembering the blankness of their faces in the Piazza. Four of them—! Oh God! She braced herself for the hands pawing at her, the hot dripping breath forced past her mouth. The press and thrust of sweating bodies, the repeated multiple submission.

Hands grabbed her shoulders and pulled her upright, swung her legs off the bed. She stood up, allowed herself to be guided out of the room, into the other. She stood by the door, nakedly aware of the men crowding around her, the frightened flutter of her heartbeats.

As if in response to a signal, someone knelt before her. Hands plucked at her right shoe. She staggered as her foot was raised, the shoe removed. Then the other shoe. Hands crawled up her legs, rolled down her stockings, took them away from her. Her feet felt the warm, wooden floor. Something cold and hard was placed around her ankles. Locks clicked, she bit back a cry of pain as the metal cut into her flesh, and swayed slightly as her feet were locked together.

The rest happened quickly. Her hands were freed, then manacled tightly in front of her. A rope was passed underneath her arms and she was pulled back and upwards against the door, nearly suspended from it, her feet stretching to balance precariously on tiptoe.

The cuffs were cutting into her wrists and ankles. Already she could feel the blood pounding along her fingers and toes, the growth of a slow, pulsing pain.

'Now,' a voice said, 'We wait.'

Claire started, the rope jerking her body, feeling the pain of the metal against her flesh increase. The voice was new, yet familiar. She'd heard it before in different circumstances, and despite a ring of hollowness about it, she recognized the voice of Midas. She knew who Midas was. Brian Keith.

CHAPTER THIRTY-TWO

In the hotel room, the three men looked at each other. Wolweber got up, left the room, checked with his man downstairs, came back shaking his head. 'This time nearly,' Wolweber said. 'Next time we'll have them for sure.'

'That was Brian Keith,' Martin said. 'Keith is Midas.'

'Not Keith, Edgar,' Dominic said. 'Keith doesn't have the talent, the imagination or the will. Keith's doing what he's always done, being Edgar's mouthpiece.'

'I can't believe it's Edgar,' Martin said.

'I saw them leave the bank in that black Mercedes. And Landi described Midas as a man who was tired of wealth.'

'Well, what are we going to do?' Martin asked. 'They won't wait till two. We'll have to find another place.'

Wolweber creased his brow in thought as Dominic and Martin turned inquiring gazes on him. After a while he said, 'The top of the funicular in the Piazza Luini. It is not so good, but it is more quiet than the Riforma. You make the exchange at the bottom and we will cover you from the top. We'll be ready by eleven-thirty.'

Dominic knew the place Wolweber spoke of. Just behind the fifteenth-century church of Santa Maria d'Egli Agnoli, a short funicular ran up to the Via Maraini above. 'We can't wait till eleven-thirty,' he said.

'I can't do it any quicker. In any case we must wait till the funicular closes down.'

'We still have to make them agree to our choice of time and place,' Martin remarked.

Wolweber stood up. 'You'll find a way. Now I'll go and get the men ready.'

Wolweber's departure brought on a kind of loneliness,

a weakening of confidence, and the inactivity didn't help at all. Dominic fiddled with the Colt, then opened his case and fastened the Grisbi diver's knife to his calf.

'That's a vicious bit of cutlery,' Martin remarked. 'Do you pick your teeth with it?'

'It made a mess of Siccoli's face,' Dominic said, the recollection of that savage act easing his present sense of helplessness.

'I think Edgar is mad,' Martin said. 'He has everything and now he has to try politics. Politicians are the ruination of society.'

'You think Nixon would have made it as a banker?'

The phone rang.

'Have you made up your mind yet?'

'No,' Martin replied. 'You must understand we are a government department. We need time to take decisions. There are a number of people involved.'

'Wrong,' Midas said. 'There's just you and us. A letter, money, the girl and Cain.'

'It isn't that—'

'I want to talk to Cain.'

Martin hesitated, then handed the receiver to Dominic.

'Cain, you have proved very dangerous. You should have been on our side. We might have done great things together.'

Dominic concentrated on the voice, groping towards recognition.

'We do not have much time, and I am suspicious of Pelham. I do not want to be provoked into doing something you will regret. Will you make the exchange?'

'I can't.'

'Well, listen then and learn. Midas does not like to be thwarted. Claire is in this room with us. She is literally hanging from the door. Her wrists and ankles are cuffed together. Tight. From where I am sitting, I can see the metal biting into her flesh. There is one man standing by

226

her, one man crouched at her feet. When I put this phone down, they will stroke her fingers and her toes, very gently. As blood is drawn into these parts, the pain will be excruciating.'

Claire heard the phone clatter against the desk, tried to move against her bonds. Then, through the numbness that was her hands and feet, she felt a fly-light touch, followed by a not unpleasant tingling, then the pain. Pain like a bruise, pain exploding, swelling, drawing through her extremities in ribbons of fire and ice. Claire screamed.

Dominic heard the scream and went rigid. The men stroked her again. Her hands and feet must feel on fire, and again the shrill, piercing scream, followed this time by sobs. Dominic felt the anger inside him turn cold, become like a chill, blue flame. Claire screamed again. And again. But this time Dominic felt no pain, not for him or for her. There was one thought in his mind now. Tonight, Midas would die and Dominic would kill him.

'Every five minutes for the next half hour we shall continue to stroke her,' Midas said. 'Then I will have her ask you to arrange our meeting.' The line went dead.

Dominic calculated: half an hour, an hour – how long could she stand it? The longer she was kept cuffed, the more sensitive would her hands and feet become. Each time they stroked her, the pain would be multiplied a hundred times. How long could she stand it without endangering the future use of her hands and feet, how long could she stand it before her mind went?

There were footsteps outside the door. The little man with the round-lensed glasses came in. 'I have the number,' he announced with pride. 'It is a house, ten kilometres outside Lugano. It belongs to the Banco Lattoria.' He handed Dominic a piece of paper with the telephone number and address.

'Thank you,' Dominic said, ideas whirling through his mind.

The man left and Dominic turned to Martin. 'We can't wait till midnight. Even if we have to go in and get her.' He told Martin what they were doing to Claire.

Martin said, 'It's better to do the deal. If we are seen near that house, she will die.'

Dominic said, 'We don't need snipers at the top of the funicular. We don't need six uniformed men. Not if I manage to see Midas alone. Then one man would do or two. They could take him at the bottom, after the exchange. We wouldn't need to wait for the crowds to clear. We could use the crowds to hide in. Convince Wolweber,' he said. 'Tell him, if we don't do something, that girl is going to need an amputation job in an hour.'

Dominic left the room and hurried onto the street. The doorman found him a taxi to take him to the Hotel Splendide-Royal.

Dominic collected the Landi letter from the safe, took it with him up to the room he had booked. Twenty minutes. It would take Martin twenty minutes to convince Wolweber to have his men stationed at the foot of the funicular. They had agreed that if Wolweber wouldn't cooperate, Martin would come alone. If he called Midas now, it would take him half an hour to get there. He picked up the phone and dialled the number that the phone-tapper had given him. At least it saved Claire ten minutes of hell.

Burr-burr, burr-burr: the high-pitched ringing tone kept sounding in Dominic's ear like an impatient wasp going soprano. Were they never going to answer? If they didn't answer the whole scheme was blown. Burr-burr, burr-burr. Come on Midas, pick the bloody thing up. Leave my girl alone and answer the phone. I've got news for you.

'Hello,' a voice said in a guarded tone. It was Midas.

'This is Dominic Cain.'

A sharp intake of breath. Midas was undoubtedly

228

worried. 'I know your number and I know where you are.' Dominic paused to let the effect of that sink in. 'Pelham's told the Swiss police about it. They are on their way to you now.'

'And you've decided to change sides, have you Cain?' Midas asked. 'To be British and support the under-dog?'

Dominic frowned. The voice was vaguely familiar. It sounded not like Brian Keith but like someone imitating him.

'I don't give a bugger what happens to you,' he said. 'I want Claire.'

'You should have thought of that before you became so damn efficient and involved the police.'

'It's too late for recriminations. The fact is I am no longer with the police. I am no longer with Pelham. I am at the Hotel Splendide-Royal. And I have the confession. Pelham hasn't seen it. It's been in the hotel safe ever since I've been in Lugano. If you doubt me, ask Claire. She was there when I deposited it.'

Dominic heard Midas talk to Claire, heard her reply, faint and tired.

'All right, Cain, she confirms your story. What do you want?'

'I'm prepared to make the exchange and give you the irrevocable authority to the Banque Dürer for the eighteen million francs. But I want the girl. I want to make sure that nothing happens to us afterwards. So I will only deal with you. You must come alone with the girl.'

'That's impossible.'

'Midas, listen to me. I've buggered up my job running out on Pelham. The reason I did that is that he was crazy to get you. Even if it meant the girl dying. I love that girl. I want to marry her. I don't want your heavies taking pot shots at us after the exchange. That's why you must come alone. I trust you. I don't trust them.'

'You know I can't agree to those conditions. You're keeping me talking just so that I will be here when the police come.'

'No, you fool! I know too damned well what will happen when the police get there. I'm not interested in that bloody bank. All I want is Claire. When the police get there, neither of you must be there. If you're both gone, there's no offence they can prove. Leave while you can.'

'I'll bring two men,' Midas said. 'No more.'

'Right. I'll see you at the top of the Piazza Luini funicular in half an hour.'

Without giving Midas time to protest, Dominic slammed the phone down.

It was working, he thought; thank God it was working. Midas had fallen for it hook, line and sinker. All he had to do now was wait for Martin's call, telling him that Wolweber had agreed. Midas was confined to operating on the street, with as many bodyguards as he could cram into one motor car.

He paced about the room anxiously, waiting for Martin's call. Five minutes later it came. In fifteen minutes, the funicular would be covered by Wolweber's men, all in plain clothes and carrying revolvers. Once Midas got up, there was no way he would ever get down.

Dominic went to the bathroom, ran cold water over his wrists and washed his face. Midas wasn't going to get down anyway. Half an hour ago Dominic had made a decision to kill him. For the last time he checked the gun and the knife. Then he shut the door behind him and walked into the corridor. The phone in his room began to ring.

Dominic thrust open the door, picked up the phone. 'Cain?' It was Midas, from a call box. 'So you really are at the Royal.'

'Yes. Did you call the Walter and check where Pelham is?'

'Yes. I've done that.'

230

'Well, what's the problem? Do we make the swop or not?'

'We do, Cain. We do. But not at the Piazza Luini. You have twenty minutes to get to the jetty in the Parco Civico. You have made us abandon our plan and we are leaving Switzerland. We have very little time. If you are not there with the appropriate documents in twenty minutes, we will execute the girl.'

'But twenty minutes isn't enough!'

'It is, if you leave now.'

The Parco Civico was at the other end of the town, a ten-minute taxi ride, twenty minutes if you walked fast. The gates were locked at sunset, and the park would be totally deserted by now. Dominic quickly dialled the Walter and asked for Martin. The receptionist was sorry, Mr Pelham had gone out. Wolweber was no longer at the police station. Dominic scribbled a note and left it with the concierge downstairs. Then he set out alone for the park. Strapped to the top of his thigh, concealed by his leather coat, was the Grisbi diver's knife. Stuffed in his pocket was the Colt and snug at the top of his waistband was Siccoli's baby Biretta.

CHAPTER THIRTY-THREE

He slipped into the Parco Civico over a side gate, ran along the wall till he reached the tarmac path that skirted the lake and led to the jetty. The gardens were dark and deserted, full of shady trees and ghostly busts of bearded poets and philosophers. The path angled gently towards the lake, to the right, bordered by flowerbeds and lawns, punctuated by dim lighting that cast pale shadows. A municipal park – a fitting end to the ideology of Midas, Dominic thought – and wondered: *whose* end?

He saw the jetty through a clump of trees, a concrete, semicircular promontory jutting into the lake, bordered by a knee-high wall. It was illuminated by four lamps with metal shades shaped like the hats of Chinese coolies, set equidistant along the wall, throwing a sad, silvery-blue light over the jetty. In the middle of the jetty, bathed in the sad, silvery-blue light, Dominic saw two figures. Edgar, very erect and Napoleonic, and Claire, bound, gagged, blindfolded and kneeling.

Dominic left the path and moved across the lawn, heading for a clump of trees, beside the jetty. He didn't believe that Edgar had come alone. Somewhere amongst the trees and the darkness were his armed bodyguards.

Dominic reached the clump of trees and stood still. He was ten yards from Claire and Edgar. Edgar was an easy shot, even in that light. But killing him now would mean sacrificing Claire. Dominic kept very still and studied the scene.

The path skirted the jetty and beyond it were trees and darkness. If Edgar had been able to use only one car, there would be no more than three others. If he was intelligent, he would have placed them in a semicircle, one directly in line with the centre of the jetty, the other two at an angle bisecting that centre line, so that the jetty was covered by a wide arc of fire and there was no risk of them shooting each other. The main thing, Dominic decided, was to break that circle.

He cupped his hands to his mouth and shouted, 'Edgar, free the girl!' and moved to his right, amongst the trees, nearer to the lake. 'The deal is the girl comes with me. I can't take her like that.' Again he moved. He had to keep moving. He couldn't afford to let them pinpoint him.

Edgar had sarted at the sound of his voice, and looked hesitantly about him. 'Have you got the documents, Cain?'

Dominic remained where he was. 'Free the girl and I'll tell you.'

Edgar looked around him as if checking his men were in position. Then he removed the blindfold and gag, loosed the bonds, and helped Claire to her feet. First blood to us, Dominic thought. He had the initiative, and the longer these preliminaries lasted, the better chance there was of Martin finding his note and getting there with Wolweber's men.

'Claire, are you all right?'

'Of course she's all right,' Edgar shouted. 'Give me the documents and go.'

Claire stood there blinking, rubbing her wrists and peering through the darkness towards him. Her face was pale and strained and there were dark shadows around her eyes.

'I want to see her walk,' Dominic shouted. 'I want to be sure she's okay.'

'Don't waste time, Cain.'

'Make her walk to the end of the jetty and show me.'

Edgar shrugged, took Claire's elbow and led her very slowly towards the boundary wall. Claire walked with difficulty, as if there was no strength to her legs, hanging onto the arm Edgar offered her. Given time and motive enough, Dominic decided, she would be able to run. Then

234

he broke from the clump of trees and ran towards the lake. The path was separated from the lake by a low wall. Dominic clambered over it and dropped eight feet onto the lake shore. The shore was narrow and rocky and smelt of a rotten wetness. There was the sound of slopping water and it flowed over his feet and ankles as he ran to the outward jutting wall of the jetty.

The wall of the jetty rose sheer for about six feet. After that there was a wide ledge and then the concentric boundary wall. Dominic stood on a rock, leapt and scrambled onto the ledge. He crawled along it till he came to the middle of the jetty and lay flat, the Colt Python in his hand.

Claire and Edgar reached the wall and looked over.

'Keep very still,' Dominic said softly, 'or I'll blow your fucking head off.'

'You're mad, Cain,' Edgar said. 'Give me the documents and go.'

'Claire,' Dominic said, 'jump over the wall.'

She looked at him with a kind of resignation. 'Dominic,' Claire said, 'Edgar isn't Midas. He's a prisoner like me. There are three of them behind us.'

'They've got us covered with rifles,' Edgar said. 'If you don't show up pretty soon, they're going to shoot us.'

'Then jump,' Dominic said urgently. *Both of you! Now!*

The intensity of his voice gave them strength to act. They swung over the wall and fell, Edgar kicking away Dominic's legs, almost dragging him down with them. A rattle of automatic fire screeched off the wall and buzzed into the night. Dominic raised Siccoli's Biretta and fired two shots. After that there was silence.

'Midas!' Dominic shouted. 'I'm coming over. Tell your people not to shoot.'

There was another silence. Then a voice said, 'All right, Cain.'

From below him, Claire said, 'Dominic, don't. You're crazy.'

235

'Get going,' Dominic said. 'Keep to the lake side. Don't go in the park. I'll see you soon,' and leapt over the wall.

'You bloody cheated!' Dominic shouted. 'I said you were to come alone and you brought men with you. You set Edgar up for me. Do you think I don't know who you are? Do you think Landi didn't know?'

Dominic waited and counted to ten. Then he shouted, 'Edgar and the girl are walking to the town. Keep your men where they are. If anyone moves I'll go with Edgar and you'll never see the documents or the eighteen million francs again.'

A voice cried, 'Everyone stay where they are.'

Dominic waited, staring at the blackness beyond the path, his nerves tense as stretched violin strings, trying to see where the men were, if there was anyone after Claire and Edgar, straining his ears for the slightest noise which would betray the fact that they were going to shoot him.

'We wait three minutes,' Dominic cried. 'Then you, Midas, come and get the documents. Don't think you can kill me and take it off my body. I might fall into the water, or I might have brought the wrong documents.'

One minute passed, two, each second stretched out like eternity. Any moment Midas's nerve could break or one of the men could panic. Dominic's eyes hurt with the strain of staring, his palms gripping the roughened brick were damp with sweat. He concentrated on controlling his breathing and slowing his pulse rate, steeling himself for what he had to do next.

'All right, Midas, come and get it. But make sure you come alone.' He took the documents from his pocket and let them dangle temptingly from his fingers in their white envelope.

Something moved away to his left. A man in a dark suit. Dominic moved his right hand underneath his coat, rested it on the hilt of the knife strapped to his thigh.

236

He watched while the figure crossed the path, a tall, bulky person, a gleam as the light caught a bald patch on his head. Dominic eased the toggle back and freed the knife from its scabbard. Brian Keith walked onto the jetty.

'Dominic Cain,' he said, 'You are a pain in the arse.'

'Number two trying to be number one, right? You would have been head of the bank in two years. Why do all this?'

'Because it's bloody necessary,' Keith said. 'For poor bastards like me this kind of thing is always necessary. It's either this or slaving every day of our lives so that idiots like Edgar can shoot grouse and drive a Rolls-Royce.'

'The politics of envy are the politics of revolution,' Dominic said.

Brian Keith was only five feet away from him now, his eyes fixed on the envelope. Dominic held it up a little to his left. Keith gave Dominic a small grin. 'We should discuss the politics of envy sometime. I would like that. But for now, the documents.'

'Of course,' Dominic said, thinking that, right at that moment, he liked Brian Keith.

Brian came up, moved to Dominic's left to take the envelope. As he reached for it, Dominic let it slip from his fingers. Instinctively Brian leaned forward, grabbed, bent at the waist. Almost as instinctively, Dominic moved quickly to the left and brought the knife up from under his coat, whipping it in a vicious arc, forwards and upwards, pushing it as it jammed against flesh, twisting it, pulling it up and up, ripping through Keith's stomach with the wet and ugly sound of tearing cloth and flesh.

Keith gasped, his eyes going pale. He flung his hands around his middle in a flabby embrace, as Dominic took the knife away with a soft, sucking sound like an obscene kiss.

Quickly Dominic caught him by the shoulders, keeping Keith's dying body between him and the men in the darkness of the trees.

'That was for Lew Carmody and Abe Stone,' Dominic said.

Keith's tongue was beginning to protrude, his eyes were rolling. 'I didn't—' he gasped. 'Oh God!'

Dominic propped Keith upright against him. 'You men over there,' he shouted, 'this is Dominic Cain! I have your leader. I want you to come onto the jetty with your hands raised over your heads and balancing your guns in them.'

Keith tried to wriggle away, but Dominic held him. 'You have five seconds,' Dominic shouted. 'Or else he dies.'

Two men emerged from the trees and walked across the path, their upraised arms supporting automatic rifles.

'Stop there,' Dominic called. One of the men was Kit Garnham. 'Throw the rifles down.' Dominic wondered if he should bring out the Python, then decided that left him with one thing too many to do. Keith's legs were going. Already he was resting his head on Dominic's shoulder, and his body was beginning to smell.

'I have made a deal that you can go,' Dominic shouted. 'Go now, quickly. Get away from Lugano. In ten minutes this place will be surrounded.' Garnham and the other man left, without a backward glance at Keith.

Dominic waited two more minutes, then laid Keith on the ground. There was no one in the darkness waiting to take a shot at him. He picked up the rifles, took out the magazines and then he began to run along the path by the lake.

He saw Claire and Edgar walking along the shore and shouted to them to use the path, and kept on running, knowing the sooner he met with Wolweber, the sooner he would be able to get a doctor to Keith.

He had nearly reached the tall gates at the entrance when he saw a figure limping furiously towards him.

'Dominic, I came as quickly as I could.' Martin followed Dominic's stare, looked around and shrugged at the fact that he was alone. 'I couldn't raise any help from the Department. I'm sorry.'

'It's all over,' Dominic said.

'Did you find Midas?'

Dominic nodded.

'So it is all over, then. I might as well have Landi's confession, for the Department.'

'I'm not working for the Department,' Dominic said quietly. 'This goes to Haden.'

'Don't be absurd, Dominic. You work for the Department. You're on loan to Haden. That confession belongs to the Department. I want it.'

'No,' Dominic said, and made to push past Martin. 'Go and play your bloody silly bureaucratic games elsewhere. I've got something urgent to do.'

'I want it,' Martin repeated and Dominic stared in surprise as a gun bulged angrily in Martin's hand. 'Give it over, there's a good chap.'

Dominic stared at him in wild disbelief, a confused welter of thoughts rushing through his head. Chagny, sodium amytal, Lew Carmody, the assistance from the Department that hadn't come, the phone call to London that had not been made, the prolonging of the capture of Claire and the subtle torture that had nearly forced him to deliver the documents to Midas.

'You,' Dominic said.

Martin smiled. 'So you know. It *wasn't* in Landi's confession, was it now? You would have made a great poker player, Dominic.'

Dominic remembered. 'That day in Chagny you weren't going to take them out, you were going to warn Thirstone that I would kill him. You and I were the only ones who knew what Lew Carmody was doing, we were the only ones who knew that Carmody knew too much. So you had him killed. You were the one who tipped off de Marco and

239

Grady. And all that bullshit about government pressure and help from the Department! Christ! Brian Keith must have died laughing when I told him you were calling London, when I told him I had double-crossed you. And all the time you were supposed to be calling London you were master-minding the whole operation.'

Martin shook his head sadly, 'I tried so hard to get you off the job, Dominic, but you wouldn't listen.'

'But why, Martin, Why?'

'Because I don't believe any more. I don't want the things you want. I'm tired of living in chains.'

'The only chains are the ones you forge yourself,' Dominic said.

'Give me the documents,' Martin said, and raised the gun.

Dominic stepped up to him, gave him the envelope. As he took it, Dominic swung his foot out and sideways, and swept Martin's damaged leg from under him. Martin swung sideways in the air, crashed down on his shoulder, the gun skidding across the tarmac. Dominic stepped over him and took out the Python. His eyes were flat and expressionless.

'Dominic,' Martin cried. 'We're friends.'

'I owe you for that too,' Dominic said, and clicked back the hammer.

Claire shouted, 'Dominic, don't! Dominic, for God's sake *don't*!'

Dominic hesitated a moment, before he pulled the trigger.